THROUGH
A
GLASS
DARKLY

THROUGH
A
GLASS
DARKLY

Val Gielgud

PERENNIAL LIBRARY

Harper & Row, Publishers, New York
Cambridge, Philadelphia, San Francisco, Washington
London, Mexico City, São Paulo, Singapore, Sydney

I must state in the most unequivocal terms that none of the characters in this story are to be identified with any living person. Further—obviously I cannot pronounce as to whether it is for the good or ill of the great army of Viewers—the Gargantua Television organisation, its personnel, its policy, and its programmes, are the fictional products of the author's imagination.

V.G.

A hardcover edition of this book was published in 1963 by Charles Scribner's Sons. It was first published in England under the title *The Goggle-Box Affair*. It is here reprinted by arrangement with Charles Scribner's Sons.

First PERENNIAL LIBRARY edition published 1986.

Library of Congress Cataloging-in-Publication Data

Gielgud, Val Henry, 1900–
    Through a glass darkly.

    I. Title.
PR6013.I295T5   1986   823'.912   86–45103
ISBN 0-06-080822-5 (pbk.)

86 87 88 89 90   OPM   10 9 8 7 6 5 4 3 2 1

For Judy, who liked it

PART ONE WHO?

O—who hath done this deed?
Nobody—I myself. . . .

—OTHELLO

———————————————

CHAPTER 1

INCEPTION OF THE CASE

It became a case on the evening of Friday, 30th, December, 196-, when the appropriate file was started in the appropriate office at New Scotland Yard. Before that it had only been one of those nine days' wonders, so beloved and exploited by the popular Press.

On that date the Metropolitan Police Commander, who at the time was acting head of the Criminal Investigation Department, lunched in the Savoy Grill Room with a Private Secretary (Additional, Unpaid) of a certain Minister of the Crown. The luncheon was excellent and expensive. The wine was admirably chosen. The Commander—who had been the Private Secretary's fag at his public-school—had not been particularly surprised by the invitation, though it had been couched in terms rendering refusal difficult if not impossible. Out of genuine friendship, as well as mutual advantage, the two men had preserved regular contact over the years, and indeed lunched together about every three or four months. But, as a rule, the Commander was invited to the Private Secretary's Club: a modest establishment in Brook Street—too full of intellectuals, in the Commander's opinion, for a simple policeman—notable for its conversation rather than its cooking. He concluded, rightly, that more lay behind the Savoy Grill and a vintage Margaux than the mere preservation of good-fellowship.

When he was not so much invited as adjured to choose his own liqueur brandy, the Commander's suspicion became certainty. (Lest any pillars of the Establishment be rocked I propose to return to the ingenious nomenclature of schooldays. The Private Secretary had been known as "Beetle"; the Commander as "Kitten." Should anyone be curious as to the why and wherefore, suffice to say that at school the Private Secretary had worn round steel-rimmed spectacles and read Kipling; while the Commander had concealed effective claws beneath the velvet glove of a charming personality.) Having refused a cigar—he did not smoke—the Commander also declined a bell-glass for his brandy, looked round the crowded room, put his elbows on the table, and leaned forward.

"Well, my dear Beetle—what's the form?"

The Private Secretary made distinctly heavy weather of lighting his cigar. The result was a satisfactory smoke screen. "I don't know what you mean by 'form,'" he said a trifle querulously. "I do know that you've told me more than once that if I wanted to tell you anything in confidence the best place to do it was at a table in a crowded restaurant."

"Certainly. When everyone else is pitching his or her voice a little higher than normal in the hope of being heard no one is going to be able to hear what is said by two people talking in average conversational tones. Go ahead. What is it?"

The Private Secretary blinked and looked at the ceiling.

"I want to borrow one of your men," he said.

The Commander grinned.

"You mean, my dear Beetle, that your Minister wants to borrow one of my men?"

"I wish," said the Private Secretary irritably, "that you wouldn't jump to conclusions."

4

"I wish," said the Commander, still grinning, "that you'd forget that you were once in the Diplomatic, and get to the point. I've some work to do this afternoon."

The Private Secretary drew heavily at his cigar; coughed; picked up his glass of brandy; put it down again; leaned in his turn across the table. The elbows of the two men were almost touching.

"I want," said the Private Secretary quietly, "someone of intelligence and discretion beyond the ordinary to investigate the death of Simon Hargest."

"Hargest? My dear Beetle—what on earth for? The inquest and post-mortem were perfectly in order. The verdict was perfectly clear; suicide while the balance of his mind was disturbed. There was any amount of evidence to show that Hargest had been overworking himself fantastically for months—"

"I know all about that, Kitten. Can you find me a man? Not one of your usual admirably efficient routine characters who know all the answers; started as Dixon of Dock Green, and graduated as Perry Mason. I want an intelligent freak— for choice someone who's been farther than Blackpool or Margate on his holidays."

"You always were a bit of a snob, Beetle."

"And I always admitted it, Kitten. Well?"

"You've got to tell me more. You know that as well as I do. Why go on beating about bushes?"

"Habit, I suppose," said the Private Secretary, and put down his cigar. "What do you know about Simon Hargest?"

The Commander shrugged his shoulders.

"I know what everyone knows, Beetle. He was an immensely rich and successful tycoon at the age of forty-three. He was a scholar of Trinity Cambridge; read for the Bar; chucked the law to go into business; did a good job with Military Intelligence during the war, mostly in the Middle East; got a seat in the House immediately afterwards; made his name as one of the leading lights among the promoters of Commercial Television; and became Managing Director of

Gargantua TV—last of the big organisations to get an ITV licence, and the first to have the sense to profit by its competitors' mistakes. What he forgot, apparently, was that when you're working under that sort of pressure and can't sleep it's liable to be fatal to mix too many barbiturates with too much alcohol."

"You certainly do your home-work, Kitten."

"I'm paid for it," said the Commander. "I believe that you aren't."

The Private Secretary's answering smile was rueful. "True enough. I suppose I'm almost the last of the amateurs. It makes it difficult for people to take me seriously."

"I'm not rising to that," said the Commander. "Will you please either smoke that cigar or stub it out—the smoke's getting in my eyes—and get to business?"

The Private Secretary stubbed out his cigar; picked up his glass of brandy, and put it down again. With his bald head, his jowls, his fat cheeks, his white pudgy hands he gave an overwhelming impression of softness: of over-feeding and good-living. The Commander—who took a cold bath and rode daily for an hour before breakfast—had some difficulty in believing that on more than one occasion "Beetle" had beaten him smartly on the hinder parts for having failed to produce toast to his fag-master's satisfaction. But memory of those beatings remained. They had been laid on scientifically, and proportionately painful. He also remembered the eyes of "Beetle" behind spectacles that in those days had been steel-rimmed: watery grey eyes, coldly dispassionate, somehow frightening. The spectacles were now horn-rimmed and triangular but the eyes were the same.

"Get it over with," said the Commander, assuming a lightness of heart he didn't feel. "You're breaking my heart."

"Nobody believes that I've a heart to break," said the Private Secretary, showing for once quite human exasperation. "I'm just the necessary cog-wheel, the indispensable channel of communication, the discreet and almost faceless go-

6

between. When I go to the bathroom to shave in the morning I wonder sometimes if I shall see anything in the mirror."

"You can always look at your indecently large bank-statement, Beetle."

"And muse upon the proverbial deceitfulness and impermanence of riches—I suppose I can. It doesn't cheer me up very much."

"I'd exchange my job for your income any day, my dear Beetle."

"The job I want from you, Kitten, is to find me a man of the right calibre and discretion to look into all the details and circumstances of Hargest's death, and ultimately to report to me through you. He must, of course, think that it's nothing more than a routine inquiry—that you're being over-conscientiously fussy, if necessary."

"Thanks. Well, I suppose I must play ball. I've a chap in mind who might do: bright enough—inclined sometimes to be too bright; has been abroad a good deal; was attached to Interpol for a time; never really happy with the daily round and common task."

The Private Secretary nodded. "He sounds as if he might fill the bill."

"Will you see him, Beetle?"

"Good God—no!" The Private Secretary sounded honestly shocked.

"What about expenses? I don't imagine he can do this job on his normal pay, and I've no secret fund for this sort of caper."

The Private Secretary grinned. "You'll have to trust me for the necessary cheque when you want it, Kitten. You'll get no promise in writing."

"I wish," said the Commander, "that I'd never accepted your damned invitation to lunch. You're simply exploiting my good nature—and the fact that I've been fool enough to go on knowing you for far too long."

"That," said the Private Secretary, "was the object of the

exercise. Have another glass of brandy?"

"Thank you," said the Commander with feeling, "I will. And, as you've already vulgarly reminded me that you can easily afford it, you can make it a double."

CHAPTER 2

GREGORY PELLEW TELEPHONES

About half past six in the evening of the day when "Beetle" and "Kitten" had lunched together, Detective-Inspector Pellew was sitting in his office at New Scotland Yard. On his desk was a cup of tea, which he had allowed to get cold; an over-filled ashtray; a large sheet of paper on which he had scrawled voluminous notes; and a copy of *Who's Who*, open at the page containing the entry relating to the late Simon Hargest. Scattered on the floor was a file of newspapers in which he had read various—and varying—reports and comments concerning Hargest's death and the subsequent inquest thereon. He felt exhausted, exasperated, and exceedingly puzzled. He admitted wryly to himself that he had very little idea as to what to do next.

The whole business was so damned queer. In the first place the procedure was utterly irregular—and at the Yard irregularity of procedure was, to say the least of it, unusual. And when it occurred it was frowned upon. The head of the C.I.D.—even if only "acting"—was not in the habit of giving instructions personally to individual detective-inspectors. And, while Pellew had had the sense not to argue about them, the instructions he had received had been such as to make him blink and question the accuracy of his hearing.

"I've been looking at your personal file, Pellew," had been the Commander's opening gambit. "It's an interesting one. As far as I can judge if you hadn't tried so hard to be clever, and if you'd had rather better luck, you'd have been well on the way to the top by now. Any comment?"

"I don't think so, sir."

"I get the impression that you're happiest with what this generation would call 'off-beat' activities. That business in Sicily, while you were on attachment to Interpol—you speak a language or two?"

"French pretty well. I can get by in Italian."

"Good marks for initiative and discretion—considerable reservations about reference for irregular methods of working—a liking for rather Bohemian society—not the Chelsea Set, I hope?"

The Commander smiled, and Pellew permitted himself to smile back. "No, sir."

The Commander got out of his chair, walked over to the window, appeared for at least thirty seconds completely absorbed in the view across London River, and turned round abruptly.

"I've a job for that initiative and discretion of yours, Pellew," he said. "And I fancy that irregular methods of work may be a positive advantage for once. I want you to look into the circumstances of Simon Hargest's death. You know about it, of course."

"I know what everyone knows about Hargest, sir. I read about the inquest in the papers. I've just come back from a fortnight's leave in Paris."

"You're lucky. What I want you to do is to find out what everyone doesn't and didn't know about Hargest. Did he in fact kill himself, and if so, why? If he didn't—"

"Has something come up since the inquest, sir?"

"Nothing—as far as I know. All I can tell you is that a

further inquiry has been called for at an exceedingly important level. You're probably wondering why I'm not putting the business in the hands of the Special Branch. The reason is that the whole thing's unofficial. You'll have to work without the help of the organisation here. Your status will be that of a private agent, and you'll report only to me. I'll take care of your necessary expenses personally, and square things with your department. Incidentally, as it's unofficial, you're at perfect liberty to refuse the assignment. And whether, even if you get results, it will do you any professional good I simply don't know. Well?"

"I'll do my best," said Gregory Pellew.

"Thanks. Then for two months as from to-morrow morning you can forget about this place. Communicate with me at my private address if you want me. I'll find the story to account for your absence. Good luck."

Pellew had gone back to his office with the conviction that in this case the best of luck would be inadequate. And with every newspaper that he read, with every note that he scribbled, that conviction was only strengthened. Where the devil was he to begin? Hargest was dead and buried. The cause of his death was known and had been accepted. There was no shadow of a case for an exhumation, and in any event Pellew by his instructions was barred from investigating along conventional lines—even from discussing possibilities with any of his colleagues who had been concerned with Hargest's death. Who the deuce was interested in stirring things up again? Pellew did not believe that it was the Commander. Could it be a comparatively new broom of a Home Secretary, throwing his weight about? There was no means of telling, and it was not Pellew's business anyhow.

One thing of course he could do—and did. He took a brand-new file from a drawer in his desk, marked it with a large and sprawling H, and put into it a selection of cuttings, which he sliced from his newspapers, and his own sheet of notes. Then he resumed his gloomy study of the column in

Who's Who. Obviously he must go to Hargest's background —and the infernal fellow had had as many activities as a chameleon.

However, if the backgrounds had been tiresomely varied they had also been reasonably widely spaced. It was almost impossible to believe that a man who committed suicide in his late forties had done so as a result of anything he had done as an undergraduate at Cambridge, or as a barrister in his twenties. (For the moment Pellew was determined to accept the verdict of suicide. To do otherwise was to allow the attraction of melodrama to outweigh common sense.) Work in Military Intelligence started every kind of line of thought. But "Intelligence" had covered a multitude of nicely cushioned wartime jobs. And apart from memoir-writing generals most people seemed to have thrown 1939–45 together with 1914–18 into the discard of a valley of very dry bones. There remained tycoonery in general and the managing directorship of Gargantua Television in particular with all that they implied.

(Pellew, who admitted against the grain a weakness for *Whack-o!* and *Monitor,* felt in his secret heart that responsibility for any large-scale TV output was more than enough to drive anybody round the bend.)

At this point in his thinking Pellew, who was lighting a pipe just refilled, allowed the match to burn his fingers and swore. "When the balance of his mind was disturbed" was a phrase implying the passing of the limits of mental strain— likely and reasonable enough in the case of a modern business man with multifarious financial interests to which he had added television, possibly without realising what demands that many-headed monster would make. But the same phrase could also imply the passing of the limits of *emotional* strain: circumstances arising out of an unhappy marriage, a disastrous love affair, or blackmail. Marriage just over three years old—to Clarissa Jane, daughter of Colonel and Mrs. Charles Sibthorpe—no children—was mentioned in *Who's Who.* More than one picture of the widow had appeared in the most popular of the dailies. Pellew studied them carefully. They told him nothing except that Mrs. Hargest was rather tall, ash-blonde, more than averagely good-looking, and had a nice sense of clothes and how to wear them. But he reminded himself that, while Gargantua Television and its staff—or at any rate those members of its staff with whom Hargest had been most intimately concerned—and other business associates were the most obvious subjects for investigation, he must not forget to inquire into Hargest's domestic background and the possible existence of a skeleton in the closet.

Pellew closed *Who's Who* and opened a copy of the Gargantua Staff List which the Commander had given him as he left the latter's room. The organisation was vaguely based on that of the B.B.C., comprising three divisions: Administration, Engineering and Programmes. Including the Managing Director there was a board of five. In Hargest's own office were shown a Personal Assistant and two secretaries. There must be the obvious starting point. But how in the first place was Pellew to get in there without any official *laissez-passer* from the Yard? And where did he go from there? He looked down the closely printed list of names with deepening gloom.

Then his eye caught one name at which he stared incredulously for several moments. Perhaps luck was going to be with him this time. He grabbed the Directory E–K, riffled hastily through the pages, reached for his telephone and dialled a TEM number.

"Could I speak to Lady Hannington?"

"Speaking."

"Gregory Pellew here, Lady Hannington."

"How nice. But I suppose you want Humphrey, Mr. Pellew?"

"Would he be in after dinner this evening? And if so, could I come round?"

"You could not, Mr. Pellew. We dine at eight, and we shall expect you. Good-bye."

13

Pellew grinned as he hung up. Lady Hannington had not changed for all that she was now a dowager, and had exchanged Hares Green for London to live in. The horizon was distinctly brightening. Whatever else he might have to look forward to in the immediate future Pellew could be certain of a capital dinner that night.

CHAPTER 3

LADY HANNINGTON ENTERTAINS

When the news appeared in *The Times* that Humphrey the Viscount Clymping had quietly married abroad a young actress of no particular distinction, that large circle of his acquaintances who had enjoyed Humphrey's more spectacular pranks for some years felt gloomily that it was beyond a joke. When, a fortnight later, the same newspaper announced with appropriate regret the death of the Earl of Hannington "after a long illness borne with exemplary fortitude" it was generally felt that, as a matter of naked necessity rather than policy, reform of the House of Lords would have to be put in hand forthwith. Otherwise the opportunities now opened before Humphrey would be bound to prove irresistible.

The said acquaintances, however, failed to reckon with two women of character and determination: the late earl's widow, and the new earl's wife. The former said with her usual sweetness that she declined to be known as the dowager. Everyone knew her and spoke of her as "the Countess." She liked it, and was too old for a change. Further she considered that the only woman who in her experience had worn the title of Dowager without implication of dowdiness or decrepitude had been the late Queen Alexandra. She had been inimitable, and Lady Hannington did not propose to attempt the impossible. Humphrey's wife, on the other hand, had made it one of her conditions before marrying him that after marriage he would make no use of his title. She proposed to continue her acting career, from which she derived a good deal of pleasure, and she did not believe that an actress benefited in this day and age from being "Lady" anything, except perhaps in television circles. Also she and Humphrey would be hard up, and a title only meant an extra ten per cent on bills. Humphrey said flatly that they would be known as Mr. and Mr. Humphrey Clymping, and that he did not propose to argue the point with the Lord Chancellor, the editor of Debrett, or William Hickey. He had no intention of taking his seat in the Lords. People could like it or lump it.

All this was diverting, exasperating, or mildly scandalous, according to taste. But more was to come. Lady Hannington disposed—fortunately at a handsome profit—of the house at Hares Green, where she had nursed her husband till his death, and from which she had presided distantly but efficiently over village affairs. She then secured the lease of a dilapidated but picturesque residence within a stone's throw of Seven Dials. To objections that the house was too big, and that the neighbourhood was hardly suitable for an elderly gentlewoman living alone, she retorted crisply that she found the locality both convenient and interesting, and that the house might be too large for one; it was certainly not too large for three. Humphrey and his wife would live with her. Any jokes about mothers-in-law would be extremely ill-received. She and Kate took extremely good views of each other. People raised eyebrows, shrugged shoulders, but in decency could say no more.

A good deal more was said none the less when Humphrey Clymping not only got himself a job but got that job with Gargantua Television. He got it by reminding Simon Hargest of an evening at Oxford when Hargest had come up as guest of honour at a club dinner. The dinner had been indifferent, and Hargest had been bored. Humphrey, who had been even more bored, succeeded in winkling Hargest neatly out of the company of youthfully solemn and self-conscious would-be politicians and the dreariness of a hotel private dining-room and into the agreeably relaxed atmosphere of his own rooms in the High. Hargest was not only grateful. He was impressed by his host's vitality and his amusing line of talk. He was also mellowed by an excellent brandy. A good memory was not least among the reasons for his success, and he prided himself on choosing members of his staff for qualities apparent only to himself. Humphrey found himself one of the unit which handled a regular topical programme item called *Here To-day, Gone To-morrow*—one of Gargantua's most successful features. He shaved his beard, carried a briefcase, became a slave to an almost morbid sense of punctuality, and was only saved from pomposity by his wife's affectionate sense of humour, and his mother's refusal to take him seriously.

He received with enthusiasm the news that Pellew was coming to dinner. He liked and admired Pellew. Also Kate was playing a small part and understudying in a Shaftesbury Avenue theatre and did not get home until after eleven. Fond as he was of his mother Humphrey found trying her remarkable capacity for finding him odd jobs to do about the house during evenings when he had not the excuse of his wife's society to avoid doing them.

"I thought Greg was in Paris," he said. "I wonder what he's up to this time."

"If you wait," said Lady Hannington sweetly, "you will almost certainly see."

Humphrey grinned, and mixed the dryest possible martinis.

Pellew was not disappointed in his dinner: *vichyssoise;* a roast of baby lamb with new potatoes and fresh garden peas —Lady Hannington had been careful to preserve certain desirable contacts with Hares Green; raspberries and cream; a bottle of Cantenac-Brown '53. He pleased Lady Hannington

by confining conversation during dinner to suitable appreciation of the house, mild bantering of Humphrey for having
joined the working-classes, and a sardonic description of the
UNESCO building in Paris as "the Earthly Paradise for International Eggheads."

After dinner they adjourned to Lady Hannington's own
sitting-room with its Edwardian furniture and chintzes, the
indifferent portrait of the late earl in full-dress yeomanry
uniform above the fireplace, its many small tables with
spindly legs and a multitude of tiny silver boxes. Lady Hannington made and dispensed Turkish coffee. Humphrey
poured out brandy.

"No brandy for me, dear," said Lady Hannington.
"Humphrey doesn't approve, Mr. Pellew, but I prefer Marie
Brizard anisette. A little sweet, perhaps, but I find it smooth
and settling."

"That sounds like the stuff for me—at this moment," said
Pellew.

"Are you in trouble, Greg?"

"Of course he's in trouble," said Lady Hannington. "Why
else should he have asked himself to dinner? Not that we're
not delighted to see you, Mr. Pellew."

Pellew asked for permission and lighted a cigarette.
"Frankly, I want your help, Humphrey. It's a complicated
out-of-the-ordinary sort of business, and if you come in with
me you'll have to do a good deal of blind riding. To begin
with I've got to ask you to promise me that nothing I tell you
goes beyond these four walls."

"Of course, Greg."

"Perhaps," suggested Lady Hannington, "Mr. Pellew
would rather talk over his problem alone with you,
Humphrey?"

"You wouldn't mind, Lady Hannington?"

"I should mind very much. I've the insatiable curiosity of
the Elephant's Child. I should understand all the same."

Humphrey got up and kissed his mother, who patted his
cheek.

"I wouldn't dream of leaving you out," said Pellew. "I don't forget how helpful you were over the Heseltine case. And you probably knew Simon Hargest."

"I met him once, Mr. Pellew. I arranged it soon after Humphrey got himself mixed up with the goggle-box business. I wanted to see what the man he was working for was like."

"And what was he like, Lady Hannington?"

"He impressed me. He obviously knew his own mind. He talked sense and he didn't waste words. So many successful men are such bores. Mr. Hargest didn't bore me for a minute."

"What did you talk about, Mother?"

Lady Hannington reflected, and finished her anisette. "I think I will have one tiny half-glass more, dear. Thank you. As far as I remember we talked about the deplorable state of the English Theatre, on which we agreed; the breeding of Siamese cats, about which we disagreed profoundly; and Elizabethan music, of which he knew a great deal more than I did. Yes—a definitely civilized person."

"I see," said Pellew frowning.

This was a very different picture of Hargest from that which he had formed in his mind after reading that column in *Who's Who:* the brilliant ruthless careerist tycoon with a foot in every sort of camp and a finger in every sort of pie.

"But Hargest's dead," protested Humphrey.

"Don't be obvious, dear. He was only forty-nine, if I remember. Perhaps Mr. Pellew is interested in why Mr. Hargest died."

Pellew smiled gratefully. "That saves me a lot of trouble, Lady Hannington. You've hit it in one." He gave a brief résumé of his conversation with the Commander, and went on: "So you see, Humphrey, I must get some means of entry to the Gargantua set-up, and I need anything I can get in the way of information about Hargest's recent activities, and the people in Gargantua with whom he actually worked in close contact."

"So that's where I come in," said Humphrey slowly. "Quite an assignment. I've often thought it would be fun to try being a 'private eye,' and you say you're off the official hook?"

Pellew nodded.

"Just so. The first part's easy. We're always exploring rather wild ideas as programme possibilities for *Here To-day, Gone To-morrow*. I can pull you in on one of those: The Psychiatrist and the Criminal, Sex and the Juvenile Delinquent—"

"Now, dear, don't be naughty."

"I'm being practical. And if we can't think of a title with a good gimmick, you can bet that Kate will."

"I would advise you to ask her," said Lady Hannington dryly. "As for the second part," Humphrey went on, with the suspicion of a wink at Pellew, "I'm afraid I'm not going to be very helpful. I've only been in the show for a few months, and the new boy didn't see much of the top brass—though Hargest was always very decent to me when I did run across him. I fancy Rollo Gunn's our best bet as a line of approach. He's quite a pal of mine."

"Hargest's Personal Assistant?"

"That's the chap. You know him, Greg?"

"I've done my home-work, Humphrey. What about the two secretaries?"

"The plain and the pretty—out of my star, alas! Especially the latter, though I might have had a chance with her if I'd stuck to the title. She's quite a piece—knows the price of everything and the value of most people. But you can get at them through Rollo."

Pellew lighted another cigarette, and screwed up his eyes behind the smoke. "Just two more questions at this stage, Humphrey. Hargest had been away from his office—abroad, I gather—for about a fortnight before the tragedy. He came back to London forty-eight hours before his death. Where had he been?"

"I can answer that one. West Berlin. Hargest was completely sold on Eurovision and all that carry-on. He was always saying that the B.B.C. had scooped that particular pool, and that something had to be done about it. He'd arranged a conference in West Berlin with about half a dozen of the most vitally interested countries. I happen to know because at one time there was some question of my going with him."

"Why West Berlin?"

"Ask me another. Paris—Rome—points South—and I'd have gone like the proverbial shot. But I don't love Germans, Greg—not even Western Germans, bless their little Lutheran hearts. And I don't speak their filthy language. I included myself out."

"A pity—in the circumstances. Now my second question: what do you know of Hargest's domestic background—apart from the facts that he was married and had no children?"

"I wasn't on domestic-fireside terms, Greg. Sorry."

There was a little silence which was broken by Lady Hannington.

"Perhaps after all, dear, I will take the other half of my glass of anisette. Mr. Pellew, I met Mrs. Hargest one day at lunch. I thought it might be as well to know the wife of my son's employer. She struck me as a nice-looking girl—perhaps woman would be more accurate. A good figure and remarkably bright blue eyes. Amiable and well-mannered enough but not brainy. I got the impression that she was not particularly happy."

"Really, Mother!"

"Well—I did. Mr. Pellew is quite intelligent enough to take my opinion for what it's worth."

There was another little silence.

"Waiting for the gossip-scandal of the alcove, Greg?"

"I suppose I am," said Pellew. "I don't like that sort of thing, Humphrey. It's a necessary strand in the pattern all the same."

"Then I'm afraid I can't help you," said Humphrey Clymping. "Office chit-chat was always speculating why

Hargest should have a secretary as alluring as Miss Pretty and treat her like a piece of strictly utilitarian furniture. The amount of overtime she and Miss Plain worked between them would have made the T.U.C.'s hair curl. Between Simon Hargest and the casting-couch there was no relation whatsoever—believe you me!"

"I believe you, Humphrey. Don't overplay the hand."

"Point taken. But there's just one thing, Greg. Hargest got me my job, and I'm taking a salary from Gargantua. I can't work—not even for you—against Hargest's reputation or Gargantua's interests, can I?"

"Fair enough," said Pellew. "Frankly, I've no idea what this business may imply in the long run. Just remember first that for the time being I'm not a policeman; secondly that you remain a free agent. You can opt out any time you like."

"I'll do my best not to take you up on that, Greg."

"*Entendu*. And I think that's about enough in the way of business for one evening. If I come along to Gargantua in the morning will you effect the necessary introduction to your Mr. Gunn?"

"I don't think you'll like him, Humphrey."

"Why do you say that?" asked Pellew sharply.

"I don't know—well, I suppose I do. I find him amusing; and he needles the administrative boys by putting their more pompous memos into his waste-paper basket without reading them. But he's a sarcastic devil—rather oppressively Wyke-hamist. He may try to patronise you."

"Do you know why Hargest chose him for this job?"

"Together in Cairo in the war, I believe."

"What had he done in the interval, Humphrey?"

"I haven't the remotest idea, Greg. And don't start talking about going. We could both do with some more brandy, and Kate's due home any minute now. I'll be in trouble, if she doesn't find you still here. Won't I, Mother?"

Lady Hannington smiled winningly.

"I'm sure Mr. Pellew will stay—won't you, Mr. Pellew?"

"You are right, as usual," said Gregory Pellew.

CHAPTER 4

GARGANTUA AND ROLLO GUNN

The building that housed Gargantua Television was the latest and loftiest of those vast and architecturally characterless oblongs which are rapidly providing London with a new skyline. It had risen upon one of the many South Bank sites which at one time or another had been assigned to the National Theatre. Through the opulent glass of at least twenty of its stories it was possible for its occupants to look down literally upon such old-fashioned landmarks as the Old Vic, and Lambeth Palace, not to mention the Festival Hall and Lord Morrison's Waterloo Bridge. It was streamlined, air-conditioned, unashamedly functional from the power generators in the basement to the self-service staff canteen on the roof. It was entirely administrative. The Gargantua Studios were housed in another great building, which had once been an airship-shed, on the northern outskirts of London. Absence might not actively create fondness for administrators on the part of studio personnel. That it tended to reduce friction had been one of Simon Hargest's sensible ideas.

Pellew's inquiry at the reception-desk was received with a smile as efficient as the make-up on the face of the blonde young woman behind it. After no more delay than was necessitated by a briskly conducted telephone call he was shot skywards in a non-stop lift which gave the impression of being jet-propelled. He was still trying to get his breath back when he found himself in Humphrey Clymping's office: an oblong box of a room containing a desk, three chairs, two telephones, four filing cabinets, and—with some difficulty —Humphrey. Through an open connecting door Pellew could see about half a slightly smaller oblong box in which a secretary was sorting an impressive pile of scripts Roneoed on bright yellow paper.

"Hallo, Greg. Glad to see you on time. Find out if Mr. Gunn's ready for us, Maggie, will you?" Humphrey closed the connecting door, waved a hand vaguely at the two unoccupied chairs, and took a box of cigarettes out of a drawer. "Well, how does it all strike you?"

Pellew lighted a cigarette, and considered.

"Quite hideous. Madly efficient. Rather frightening," was his verdict.

"And all Simon Hargest's own work. That should tell you something about him. I've blazed the trail, Greg. We'll be seeing Rollo any minute now. Whether he'll be co-operative is another story. He's intelligent, and I think he's spotted that there must be something fishy about you."

"Fishy?"

"More than meets the eye, at any rate. He pretty well said as much."

"What did he say?"

"He remarked that programme ideas covered other sins apart from phoney expense accounts. You've been warned."

A buzzer buzzed, and Humphrey picked up a telephone.

"Thanks, Maggie. We'll go right along. Rollo's working in Hargest's office for the time being. That may be helpful as it gives you the chance to look at that part of the background. It's only at the far end of this passage."

The private office of Gargantua's Managing Director had nothing box-like about it. It was more like a suite in a luxury

hotel. It was cushioned from the passage by a room in which
the two secretaries worked: a room roughly six times the size
of Humphrey Clymping's, with a thick pile carpet, and furnishings that were comfortable as well as functional. The
inner sanctum was reached through a door over which were
red and green lights to indicate ENGAGED or FREE. One of
the secretaries—the pretty one—got up as Humphrey and
Pellew came in. The plain one continued to work on a noiseless typewriter without lifting her head.

"Sally Anstruther—Miss Jukes—Mr. Pellew," said
Humphrey. "Can we go in?"

Miss Jukes nodded abruptly. Pellew was conscious of rim-
less pince-nez, mouse-coloured hair, a squareish sensible face,
large ugly hands and a white ruffled blouse. Miss Anstruther
undulated rather than walked to the inner door, and opened it
with the air of a mannequin making her entrance for the
showing of a Collection. A dark tailored suit displayed to
advantage a magnificent figure and beautiful legs. A pale
creamy complexion, greenish eyes with lids discreetly shadowed, too-vivid lips, a heavy charm-bracelet round her left
wrist, black hair elegantly waved, completed a picture that
would have done credit to the cover of *Vogue*. "Mr. Clymping
and Mr. Pellew to see you, Mr. Gunn." The voice was
agreeably low, which made startling an intonation unmistaka-
bly cockney.

The door closed behind them. At the far end of the room
Rollo Gunn was sitting behind the desk that had been Simon
Hargest's. He did not get up. Behind him what was probably
the finest of all views over London went apparently disregarded. In the wall on his left were two doors, which,
as Humphrey explained afterwards, led respectively to a
bathroom-cum-dressing-room, and to a private lift giving
access to an unobtrusive and equally private exit from the
building at street level. Apart from the vast window and the
three doors the walls were lined with book-shelves from floor
to ceiling. There was an Aubusson carpet on the floor. There
were three comfortable arm-chairs, and a low round table

covered with newspapers and magazines. With a certain surprise Pellew noted the absence of either television-set or cocktail cabinet.

"Do sit down," said Rollo Gunn. "I gathered from Clymping that you want to see me, Mr. Pellew. Perhaps you'll tell me why?"

The voice was thin and precise, like everything else about Rollo Gunn: his greyish lips, his nose, his wrists, his eyebrows and his clothes.

"I'm pretty busy," he went on, "as I'm sure you'll appreciate—especially with things as they are at the moment. It'll save time if you'll come straight to the point."

Humphrey looked uneasily at Pellew as they sat down. But Pellew was crossing his legs, apparently quite at ease, and taking a pipe out of his pocket.

"Smoke by all means," said Rollo Gunn. "I may as well tell you, Mr. Pellew, that I had a word with Scotland Yard after Humphrey had talked to me about you. I have an excellent contact there. I know something of your record—which is enviable I admit—but I understand you still belong to the police. So I'm naturally curious."

Pellew by this time had got his pipe going satisfactorily. "Your 'excellent contact,' Mr. Gunn, is not quite up to date. At the moment I am not in the police service. I am making some inquiries privately on the part of a certain insurance company, which must, I'm afraid, be nameless."

Rollo Gunn frowned. "Why didn't you tell me that, Humphrey?"

"Because Humphrey didn't know," said Pellew quickly. "I'll be quite frank with you, Mr. Gunn. It appears that the late Mr. Hargest took out a considerable insurance policy on his life some ten years ago. It was taken out in favour of an individual, who also must be nameless, unknown to Mr. Hargest's family and friends. You see that the whole matter is rather delicate. A considerable sum of money is involved. Suicide would, of course, render the policy invalid."

"I don't understand," said Rollo Gunn impatiently. "The verdict was suicide, and could have been nothing else."

"The individual concerned happens not to agree," said Pellew. "The company is anxious to make sure that there is no likelihood nor possibility of the case being reopened."

There followed a considerable silence, during which Rollo Gunn doodled with a blue pencil on the blotting-pad in front of him; Pellew gazed up at the ceiling through the fumes of his pipe; and Humphrey Clymping wondered just how thoroughly Pellew had prepared this new explanation and thought what a wily devil he was.

"This unnamed individual," said Rollo Gunn at last. "A woman?"

He no longer sounded sarcastic, and Pellew noticed it. "That much I *can* tell you," he replied. "It probably explains the attitude which is anything but reasonable towards the company. It's not a pleasant business, but in the face of the verdict my inquiries are hardly likely to amount to more than a routine inquiry and subsequent confirmation."

There was another silence. Then Rollo Gunn got up from behind the desk, and began to walk up and down the room. It was as if he wanted to talk to himself rather than to his visitors. "Simon Hargest was a great deal more to me than an employer," he said. "He was my dearest friend—and I don't make friends easily. I met him in Cairo during the war, and we worked together. We were two of the chair-borne brigade to whom Montgomery took so much exception. We appreciated such comforts as we could get. We didn't wear funny hats. And we did burn secret files when, in our opinion, there was danger of their being captured by the enemy. I don't pretend that either we or our work were very important. Anyway the war's a long time away—and to me it seems a damned long way further than that."

The sarcasm was creeping back into his voice. "For some years after the war ended I was a bit of a rolling stone. Mostly in America. But Hargest always kept in touch with me—God knows why. In fact, he kept me going more than

27

once when I was on my uppers. I was in a position to supply him with a certain amount of the information he wanted about commercial TV in the States, when he was beginning to lobby for it in this country. I suppose that's why he made a job for me when he started to organise Gargantua." He halted beside Pellew's chair, and stared down at him. "You'll see why I'm upset by what you've told me, Mr. Pellew. I was fond of Hargest. I owed him more than I could ever repay. I don't like the idea of some scandal being stirred up about him now that he's dead by some gold-digging bitch of a woman. Besides, there's Jane Hargest to consider. She's all to pieces as it is. If she doesn't know about this new development, you're not going to drag her into it?"

"I shall have to see her," said Pellew slowly.

"Then find an excuse, and a good one. She was devoted to Simon Hargest—and I believe he was to her. What do you know of this other woman?"

"Nothing. You had no idea that there might be some entanglement of this kind, Mr. Gunn?"

"I certainly hadn't! And I tell you I find it exceedingly hard to believe. Hargest was far too busy a man to have the amount of spare time necessary for romantic intrigue. Besides, he wasn't the type. In this TV racket he was continually in contact with good-looking girls—budding starlets, chorus girls, model girls, typists, the lot. He never looked at one of them twice. I very much doubt if he realised that Sally Anstruther there in his outer office is one of the loveliest girls in London, though all of us in Gargantua knew that she'd have put her eyes on stalks for him."

Gunn went back to his desk and turned round. "Are you sure that we're not jumping to conclusions about this policy, Mr. Pellew? The beneficiary might be an elderly relative, an old servant—"

"Apparently not," said Pellew.

"Then I don't understand it," said Rollo Gunn querulously.

Pellew, who had been intent on relighting his pipe, looked up at him.

"I mustn't take up too much of your time, Mr. Gunn. There are just two other things."

"Well?"

"I shall probably have to ask a few questions of various members of the Gargantua staff—Mr. Hargest's secretaries, for example. I think I can promise you to be reasonably tactful about it. Can I have your official permission?"

"I can't stop you, can I?"

"You can make it considerably more difficult," said Pellew with a smile.

"Well—so long as you don't interfere with them during office hours."

"Many thanks."

"And the other thing?"

"What can you tell me of Mr. Hargest's relations with his board of directors?"

Gunn's lips tightened. His expression was the reverse of encouraging.

"Between these four walls—just a lot of rabbits, only interested in how deep they can get their noses into the parsley! Hargest did the work, and had the ideas. They signed on the dotted line—and were a good many pennies the better. It saved him trouble to deal with a set of rubber stamps with foolish faces, and I don't suppose he wasted an ounce of effort or an hour of his time on them any day of the week."

"All of them?" persisted Pellew.

"Except the Chairman. Quite another pair of shoes. Sir George Farley of Lombard Street and points East. Shrewd and tough as they come."

"Was there any trouble between Sir George and Hargest?"

"Never to my knowledge. Sometimes I thought they were a bit too thick. You don't get much room for manoeuvre in any set-up when the Chairman and the Managing Director always see eye to eye. But that's the way they both seemed to like it."

"Forgive me, Mr. Gunn—this is really an impertinence —but are you to be the new Managing Director?"

"Not even remotely in the running. I'm an efficient subordinate, but I can't run any show, let alone a show this size. And Sir George doesn't like me. My background was too far away from the City of London for too long."

"Do you like Sir George?"

"I admire him. Like? I don't know him well enough to say."

Pellew hoisted himself out of his chair. "I'm most grateful to you, Mr. Gunn. You've been very patient and helpful. I'm sure I can rely on your keeping the subject of this meeting to yourself?"

"I'd like to forget it altogether," said Rollo Gunn. "Please remember that the last thing we want is to start anything in the way of gossip in Gargantua on the subject of poor Hargest's private affairs."

"I can promise you that. Come along, Humphrey."

From behind the big desk Rollo Gunn made Pellew a formal little jerk of a bow. He did not hold out his hand. In the outer office Miss Jukes was still typing as if her life depended on it. Miss Anstruther sped them into the passage with another dazzling smile. They went back to Humphrey's room in silence.

"Coffee-break for you, Maggie—and don't bother to come back for half an hour," said Humphrey to his secretary.

"Thank you, Mr. Clymping. By the way, Mr. Rathbone wants to see you. He said it was urgent."

"Mr. Rathbone always says everything's urgent. It may be for him. It's definitely not for me. Tell Mr. Rathbone to get an idea of his own for a change, give him my love, and tell him I'm half-way to the South of France or Buenos Aires, and that you don't know when I'll be back."

The girl vanished. Humphrey dropped into a chair which creaked under his weight, and looked at Pellew with mock disapproval. "You and your bogus insurance carry-on, Greg!

Ingenious, I hand it to you. But you might have warned me. I might easily have put my foot in it."

"You might. You didn't. I apologise, Humphrey. I only thought of it on my way here this morning. I expected that Gunn would have contacted the Yard. I had to have a 'cover' that held water. Admit I kept my lies to a minimum."

"Greg, your example would corrupt an archangel."

"Which, as you are emphatically no angel, arch or otherwise, is irrelevant. Who is this Rathbone character who seems so anxious for your society?"

"He presents *Here To-day, Gone To-morrow*, but he hasn't the charm of the B.B.C.'s *To-night* team. He grins like a dog, and runs about the city. Talks about his work as 'a mission,' and refers to TV as 'the greatest medium ever of sociological significance.' He is my immediate boss, my heaviest cross, the largest fly in my ointment. Let's forget about him."

"I gather you don't like him much."

"I hate his guts, Greg. Unfortunately he is extremely efficient after his own fashion. I doubt if *Here To-day* would survive without him. So I endure. Contrariwise, what did you think of Rollo Gunn?"

"You mustn't tempt me to make rash judgments on inadequate experience. But I fancy he's a worried man, and an unhappy man."

"He's probably worried," said Humphrey, "because his sponsor is no longer with him, he's got no chance of the managing director job—as he told you himself—and the new Amurath will probably want a new personal assistant of his own choosing."

Pellew nodded.

"But unhappy?" Humphrey continued. "I don't see it. He's an uncomfortable prickly type, with a thin skin and a highly-geared defence mechanism—"

"He's not lovable, Humphrey, and he knows it. I see a beautiful Biro and a virgin scribbling pad on your desk. Would you mind writing down for me a list of questions to which I'd like to know the right answers."

"Right you are. Go ahead."

"*One.* Why was the Eurovision conference held in West Berlin of all places, and why did a man in Hargest's position have to go to it himself?"

"I told you, Greg. Hargest had a special 'thing' about Eurovision. He was always talking about its importance. He'd fixed this particular meeting. He'd been invited to chair it. He had to go."

"West Berlin still nags at my imagination. It's a brash and comfortless city. However—

"*Two.* Was Gunn as genuinely attached to Hargest as he made out? The patron with the helping hand permanently outstretched usually gets service. I doubt if he gets real gratitude, still less affection. Comment?"

"I can only say that they always seemed friendly when I saw them together—which wasn't often."

"*Three.* What was the function of the Anstruther glamour-puss in that office, if Hargest was the icicle Gunn implied?"

"Window-dressing, Greg. Most of Hargest's callers were male, and probably reacted favourably to the sight of an unusually attractive girl. Besides Sally's no fool, and lots more efficient than she looks. But I don't mind taking her out to dinner, at your expense, and seeing what I can find out."

"You're forgetting, Humphrey, that you are now a respectable married man. I shall take Miss Anstruther out to dinner —if she'll come."

"She'll come all right," said Humphrey gloomily, "if you pick the right income-group restaurant."

"*Four.* Were the relations of Mr. and Mrs. Hargest as idyllic as Gunn seemed to think?"

"I haven't a clue."

"Then it'll be your job to try and find one, Humphrey. You can fake up an excuse to go and see Mrs. Hargest, can't you?"

"I suppose so."

"You'll presumably be entering a house of sorrow, but I

trust you'll manage a more cheerful expression than that to take with you."

Humphrey grinned.

"Yes—but don't overdo it. *Five*. What was the real situation between Hargest and his Chairman? As described by Gunn it sounded almost too good to be quite true."

"If you want him interviewed, Greg, you can do it yourself. He may have been a lamb with Hargest. His reputation is definitely that of a tiger."

"I shall go and look him straight between the eyes. It may not be pleasant, so I'll try and get it over with straight away. I imagine your Mr. Rathbone will be occupying your energies for the time being?"

"He will—blast him! Work on *Here To-day*, like a woman's, is never done—and Hamish Rathbone never tires of rubbing in the fact. To do him justice he does at least ten hours regular on it himself, and probably dreams about it all night."

"By the way, add Miss Jukes' name with a large query after it to that list."

"I don't know a thing about her. I expect I can get her personal file through Gunn, if you like."

"I do like. I think that's all for the moment."

Humphrey put his feet up on his desk with a crash. "Before you go, Greg—what about the actual circumstances of Hargest's death? Is there any genuine reason to doubt that he killed himself?"

"Absolutely none, on the face of it. He came back from Berlin on the Wednesday evening. During the Thursday and Friday he was working here as usual. On the Friday evening he dined at home with his wife, and went to bed early— about ten—saying that he was still feeling tired after his journey, and would sleep in his dressing-room. He was found dead on—not in—his bed the next morning, wearing pyjamas, a dressing-gown and bedroom slippers. On the bedtable was a half-empty bottle of whisky and a silver box which had contained sleeping-pills. The post-mortem—and it was carried out by an absolutely reliable medico—confirmed that the cause of death was a large quantity of alcohol taken on top of a heavy dose of barbiturates. The body was perfectly healthy, and there was no trace of violence. No, Humphrey. I think we can take it that Hargest did it all right. What we're after is why—not how. And there are more ways of murdering a man than by bashing him over the head, cutting his throat, or putting arsenic in his coffee. There's what Captain Liddell Hart calls 'the strategy of Indirect Approach.' It's still ninety to one on his having cracked up under the strain of overwork or an emotional brain-storm, or a combination of the two. Is the answer in that penthouse of his in Chester Square, here in Gargantua, or in West Berlin?"

"As simple as that," said Humphrey sarcastically.

The door behind Pellew was flung violently open. A fat young man with bright red hair wearing a bright green polo-necked sweater, dark green corduroy trousers, shabby suède shoes, and a most unamiable expression stood in the doorway and glared at Humphrey Clymping.

"What did I tell you?" said the latter resignedly. "Anything I can do for you, Hamish? By the way, meet Gregory Pellew."

Hamish Rathbone ignored the introduction.

"You can do quite a lot," he said savagely, "if I can drag you away from your urgent personal affairs. The whole programme's in the most god-awful mess!"

"Was it ever anything else?" inquired Humphrey.

"When I had people working on it who worked! Dermot can't get back from his bloody lighthouse assignment because a storm's blown up in the Bristol Channel. Eric was late getting to London Airport and missed the interview with Miss Universe. And we seem to have lost Andrew altogether. We're three items short, Humphrey, and I'd be glad if you'd start something pronto!"

Humphrey Clymping got up lazily, and stretched hugely. "I shouldn't panic if I were you, Ham. The lighthouse story

34

was always a rotten one. You can bet Miss Universe is as dumb as they come. And Andrew's total loss will save us in drinks a lot more than he's worth."

Rathbone snorted angrily, but Humphrey went on before he could speak: "My car's in the park—you know that rather vulgar scarlet convertible job. Run along down to it, and I'll join you in five minutes. We'll think up ten good notions on the way out to the Studios."

To Pellew's surprise Rathbone nodded and went out, slamming the door behind him.

"You see, Greg—that's my line—holding up the pillars of the temple like Atlas—or was it Samson? And you expect me to be your Man Friday into the bargain."

"I do. Don't forget that variety of occupation makes men out of beasts. Take that list of questions with you, Humphrey, and let your mother see it when you get home. I want to keep her in the picture. I'll try to look in on Seven Dials sometime to-night, probably rather late. Now go and look after your excitable young friend. I'll find my own way out."

Humphrey Clymping picked up his brief-case, put a battered tweed hat on the back of his head, clapped Pellew affectionately on the shoulder, and departed.

A few minutes later Pellew followed him into the passage. But instead of turning left towards the lifts he turned right towards the Managing Director's outer office, and knocked on its door. Luck was with him. He found Sally Anstruther alone. Miss Jukes was, presumably, engaged with her employer. It might have vexed Humphrey—though it would not really have surprised him—had he known how short a time it took Pellew to persuade Miss Anstruther to dine with him that evening at the Mirabel. Miss Anstruther liked men who knew one restaurant from another. She also liked men with good figures, greying dark hair, and no suspicion of glint in their eyes. And, when he cared to exercise it, Gregory Pellew had considerable charm, and knew more about women than most people, certainly than Humphrey, had ever guessed.

CHAPTER 5

SIR GEORGE FARLEY

Pellew did not bother about "cover" as far as interviewing Sir George Farley was concerned. As he saw it, this was strictly a case for recognised Establishment technique: a telephone call to the Commander's private address, to be followed by a second call from the Commander to Sir George, asking him to see Pellew on a strictly private matter. There was, of course, the risk that Sir George might discuss the interview later with Rollo Gunn. Pellew decided such a development unlikely and the risk worth taking. Within half an hour of his leaving the Gargantua building he learned that he could see Sir George in his City office at three that afternoon.

Apart from his chairmanship of Gargantua TV Sir George was senior partner of an old private bank—the type of concern which looks after the affairs of old-fashioned country families—and director of half a dozen companies both successful and highly reputable. It was in his private room at the bank that he received Pellew: a sombre panelled room with Empire furniture, and a single picture above the fireplace: a good early eighteenth-century portrait of the bank's founder, clean-shaven, prim-faced, and evidently Puritan.

Sir George presented a remarkable contrast to his predecessor. He wore a fine snow-white dragoon's moustache, and his eyebrows twisted upwards as though in sympathy. His fat cheeks were mottled inclined to mulberry. He had a thick neck and thick legs with a square body and square shoulders. The first impression that he made was rather that of the conventional general of musical comedy: one of explosively harmless terrorism. He might almost have been expected to burst out with "The Army's going to the dogs, sir! Pass the port!" On the other hand his chin was good, his nose better. His hands—they were manicured—looked capable. If his eyes were globular, their glance was shrewd.

He gave Pellew a chair; handed him a Manila cheroot; and took up a solid stance under the portrait, as though warming his hinder parts at the nonexistent fire.

"Want to talk about poor Hargest, hey? Well, Mr. Pellew, you've come to the right man. Glad to know someone's still interested. Bad business—that inquest. Damned fool—that coroner. I'd been thinking of making some inquiries myself. Don't know what Gargantua's going to do without him. No one's supposed to be irreplaceable nowadays—I know that. But Hargest was. He made the show. He ran the show. Worked like a slave, and loved every minute of it. Capital company into the bargain. Liked his food and could take his liquor. Damned sorry for that wife of his—a pretty woman. D'you know her?"

"Not yet."

"Hum—I see. You'll handle her with kid gloves, hey? She's badly broken up. But it's Hargest you want to hear about, hey?"

"I'd be grateful for anything you can tell me, Sir George."

"Hardly know where to begin. Met him first when he was standing for the House. I was an M.P. then—had been for fifteen years—God knows why, damned talking-shop!—and Hargest's constituency was next to mine. Central Office asked me to rally round and give him a hand. Did my best—not that he needed it. Had the place in his pocket in a fortnight,

38

and increased the majority by over five thousand. Wonderful gift of the gab, and a grasp of detail I've never seen equalled in my life. Never forgot a face, and always knew his own mind. I was glad and proud to make friends with him. That cheroot all right, hey?"

"First-rate, thanks."

Sir George grunted approvingly, and twisted his moustache. "Hargest pulled me in on the party when he was looking for the financial backing for Gargantua. We'd both been in the movement that lobbied for commercial television—and there weren't many of those boys like Hargest I can tell you! All most of them were after was a chance to get butter on one side of their bread and honey on the other. And they didn't care how sticky they got their fingers either!" He paused, and lighted a cheroot for himself.

Pellew, whose opinion of Sir George was improving with every sentence, took his courage in both hands. "Don't think I'm being offensive, sir," he said, "but I'm bound to ask you one question. You'll see its obvious relevance I know."

"Fire away. Is Gargantua quite sound? Is that it, hey?"

"That's just it."

"I could refer you to the price of the shares, Mr. Pellew. I assure you they give a perfectly true picture. There was nothing on that front for Hargest to worry about. Sound as a bell, and expanding all the time. He knew his job. Learned from the other fellows' mistakes, and wasn't scared to admit it when he made his own. His private finances were more than all right, too. He banked here with us. I know."

"Had he any particular formula for success—apart from general outstanding ability?"

"Hargest didn't like slogans. Said they were invented to save people the trouble of thinking. Thought up two capital ones all the same. Top-grade TV Advertising for Top-grade Goods; and Less Television and Better. D'you know Gargantua started operations with only a news service plus two hours of programmes an evening? We only carry six hours now: one first-rate play, one first-rate variety show, one first-rate concert, one outstanding topical affairs programme—those are the highlights of every week, and audiences of genuinely interested viewers can't afford to miss them. No third-rate imported westerns. No dug-up British films which failed to get distribution when they were originally made. No second-hand imitations of our competitors' successes. Gargantua finds or makes its own. All Hargest's policy, Mr. Pellew. He made us start slow and build sure. He didn't talk hot air about the Significance, and the Importance, and the Golden Future of Television. But he believed in all three, and worked for them."

"Certainly not the accepted approach," said Pellew slowly. "He must have had difficulties in getting it accepted."

"Not by me," said Sir George cheerfully. "Thinking of the other directors, hey? Hargest and I knew how to keep them in their places."

"Actually I was thinking of the programme staff, Sir George. Most of the TV characters I've met have been sold on the ideal of twenty-four hours' output a day plus giving the morons what they want."

"Hargest had studied the beginnings of the B.B.C.," said Sir George. "Reith knew a thing or two—though he mayn't have been all that tactful in putting those things over. You can get decent standards accepted, if you stick to your guns. Good programmes can be popular programmes, with the right men in charge, enough money, and enough rehearsal. Standards pay off in prestige and goodwill. All that was true of broadcasting in sound. And TV is broadcasting—though a lot of idiots try to turn it into the Home Bioscope or Hollywood in the Parlour. We've had some of 'em in Gargantua."

"Had? You mean Hargest got rid of them?"

"Never suffered fools gladly. Hired generously, and fired ruthlessly. Smallest proportion of duds in an organisation I've ever known."

"But there are some."

"Irreducible minimum." Sir George shrugged his shoulders. "Might be worth your while to go down to the

Studios, hey? Take the temperature there for yourself. Care for a note to the Programme Director?"

"Many thanks."

"Heard of him, perhaps? James Ballantyne. Queer sort of fellow. As much a fanatic about programmes as Hargest was about Gargantua."

"Did he and Hargest get on?"

"Yes—and no. Ballantyne's a clever devil, knows his technical business from A to Z, and is as keen as mustard. But he likes his own way."

"Like Hargest?"

"I'd say more so. Hargest knew when to go slow. Ballantyne seems to enjoy bashing his head against walls. Also he's touchy—status and that sort of nonsense. Redbrick background, and a bit too proud of it."

"I must meet Mr. Ballantyne."

"Do. But don't get any wrong ideas, Mr. Pellew. Ballantyne and Hargest didn't run easily in double harness. Hargest had notions for programmes, and they were seldom the same as Ballantyne's. There were occasional fireworks. Never saw a sign of personal bad feeling all the same."

Pellew scratched his jaw.

"Sir George—you can't think of any individual hired and fired by Hargest who might have left Gargantua with an exaggerated sense of personal grievance?"

"'Fraid I can't. Memory for details not what it was. You might try Mr. Gunn. He was Hargest's liaison with the personnel manager. He'd probably know."

"Many thanks. I won't bother you again unless I have to."

"Happy to see you, Mr. Pellew. But discretion the better part, hey?"

"I quite understand, Sir George. I assure you this isn't the sort of assignment I'd have chosen for myself."

"That Commander fellow at the Yard seems to think quite a lot of you, hey? I'm inclined to agree with him. Let me know how you get on. Where shall I send you the note for Ballantyne?"

Pellew gave the address of the unpretentious three-roomed flat off the Marylebone High Street, where he slept, breakfasted, and occasionally spent an evening. Then he went on his way, his fingers tingling from Sir George's uncommonly powerful handshake.

He was wondering, with a certain pleasurable anticipation, how best to exploit his evening engagement with Miss Sally Anstruther; how far he would be justified in going to do so.

CHAPTER 6
JANE HARGEST

Meanwhile Humphrey Clymping had been spending a lively afternoon at the Gargantua Studios, for the most part in the company of Hamish Rathbone and the three other principal members of *Here To-day, Gone To-morrow* unit: a cadaverous young Welshman with the voice of a lay-preacher and an unrivalled capacity for beer; a middle-aged lady, widow of an Oxford don, who combined the appearance of the White Queen with an encyclopædic memory; and a former gossip-column writer, whose paper had recently died on him, leaving him with a permanently disillusioned expression and exaggerated ideas on the subject of expense-accounts.

Suggestion after suggestion was brought up, mulled over, argued about, and discarded. Innumerable cigarettes were smoked. Quantities of the strongest possible tea were consumed. Telephones tinkled. Buzzers buzzed. Special messengers were dispatched on fruitless errands. Stenographers were reduced to tears—in one case to hysterics. Wild-eyed studio managers and phlegmatic scenic designers looked in, and for the most part hurriedly went on. Everything, in fact, was perfectly normal.

Just before five o'clock Humphrey found himself alone. Hamish Rathbone had been summoned to the august presence of Mr. James Ballantyne. The Welshman had been sent off to the Carlton Towers to interview a celebrated Negro band-leader. The White Queen had departed unobtrusively to verify references in a library in the basement. And the ex-gossip writer had flown, like a homing pigeon, to Fleet Street where he would arrange a debate on *The Housewife and Her Hat* between the editor of a woman's magazine and the most recently wedded viscountess.

Humphrey looked with disfavour at the dirty cups, the loaded ash-trays, the scattered and crumpled sheets of scribbling paper, finally at the watch on his wrist. Then he opened the window and drew a deep breath. By contrast his designed call upon Simon Hargest's widow, on first consideration so disagreeable, seemed positively desirable. He could just about make it. Humphrey believed—regrettably enough—that traffic regulations were made for men, not men for traffic regulations. The red convertible shot southwards along the road into London at a speed which would have curled the average driver's hair. Humphrey was an excellent driver. He waved cheerfully at lorries. He sang at buses. He grinned at pedestrians. He drew fresh air gratefully into his lungs. Despite rush-hour traffic he reached Chester Square as Big Ben was striking a quarter to six.

A lift, noiseless and automatic, carried Humphrey to the top floor of one of those blocks of super-luxury flats which are seen more frequently on the films than in real life. Mrs. Hargest's door was opened by a trim little sloe-eyed maid. Humphrey felt that her glance of inspection did not approve. He would have done better to have changed his clothes on his way from the Studios. Lady Hannington would certainly have thought so.

Was Mrs. Hargest at home? Mrs. Hargest was at home —but she was seeing no one. Humphrey smiled his most distracting smile, and gave his name. Perhaps the maid would be kind enough to take it to Mrs. Hargest? He had come straight from the Gargantua Studios, and his business was rather urgent. The last thing he wanted to do was to bother Mrs. Hargest, but if she would spare him ten minutes he would be more grateful than he could say.

The maid hesitated. If Humphrey had offered her the pound note which he had kept handy in his pocket, she would have shut the door in his face. But she looked at his smile, she looked at his eye-lashes, hesitated again and was lost. She would see what Mrs. Hargest said.

Humphrey was left to cool his heels in a small but charming sitting-room, distinguished by three good modern French paintings admirably set off by a wall-paper of pale Japanese gold. He walked over to the big double window, which offered a superb view southeastward across the roofs of Belgravia. In the far distance the top stories of the Gargantua Building were just visible.

Slant-wise across one corner by the window stood an elegant French escritoire, and on it a cabinet photograph in a silver frame of Simon Hargest. Humphrey studied it carefully and curiously. Odd—it looked dead; as dead as its original. Yet in his limited experience of Hargest no man could have been more vital. Of this vitality the photograph held no hint. It was a collection of features—nothing more. The features were good: straight nose; firm chin; lips neither too full nor too thin; small ears set close to the head; eyes widely-spaced. But the expression said nothing. The face was a mask. A studio portrait tended to be flat and dull and consciously posed. But Humphrey, remembering Hargest as he had seen him that night at Oxford overwhelming undergraduates with his charm, and as he had seen him more recently in the Gargantua offices ruling the whirlwind and directing the storm, stared at the photograph incredulously. Personality was just not there. . . .

"Mr. Clymping?"

Humphrey swung round. He faced a slim woman dressed entirely in black relieved only by a single string of pearls. She had very fair hair; enormous blue eyes; a thin neck that reminded him of the tragic Princesse de Lamballe. She gave an impression of extreme fragility; that wrists and ankles could almost be snapped like match-sticks. Her hands were small and very white, with restless fingers.

"Do sit down, Mr. Clymping. Perhaps you'd care for a drink?"

"No, thanks. I feel I owe you an apology, breaking in on you out of the blue like this."

"I imagine it's something to do with Gargantua. The world's work has to go on. I know that. I learned from Simon."

Tears were very close behind her grave quiet tones. Humphrey, already feeling a considerable cad, found this patient courtesy, this childlike determined behaviour, almost unendurable.

"I won't keep you long, Mrs. Hargest," he said quickly. "I wondered if you'd come across a memorandum on programme staff reorganisation among your husband's papers: rather a bulky document marked *Confidential*. It can't be found in the office, and it was suggested that he might have taken it home with him."

Jane Hargest shook her head. "I don't think so. Simon's solicitor, and the private secretary who worked here for him, sorted out everything in his desk and his brief-case. As far as I know there was nothing about Gargantua at all. He was rather meticulous about not bringing papers home with him, as a matter of fact."

"I see," said Humphrey blankly. He had hoped that instituting search for this non-existent document might have led him to be invited to go through Hargest's desk. Not that he would have known what to look for, had he been given the chance.

He rose to his feet. Jane Hargest did not move. "Did Mr. Gunn send you?" she asked.

"No," admitted Humphrey reluctantly.

"It was your own idea, Mr. Clymping? Wasn't it rather a strange one?"

46

"I suppose it was."

"Did such a document ever exist?"

There was no longer any suspicion of tears in the big blue eyes. They were hard and wary, and her hands clasped each other tightly. "You invented an excuse to come and see me, didn't you? Will you tell me why?"

Humphrey said nothing. What at that moment he thought of Gregory Pellew is not printable.

"Not very—chivalrous, was it? But perhaps I'm rather old-fashioned. Private curiosity? Or are you playing jackal for some newspaper? I've met your mother, Mr. Clymping. I shouldn't have expected a son of hers to behave like this. Were you going to tell her about it?"

Humphrey made up his mind that the best must be made of a bad job. "I suppose it could be called curiosity," he said. "It's not as bad as it sounds. I owed your husband a great deal. I admired him very much. I did want to see you. I'd like you to believe that I wanted to be helpful. People need help sometimes at a time like this."

She dropped her head on to her hands with a smothered sob, and he saw tears trickling between her fingers.

"I'm sorry. I'll go," muttered Humphrey.

She looked up at him miserably.

"I don't know what to believe. Nothing seems real any more. We were so happy, Simon and I. Everything was so—so good. I've wanted to talk about it, but how could I? First there were the doctors and their jargon—then the police—then the solicitors—all asking me questions I couldn't answer—how could I account for what had happened? I couldn't. There was no reason. He wasn't ill. He'd always worked hard, and enjoyed it. There were no money troubles. It was so senseless—and so utterly unlike him. He was tired when he got back from Germany, but that was natural enough. He said they'd had bad weather on the return flight, and been bumped about a good deal. And those conferences are always exhausting. He was just as usual, except that he went to bed early that night."

47

"He had two days in the office after he came back. He gave you no hint of any trouble there that was worrying him?"

"Absolutely none. He didn't talk to me much about Gargantua. I think he was afraid it might bore me. I'm not clever about business affairs, and he preferred it that way. He told me once that he didn't want to spend his evenings talking about what he'd done all day. It would be equivalent to doing a lot of boring things twice over."

"Not such a bad theory either."

Jane Hargest dropped her hands back into her lap, and closed her eyes for a moment. She looked more than ever fragile and defenceless. It was clear enough why such contrasting characters as Rollo Gunn and Sir George Farley were at one in feeling protective towards her. Yet there was a vein of steel in the fragility, as Humphrey had been shown, and as he watched her he became aware of something that qualified the defencelessness: an attractiveness curiously sensual, such as is found sometimes in tubercular subjects. The delicately painted lips were perhaps too full. The blue eyes seemed to owe their brilliance to more than tears.

"Tell me," she said suddenly, "did *you* know of anything that had happened in the office which could have been worrying Simon?"

"I'm in no position to know, Mrs. Hargest. Too much of a new boy altogether. But Rollo Gunn would have known, and he didn't seem to think so."

"You've discussed things with Mr. Gunn?"

"I've got to know him fairly well," said Humphrey defensively.

Jane Hargest stood up. "Were you offering to help him, just as you've offered to help me, Mr. Clymping? Did your curiosity extend to my husband's secretaries as well as to his personal assistant? Miss Jukes, I'm sure, would have told you to mind your own business. But Miss Anstruther might be more accommodating. I must admit I've wondered more than once how that young lady dresses as she does on a secretary's

48

salary. But of course she doesn't. Not with her obvious attractions."

The counter-attack had been so sudden that for the moment Humphrey was staggered. Then he felt first aggrieved, then angry. When he had arrived in the flat he had been blatantly in the wrong. He had as good as admitted it. He had been as frank with the woman as he could. He had felt genuinely glad at the idea of being helpful to her. Now the claws had come out with a vengeance! Well—two could play at that game.

"Did you ever discuss Miss Anstruther with your husband, Mrs. Hargest?"

Afterwards he admitted that he only got what he deserved. What he got was a stinging blow across the face. He made Jane Hargest a little bow; turned on his heel; and left the flat by so much the wiser.

CHAPTER 7

SALLY ANSTRUTHER

If Humphrey Clymping could have been a fly on the wall of
Sally Anstruther's flat later that evening, his sense of grievance would have been notably—and comprehensibly—increased. For he would have witnessed Miss Anstruther and
Inspector Pellew getting along like the proverbial house on
fire.

Dinner at the Mirabel had fulfilled every expectation.
(The first thing Pellew had noticed was that Miss Anstruther
was no stranger to the head waiter.) The sea-trout, the
chicken mayonnaise, and the lemon soufflé were all equally
beyond criticism. Miss Anstruther had appreciated her mar-
tini, but refused a second; expressed preference for white
burgundy as against champagne, for brandy as against coin-
treau. She talked quietly, and she looked a picture: the sort of
picture which, in a restaurant, drives women to hurried use
of their compacts while attracting furtive glances from their
escorts. In contrast with her appearance in the office she wore
a simple black cocktail dress, and the minimum of make-up.
Her only jewellery was the gold watch on her wrist, and a
rather large oblong topaz pendant on a thin gold chain.

Pellew was in no hurry to force the pace. He was an excellent listener, and he was quite happy to sit and enjoy looking at the girl across the table; gradually to gain her confidence by what appeared to be an absorbing interest in her account of her childhood—she had been orphaned by an air-raid at the age of two—her adoption by a good-hearted elderly couple in the East End—where she cheerfully admitted she had acquired her cockney accent—her winning of a beauty competition at Margate when she was sixteen—"in those days I can tell you, Mr. Pellew, I looked more than somewhat in a one-piece"—her first job as a cinema usherette.

"Did you like it, Miss Anstruther?"

"Couldn't you call me Sally? It's more friendly."

"With pleasure. My name's Gregory."

Sally wrinkled her nose. A stuffy sort of name, disappointing. Then she remembered Mr. Peck and felt better about it.

"I liked the films all right. It was hard on your feet though. And you get tired of being pinched on the behind by chaps in the dark. So I tried the rag-trade—modelling—you know."

"I know. Was that any better?"

"It's nice wearing the clothes. But most of the girls are shocking jealous. And it's hard work—a lot harder than you'd think from the papers. You get a good many passes made too, and you haven't the time as a rule to find out whether you fancy them or not. And there's no future in it, unless you can get married. So I managed some evening classes for dictation and taught myself to type. I thought I'd like to do some sitting down for a change."

"And then?"

"I started off as secretary to the manager of one of the houses I'd modelled for. But he got a bit silly about me, and his wife didn't seem to like it. Then one day I read a whole lot about Gargantua, and I'd been watching the telly a lot, so

I thought it might be fun to work there. I got taken into the pool on trial for three months."

"How did you get on with Mr. Hargest?"

"I was sent up to him one day to do a rush job and he seemed satisfied. A week or two later one of his regular girls left, and he asked for me. Lucky—I should say I was!"

"You liked working for him?"

She bent her head over her plate, concentrating industriously upon the chicken mayonnaise.

"I loved him," she said, looking up again suddenly. There were tears in her eyes.

"You—what?"

"Nothing silly or soppy, of course. He was married, and he wasn't the sort of man to notice a girl like me—except that he was always nice and considerate. Busy isn't the word. I never knew anyone work as he did. And never got in a stew —never lost his temper. He was wonderful."

"Was that the general opinion of the staff?"

"I should say it was. Take Rollo now—Mr. Gunn you know. There wasn't a thing in the world he wouldn't have done for Mr. Hargest. Jukes, too—she keeps herself very much to herself, and most people think she's a cross between a dictaphone and a filing-cabinet. But for Mr. Hargest it was service with a smile, believe you me!"

"I believe you, Sally. But we mustn't talk too much 'shop' and waste the evening. What would you like to do after dinner?"

The girl looked him straight in the eyes for perhaps half a minute, and Pellew had the uncomfortable impression of being very shrewdly considered and summed up. Then she smiled enchantingly.

"I'm not crazy about the pictures nowadays," she said. "I can't make head or tail of most of the plays, and the others— well, when I was a kid I saw all I wanted of Kitchen-sinks with cockroaches, and girls who never washed their hair, and boys who talked your head off and never did a stroke of work

53

and thought themselves big shots. And I don't really care for dancing after a day in the office."

"You mean you're tired and would like to go home early? Admit it if you are. I shouldn't blame you."

"It's not that, Gregory. I was wondering if you'd like me to make you some coffee in my flat—"

"And if the suggestion might give me the wrong ideas?"

"No," said Sally with decision. "I've learned not to make that sort of mistake about men. I can always tell. Besides I live with a girl friend—but she's out to-night."

"I should love to come, Sally. It's a deal."

A taxi took them to one of those sprawling blocks of flats in St. John's Wood which always reminded Pellew disagreeably of Her Majesty's Prisons, so featureless was their design. He had expected an attic "just off" Curzon Street; the decayed gentility of a Kensington villa; or the dubious reputability of Maida Vale. "Come in and make yourself at home," said Sally. "You mustn't mind the mess. My girl friend's the brainy type. She works at the Poly, and never puts anything away. I'll just make the coffee." She disappeared into the kitchenette.

Pellew sank into a shabby but comfortable wicker armchair, and looked about him with interest. There was an ink-stained table by the window, with an old-fashioned typewriter and a pile of note-books. On the shelf over the electric fire was a large family of china pigs graded in descending sizes, all sharing the same blank expression. There were three bookshelves, two of them filled with more or less battered paperbacks, the third with text-books and what looked like a complete set of Galsworthy's novels. On one hard chair was a pile of fashion magazines; on another a collection of feminine garments awaited repair. The carpet was worn; the curtains were faded. Above the pigs hung an indifferent reproduction of one of Van Gogh's flower paintings. Whether Sally Anstruther was what she made herself out to be or not, her background was entirely convincing.

She came back with the coffee, and put down the tray on

the table, pushing the Polytechnic note-books cheerfully on to the floor. The fashion magazines followed them, and she sat down.

"How do you like it? Milk?"

"Black—and sugar, please."

"I'm afraid I can't give you a drink. We don't keep any in the flat."

"Principle, or precaution?"

"Too expensive. Gregory, why did you ask me to come out with you to-night?"

"I wanted to talk to you—and I thought you looked very pretty. Why did you come, Sally?"

"I suppose I was curious. And I like men a lot better than boys."

"Oh? Why?"

Sally laughed. "Boys get so silly at the drop of a hat. They've almost always got only one idea in their head—always the same idea, and they've not even thought it up for themselves. They get it from the pictures or the telly. They get red in the face, and their hands get moist. It's so boring. Of course, Toby's different."

"Toby?"

"Toby Scott. He's a producer's assistant down at the Studios. I met him when he came to see Mr. Hargest about getting a bonus he'd been given for a specially good job of work. I go out with him sometimes when he's free of an evening, which isn't often. He's mad keen about his programmes—talks all the time about camera-angles, and the artistic temperament, and dialogue building; stuff like that which I don't understand half the time. But I like him."

Pellew made a mental note to keep an eye open for Toby Scott when he visited the Studios and Mr. James Ballantyne.

"More coffee?"

"No thanks. Tell me some more about your work for Mr. Hargest, Sally."

The girl frowned. "Why do you want to know?"

"I'm interested. Hargest was a fascinating character, to

judge by what one read about him. How did you and Miss Jukes split the work?"

"Oh, Jukes did the tricky stuff, naturally. I arranged the appointments and the interviews and did the private letters. You never knew such a man for letters. And I got his theatre tickets, and reminded him to have his hair cut and things like that."

"And Miss Jukes?"

"She did the office memos and reports for the board. She went to meetings and took the minutes. And she looked after the intercom and the tape-recorder."

"Come again, Sally."

"You know what a tape-recorder is. Jukes has one in our office to keep a recording of interviews."

Pellew sat up.

"You mean that Hargest had microphones in his room, and had recordings made on tape of what was said by the people who came to see him?"

"That's it. Just for reference."

"And Miss Jukes kept them?"

"Only for a few weeks. Then they were destroyed, unless Mr. Hargest gave special instructions."

"I see. Where were they kept?"

"In a special cabinet in our office. Jukes and Mr. Hargest had duplicate keys."

"Do you think that the people concerned knew that those interviews were being recorded, Sally?"

"I haven't a clue. I expect so. We didn't talk about it, of course."

"I'm sure," said Pellew, "that you're both the pink of discretion."

"Jukes is an oyster," said Sally. "Speaks when she's spoken to, does as she's bid. I like a good natter—but I can keep my mouth shut. At least I thought I could."

And she smiled disarmingly at Pellew.

"If Miss Jukes is an oyster, Sally, I'm a sponge. It's part of my job. I think I shall have to see Miss Jukes all the same."

"Don't be surprised if she gives you the brush-off in a big way. What is your job, Gregory?"

"Well—it varies."

"If it wasn't for your manners," said Sally frankly, "I'd think you were one of those 'private eye' characters, asking all those questions."

"I know. It's a bad habit. Tell me one more thing, Sally, and then I'll go home. Why do you get yourself up like a filmstar when you're in the Gargantua office?"

"What's wrong with it? You said I looked pretty."

"You look much prettier to-night with much less war paint and much simpler clothes."

Sally pursed her lips and frowned, evidently thinking it out. "I think it started as a sort of joke really. When I got the job in Mr. Hargest's office Mr. Gunn made some crack about being glad that they hadn't got another Jukes, and that he hoped I'd dress up to my looks. And I've still got my rag-trade contacts, so I can get good clothes cheaper than you'd believe. And Mr. Hargest said something one day about my brightening the eyes of a lot of tired business men —so I suppose I piled it on a bit. And it shocked Jukes, which was fun."

"I see," said Pellew. "By the way, what did you think of Mrs. Hargest?"

"I only saw her twice—maybe three times. She has style, Gregory—the genuine article. She did make me feel a bit common and over-dressed if you like. Very quiet she was, and lovely manners. I thought she looked a bit sad. I expect she thought Mr. Hargest was working too hard and so she couldn't see as much of him as she'd have liked."

Pellew got up and held out his hand. "Thank you for coming, Sally. I've enjoyed this evening."

"So have I," said Sally frankly. "Could we have another sometime do you think?"

"I do think. Emphatically so. Can I ring you up at your office?"

"Do that, Gregory. I'm not supposed to take personal

calls, and it annoys Jukes when I do. So it's fun. Good night."

For an instant he felt more than half inclined to kiss her, rather as one kisses a child affectionately after playing a game. He was pretty sure, too, that she would not mind. However, he resisted temptation and went on his way. It was with something of a shock that he found himself thinking more about Sally Anstruther than wondering about Humphrey Clymping's activities since they had parted.

CHAPTER 8

REVIEW BY LADY HANNINGTON

Humphrey's reception of Pellew, when the latter reached Seven Dials a little after eleven that night, was the reverse of encouraging. Kate Clymping, it appeared, had gone to bed after telling her husband in no uncertain terms that in her opinion he would do better to do one job at a time and do it properly. (It must be pleaded in Kate's defence that she had had a trying evening at the theatre. When already dressed and made-up to play for the leading lady whom she was under-studying, the latter had apparently forgotten that she was supposed to be prostrated with a migraine, and had turned up five minutes before the rise of the curtain.) Lady Hannington had been even more definite, and a great deal more crushing.

"As far as she's concerned," said Humphrey, leading the way into the sitting-room, and making for the drinks on the piano with more haste than was quite decent, "I'm properly in the doghouse. In fact we both are. She doesn't think we've been behaving like gentlemen."

"Nor have you," said Lady Hannington from the doorway behind them. Humphrey continued to pour out the whisky, but Pellew turned round. He also smiled. He found it easy to smile whenever he looked at Lady Hannington. She might so easily have stepped out of *Cranford*, with her smooth, delicate complexion, her roundabout little figure, the shawl about her shoulders, and her beautifully-kept hands. The perennially auburn hair alone belied her age and spoiled the picture. And dye considered in connection with Lady Hannington seemed a thought so blasphemous as almost to deny possibility.

"And it's not the least bit of good your smiling at me like that, Mr. Pellew. You're not going to get round me with that charm of yours. I'm never surprised when Humphrey does anything foolish. And when he does things I disapprove of I'm liable to find excuses for him. I'm his mother. I confess I thought better of you. Humphrey—give me a glass of that anisette."

"I thought you'd gone up to bed, Mother."

"I had," said Lady Hannington; and sat down. "I heard your voices in the hall. If you propose to sit up half the night drinking, and discussing this deplorable affair, you'll drink less and discuss more if I'm with you."

"That," said Humphrey with a grimace, "is unanswerable." He handed the glasses, and he and Pellew sat down.

"I'm sorry if we've got into your bad books," said Pellew. "I don't like these inquiries any better than you do. All the same they have to be made."

"The Gunn man and Sir George Farley I can understand. To worry Mrs. Hargest just now seems to me frankly persecution. Humphrey deserved to have his face slapped. And I notice that of the two secretaries, Mr. Pellew, you chose to start on the good-looking one, when it must be long odds that it's the plain one who's likely to know anything useful."

"Appearances can be deceptive, Lady Hannington."

"Why not tell me that all is not gold that glitters, and that beggars can't be choosers?" retorted Lady Hannington. "What's done is done, and I hope you're ashamed of yourselves. Now what have you got out of it?"

Humphrey repeated the story he had already told to his mother of his interview with Jane Hargest. While he did so

Pellew sipped his whisky and reflected. What, in fact, had they got out of it? All that Humphrey had discovered was that Mrs. Hargest was unhappy and rather overwrought, which in the circumstances was natural enough. It confirmed the previous impression of unhappiness which she had given both to Lady Hannington and to Sally Anstruther. But while confirmation was always a good thing this was hardly a burning or a shining light. As far as Sally was concerned he had found out that she was a much simpler and nicer girl than she had seemed in the Gargantua office; that her background and manner alike seemed to deny any possibility that she might have been Hargest's kept mistress, though she had obviously been devoted to him in a romantic almost schoolgirlish way. He said as much, rather shamefacedly.

"What about that tape-recording business, Greg?"

"On the face of it it has a nice flavour of mystery and drama. One of us will have to see if anything can be squeezed out of the oyster-like Miss Jukes——"

"Not one of us," said Humphrey decisively. "It's going to be you. You've had the sweet. You can now take the bitter, and like it."

Pellew shrugged his shoulders. "I don't mind. She sounds rather an interesting character. I'm afraid I'm not well up in the conventions of high finance. It may be that it's common form for tycoons to have their interviews recorded—for reference, and to prevent any possibility of argument at a later stage as to what was actually said."

"That's all very well, Greg. But you know as well as I do what can be done with those recording tapes. I spend half my time editing the damned things for programme purposes. You can snip anything out from a pause or a cough to a paragraph, and splice the thing together again. It doesn't need a lot of imagination to see how sense and sequence can be turned inside out with a bit of ingenuity. Personally, I should look very much sideways at a tape-recording as really reliable evidence of anything. Isn't that why the Courts won't accept it?"

"That's true," said Pellew. "All the same an honest man, with no inclination towards jiggery-pokery, might easily find the system useful. I'm glad to have heard about it. We'd better take care that we don't leap to any highly-coloured conclusions."

"What about Sir George Farley?"

"He didn't show me any fangs, Humphrey. He obviously shares the high opinion everyone had of Hargest. He struck me as a nice old buffer, probably much more competent than he looks. Like your Mr. Gunn he was very concerned about Mrs. Hargest. Incidentally, what can you tell me about one James Ballantyne?"

Humphrey's eyebrows rose.

"Oho—our Jimmy-the-one—the pride and joy of the Studios—'Jim' to all and sundry from the cleaners and the call-boys upwards. A pain in the neck to the overworked producer, about as much sense of humour as a camel, but really rather a lamb. Clever as the whole *bandar-log*—though he'd probably sack me if he thought I admired Kipling. Where does he come in on the party?"

"I gathered from Sir George," said Pellew delicately, "that Mr. Ballantyne and Simon Hargest didn't always get on."

"You're telling me!" said Humphrey. "I suppose the top brass always see through a glass darkly. Didn't get on! A good deal of fur's always flying about Gargantua. It's part of the pattern. But if there was a real up-and-downer you could bet that Hargest had put his oar into programmes, and that our Jim had threatened to resign."

"Was it serious? Or just temperament and hot air?"

"With Jim temperament is mighty serious, Greg. Mark you I never saw fists being shaken or even harsh words exchanged. But I've been at programme meetings where Jim let his back hair down, and you certainly couldn't call discretion his middle name. I fancy that he thought Hargest was trying to give programmes a political slant—natural enough considering Hargest's background. And Jim's all for Entertainment, with a capital E. It's sound enough except that he's rather sold on Entertainment according to the Eggheads, which I find a bit of a bore. But that's no tree to start barking up. Those rows were all in the line of duty."

"All the same," said Pellew, "I think I shall have to take advantage of Sir George's introduction to Mr. Ballantyne. He sounds as if he'd repay study. What do you say, Lady Hannington?"

That lady had, during the last quarter of an hour, shown every sign of being asleep. Her eyes were closed, her hands folded on her bosom. She had seemed lost in the peace and placidity of a serene oblivion. On being addressed directly, however, she reacted with an energy positively startling. "I say, Mr. Pellew, that you're going the wrong way to work in this business. I'm not referring now to your manners, but to your method. Only two out of all the people and things that you and Humphrey have mentioned strike me as interesting or important. Most of what you've found out we knew at the beginning of the story: that Mr. Hargest was able and admired; that his wife is rather wretched; that his office contains some unusual characters—not that I'm the least surprised that a Television organisation should depend largely on freaks!"

"I know all about your feelings for, or rather against, the goggle-box," interrupted Humphrey impatiently. "What are your two sign-posts?"

"Just give me time, dear. The first thing is your description of the photograph of Mr. Hargest which you saw in his wife's sitting-room."

"But I told you—it gave one no impression of the man whatever!"

"Exactly. Isn't that rather significant? Here we have a man generally admitted to be gifted, vital, and successful beyond the ordinary: a man of very varied activities and very wide interests. But I don't remember ever having seen a photograph of him in a daily or weekly newspaper. And the one that you saw, dear boy—one that presumably he gave to his

63

wife, and which he liked or at any rate approved of accordingly, is as flat as a pancake and about as revealing."

"That is a bit odd, now you mention it," said Pellew.

"I recommend you to think about it," said Lady Hannington tartly. "The second thing is much more important. You've started your inquiries with the idea of discovering in the first place whether Mr. Hargest in fact took his own life—"

"That was the assignment, Lady Hannington."

"What you should have begun with," continued Lady Hannington calmly, "was the problem of why you were given the assignment at all. Surely, it's strange for a high official of Scotland Yard to take one of his best men—I won't bother to spare your blushes—away from his job, and put him on a private investigation. You said your Commander referred to 'interests at a high level.' Whose interests? How high? Until you know those answers, you're working in the dark."

"How can he know, Mother, when the Commander didn't tell him, and obviously didn't mean him to know?"

Lady Hannington held out her empty glass to Humphrey. Pellew fancied that he saw the suspicion of a wink.

"Isn't there a method called elimination?" she asked him. "There can't be many 'high levels' so lofty that they can cut through all the rules and regulations that govern the Metropolitan Police Service. A Commander at Scotland Yard isn't a second-grade clerk. He's not susceptible to anything in the nature of normal influence or pressure. He obeyed an order, Mr. Pellew—or more probably a hint that could only be construed as an order. Now who's in a position to drop a hint like that? Thank you, dear. Not quite up to the top."

"You should have been in the Service yourself," said Pellew admiringly.

"In my young days ladies and servants weren't interchangeable," said Lady Hannington. "No doubt it was snobbish and a pity. But so it was—and I'm not at all sure that it wasn't a more comfortable state of affairs than the present."

Humphrey, who had been refilling his own glass, turned round.

"Who'd you think it could have been, Greg?"

Pellew fingered his jaw and considered. "The obvious candidate," he said slowly, "is the Home Secretary."

"What about the less obvious, Mr. Pellew?"

"I suppose any Cabinet Minister is a possible."

"He'd have had to be involved in some way with Mr. Hargest, or interested in Mr. Hargest's activities, surely?"

"If by 'activities' you mean Gargantua, then the Postmaster-General's the most likely candidate. He's ultimately responsible for all broadcasting in this country, including television. He must have known Hargest. I suppose it's possible that he wants to know more about the why and wherefore of his death."

"What about the Independent Television Authority?" suggested Humphrey.

"It's an idea. I don't think so somehow."

"Not carrying the necessary weight of guns? I see. But look here, Greg, isn't Mother being the least bit in the world too clever over this? Dragging in Cabinet Ministers and top-level political secrecy and what not—it's pretty far-fetched."

"A lot of things are far-fetched—until they happen," said Pellew. "Lady Hannington's right, and I ought to have seen it before."

"But why couldn't your Commander chap tell you the truth?" demanded Humphrey exasperatedly.

"Some race-horses run best in blinkers, I believe. In my case I think the theory's mistaken. No doubt Mr. X had his reasons for having me kept in the dark. No doubt I oughtn't to try to find out who he is. I'm going to, for all that."

"Mr. Hargest had plenty of interests apart from Gargantua," suggested Lady Hannington.

"Interests likely to involve a Cabinet Minister? He'd thrown up the House, just as he'd given up the Bar. He probably had other business tie-ups with Sir George Farley—"

"Pointing to some juicy hidden scandal in the recesses of the Board of Trade?" scoffed Humphrey. "I can't see its President as the central figure of some hypothetical drama of the mysterious, any more than I can imagine the Postmaster-General as the hero of a detective novel. The thing simply doesn't jell."

"Which leaves us with the Home Secretary. I think, Humphrey dear, that you've had enough whisky for one evening."

Pellew got out of his chair abruptly; took a turn up and down the room; sat down again. "Of course they all sound unlikely," he said. "But someone did give that order or drop that hint, and there is something a long way out of the common run about the whole thing. Normally when a suicide's circumstances are investigated the people concerned are relatives—sorrowing or the reverse—or my mythical insurance company, or the police because something or someone has suggested that what appeared suicide was really murder. But in this case Mrs. Hargest didn't start anything. Nor did any genuine insurance company. Nor did Sir George Farley on behalf of Gargantua. Nor did my own people at the Yard—officially. The fact of the suicide's been accepted all round. Not even our smoke-screened X has made any definite suggestion of possible murder. So what's the bee in his bonnet? What's it all in aid of?"

"We're just chasing our own tails," grumbled Humphrey, with a wistful glance at the whisky decanter.

"But the circle's getting smaller," said Pellew. "Let's try again. Who are the people most affected by Hargest's death?"

"Jane Hargest. Old George Farley. A good many of the Gargantua staff—in particular, Rollo Gunn, James Ballantyne, the fair Sally, and the Jukes woman."

"All of whom, as far as we know, have reacted quite naturally. None of whom are in a position to get me put on the job. It isn't even as if the future prospects of Gargantua have been affected for the worse. Hargest had done his most important work when he had laid the foundations and completed the organisation. The shares haven't fallen in value. It may be that your Mr. Ballantyne sees himself with a freer hand over his programme plans for the future. I can't believe that he killed Hargest, or drove Hargest to kill himself, with that as a motive. That's far-fetched if you like. The widow, Rollo Gunn, the two secretaries, all have reason personal and material to be sorry that Hargest's dead."

"Just so," said Lady Hannington quietly. "We're back with our unknown X, who must have been seriously worried by what happened; who must have been closely connected with Hargest; who was in a position to initiate unofficial action by an official; and who had no intention of putting his cards on the table face upwards. How is this country run, Mr. Pellew? Don't tell me you're so naive or old-fashioned as to believe in democracy, except as a catchword."

"You're an immoral old lady, Mother."

"I know what I'm talking about, dear. If we had to wait for the voters, and Acts of Parliament, and the usual channels before anything was done, our whole society would run down like an unwound watch. The people who coined the phrase about the Establishment were right—up to a point. The point being that the individuals composing the Establishment are always changing, so that its goings-on aren't nearly as unfair as its detractors make out. And if it didn't 'go on' then nothing would get done. We'd be at the mercy of Working to Rule and all that that implies."

"If I didn't know you as I do, Mother dear, I should have to suspect you of being a Fascist beast," said Humphrey, and grinned. "Aren't we getting a long way from the point of issue?"

"No," said Pellew. "Lady Hannington means that our X is very much of the Establishment, and uses the sort of method which everyone in the Establishment understands and never acknowledges."

"Precisely. Thank you, Mr. Pellew."

"And Cabinet Ministers don't belong to the Establishment, Humphrey. They're too much in the public eye. One of the higher Civil Servants, a Personal Private Secretary, a member of some Secretariat or other—the essential oil that greases the works—I believe we're getting warm."

"I know I'm getting sleepy," said Lady Hannington.

Pellew apologised and rose to go. Before he went he told Humphrey that he proposed to visit the Gargantua Studios during the next afternoon and present Sir George Farley's note of introduction to Mr. James Ballantyne.

CHAPTER 9

JAMES BALLANTYNE

But Pellew was not to see Mr. Ballantyne during the next afternoon. When he rang up to announce his intention he was informed brusquely by a secretary that Mr. Ballantyne was very busy; that he always spent afternoons on the floor of the Studios; that if Mr. Pellew cared to join him for lunch *in his office*—this phrase was emphasised—Mr. Ballantyne hoped to be able to give him half an hour.

Pellew accepted the terms with a certain wry amusement, and prepared himself for a sticky interview. This uneasiness was not helped by his arriving in Mr. Ballantyne's office in a state of considerable exhaustion. Unlike the Gargantua Building on the Embankment there was no stream-lined façade of up-to-date functionalism about the Gargantua Studios. "Make-do-and-Mend" had presumably been their motto from the day when, on the inspiration of Simon Hargest, the vast bare erection that had once housed two of Britain's ill-fated airships was chosen as the workshop for Gargantua's programme output.

"We don't want the sort of studios that are the dreams of architects and lighting and acoustical experts," Hargest had said decisively. "In nine cases out of ten they turn out producer's nightmares. We hardly know the first thing yet about TV production techniques. What we want is space: space to experiment; space to expand; space in which we can put things up, and tear things down, and try again. Lots of bare floor; and unlimited power and light resources. We can go on from there."

They had gone on from there. And if no one could call the studios decorative, at any rate no Gargantua producer had ever been able to complain that he hadn't got room to swing a cat—or, which was more important, to swing his cameras round.

Pellew had been conducted across apparently endless wide-open spaces; along innumerable corridors constructed temporarily of unpainted plywood; between vast stacks of scenery and collections of "properties" ranging from medieval armour to Salford crockery; up iron ladders. He had dodged, more or less successfully, tea-trolleys, make-up assistants in white overalls, call-boys, actors in costume and actors in tweed coats and flannel trousers; cameras on cranes and cameras on "dollys"; young men in sweaters and young men in corduroys; and young ladies in horn-rimmed glasses with production scripts under their arms. He had been bumped, baffled and bewildered. He could only press on at the heels of the spring-heeled boy who guided him, and hope that a lunch eaten in an office need not necessarily mean sandwiches and tea on a tray.

That hope was disappointed. James Ballantyne's sanctum gave the impression of having been "mocked up" from some sort of attic under the roof of the Studios in their farthest recesses. It contained James Ballantyne's big desk; a typist's desk for his secretary; a number of filing-cabinets; three telephones; and four hard chairs. On the desk, when Pellew was shown in, the secretary was placing two green metal trays with two plates of sandwiches, two apples, and two large cups of thick coarse china containing tea that was far more nearly black than brown. The secretary—she looked both scared and anæmic—took one of the hard chairs up to the desk; offered it to Pellew; murmured something about "Mr. Bal-lantyne—back in two minutes—gone to wash his hands," and vanished with the anxious alacrity of the White Rabbit.

Pellew looked about him after a quick glance of distaste at the green metal trays. He hated strong tea. The most striking and interesting feature of the room was the wall behind him and facing James Ballantyne when he sat at his desk: a wall of glass from floor to ceiling with a panoramic view over the floor spaces of the Studios. Thus James Ballantyne presided over his realm, like Zeus upon the height of Olympus—but, unlike Zeus, to be seen as well as seeing if any of his subjects cast eyes heavenwards in supplication or despair. Pellew drew a deep breath. Had this been another of Simon Hargest's ideas, or was it the reflection of the personality of James Ballantyne? As symptomatic of the power-complex it was cer-tainly remarkable.

Behind the desk a door flat with the wall, which Pellew had taken for a cupboard, opened with a click. Pellew had a glimpse of what looked like the lavatory compartment of a train. In the doorway stood a little thin man with a brown leathery face, a big arrogant nose, and eyes bright and shift-ing like a cat's. Pellew almost expected to see a tail twitch.

"Mr. Pellew? Don't get up. I'm James Ballantyne. No doubt you'll be calling me 'Jim' in two minutes. Everyone does. And it saves time."

He sat down, and pulled his lunch tray towards him. He was wearing a creased blue suit, a very clean white shirt, and a deplorable tie of stripes alternating bright orange and an even brighter green. He had a mouth like a trap, and the hands of a professional pianist: square and muscular.

"Fuel—not food," he said, picking up a sandwich with one hand and stirring his tea vigorously with the other. "I once looked into the average time spent every day on the business of eating by the average executive: three-quarters of an hour for breakfast; two hours for lunch; two and half hours for dinner. Add another three-quarters of an hour for

71

tea and a coffee-break and oddments, and you get six solid hours wasted—five if some genuine business is done over lunch, which isn't often. TV can't afford that sort of waste. You agree?"

"You may be right."

"I know I'm right. There's that roof-garden restaurant at the top of the Gargantua Building that Hargest was so proud of. Four-course meals available, and vintage wines if you wanted 'em—and special cheap prices—how do you expect to get your staff back from lunch? And Hargest talked about functionalism—my foot! Well—what do you want from me? You come from old Farley?"

Pellew handed Sir George's note across the desk.

"I'd hoped," said Ballantyne, "that interference from Head Office had died with the late-lamented Hargest. I ought to have known better."

He dropped the note unopened on to his blotting-pad.

"You and Mr. Hargest didn't see exactly eye to eye?"

"People should mind their own business, Mr. Pellew. I mind mine—the planning and supervision of programmes. Hargest knew his—organisation and finance. It wasn't enough for him. He had to put a finger into my pie—poor devil! So on and off we fought like cats. But death settles all scores—so I was brought up to believe."

"Reasonably enough," said Pellew.

"But what happens?" retorted Ballantyne. "Rollo Gunn comes down and wastes the better part of a morning talking hot air about Hargest. Old Farley sends you to see me—no doubt to talk more hot air about Hargest. Hargest dead is like Banquo's ghost: promising more trouble than when he was alive. The man had his qualities and his uses. He's dead and buried, and for Gargantua TV to-morrow is also a day. Why did you come to see me, Mr. Pellew?"

"Not to talk hot air, I assure you. Sir George offered me the chance of looking over your Studios, and suggested that you might find me a chaperon who would know the ropes and keep me from being a nuisance."

Ballantyne snorted. "Anyone in particular?"

"I believe you've a young man here called Toby Scott. My mother knows his—"

Pellew broke off, praying silently to be forgiven.

"Young Toby!" Ballantyne snorted again. "Quite a good boy, if he didn't waste so much time mooning after that snooty piece who used to work for Hargest. He knows his stuff and does his home-work—not like most of these bright Oxbridge products."

"You prefer the redbrick article?" said Pellew deliberately.

"Naturally," said Ballantyne. "I am one. That was the real reason Hargest didn't like me. I didn't belong. And he didn't belong to TV. He didn't know a camera from a batten, and cared less. I don't know why he mixed himself up with Gargantua. He'd made all the money he wanted. He'd made a success of everything he touched. I suppose once a politician always a politician. He used to talk about the 'potentially civilising influence' of TV!" There was no more attempt to conceal the contempt in his voice than there had been to hide the enmity that had existed between the Managing Director and the Director of Programmes. Hargest had obviously been a very sharp thorn in Ballantyne's flesh, which he was glad to have lost. But the feeling had almost certainly been mutual. And, in Pellew's experience, acknowledged antagonisms seldom led to crime.

Munching his last sandwich Ballantyne picked up a telephone and demanded the instant presence of Toby Scott. "No reply from his office? Then find him for God's sake! If he's not in the canteen he'll be in that pub across the road—and if he's not here in five minutes I'll skin him!"

He banged down the instrument, and turned back to Pellew. "I'll use your apple, if you don't fancy it. I expect you're wondering why I let Hargest get in my hair—why I talk about him to a perfect stranger."

He took the apple and split it in half with one twist of his hands. "We could have worked together, if our positions had been reversed. I'm better at giving orders than taking them.

73

Too many people told me what I could and couldn't do, when I was young. Hargest had collected that easy assumption of obedience from others when he was wearing his bloody red tabs in the war. And what was I doing in the war you'll ask!"

"I can mind my own business, too," murmured Pellew.

Ballantyne looked at him shrewdly. "I fancy you might at that," he said. "I'll tell you. I'd developed TB. I spent most of the war in hospital in Scotland, and the rest of it in a nicely sandbagged Fire Service telephone exchange. Not so hot if compared with Hargest's fruit-salad of gongs, was it? And then he had the nerve to say he was sorry for me!"

"Perhaps he was," said Pellew with the suspicion of a smile.

"I've no doubt he was. I didn't want his blasted sympathy, not even when he wrapped it up by saying that he knew a good deal about TB because of his wife. D'you know the lady?"

"No."

"Better get to know her, if you're interested in Hargest," said Ballantyne. "She's the kiss-me-mother-ere-I-die type while knowing all the answers, unless I'm very much mistaken. Ran Hargest with her little finger. I like women with loins."

Yes, thought Pellew, while Ballantyne crunched his second apple, I bet you do. With your bursting vitality; your crying need for social reassurance; your fine white teeth and powerful hands, you would like them *à la* Rubens and no holds barred. Probably more than one at a time. And I wouldn't care to be them. . . .

At which point Toby Scott came bursting into the room after the most perfunctory of knocks. He was a cheerful-looking young man with a wide mouth, thick curly hair, and a turned-up nose. He was wearing a tweed jacket, patched with leather at elbows and cuffs, a green shirt open at the neck, and green corduroy trousers.

"You wanted me, Jim?"

"I did. Drinking in the pub with a lot of actors, I suppose?"

"Cocoa and a pork-pie in the canteen with a script," said Toby Scott amiably.

"Busy this afternoon?"

"Not specially. Why?"

"Then you ought to be," snapped Ballantyne. "Meet Mr. Pellew here. He wants to see the wheels go round. Take an hour—not more—and do what you can for him without getting in anybody's way. Glad to have met you, Mr. Pellew."

He hurried out, bawling rather than calling for his secretary; and the room seemed larger. Scott looked at Pellew, and Pellew looked at Scott; and they both grinned.

"Jim's bark is worse than his bite, Mr. Pellew. He's no end of a chap really. Likes his fire and brimstone, but delivers the goods—and how! What particularly do you want to see?"

Pellew got up. "Anything you feel inclined to show me. I'm a stranger in a strange land. No matter what I see you can count on my being properly impressed."

"That makes it easier. Most visitors want to see our secret TV colour-process—which they mustn't—or the Gargantua Graces off the set—who always have their mothers with them not to mention an official chaperon—or some 'star' who for one reason or other is taking the day off."

He led the way out of Ballantyne's office. Pellew paused at the door to look once more through the wall of glass. The general effect of space and width and height, of strongly contrasted areas of brilliant light and varying shadows, was mightily impressive. But apart from that light and those shadows you could see very little, and nothing in detail. He wondered, rather fancifully, if this Zeus hadn't built his Olympus too high for any practical purpose—except the inflation of his own ego. . . .

As Toby Scott led the way towards a "set" whereon—so he assured Pellew—the latest-made theatrical knight was giving the performance of his life in one of those plays written by

Brecht in the early thirties and discovered to be a masterpiece by the English critics in the early sixties, Pellew took the opportunity to mention to his guide that he had recently made the acquaintance of Miss Sally Anstruther. He watched with compassion the back of the unfortunate young man's neck flush up to his ears. Toby stopped and turned round.

"Did she talk about me? I suppose she must have."

"Very nicely, I assure you."

"Nicely! That's the hell of a lot of use! But that's what I am: the nice little puppy-dog running to heel when called. It's the wolf who gets Little Riding Hood, isn't it? How's it done—that's what I want to know, Mr. Pellew."

"I'm not a lady's man," said Pellew smiling.

"You must have had some useful experience, at your age."

"Experience—perhaps. Useful—almost certainly not. I'd advise you to ride your own line. I don't really know, but personally I wouldn't fancy the chances of the average wolf who showed Miss Anstruther how big his teeth were. She struck me as extremely level-headed, and quite capable of taking care of herself."

"I want her to take care of me," said Toby Scott dolefully. "You want something to go home to in this racket. The job's fine. I wouldn't do anything else. But you get fed up with landlady's chops in a bed-sitter in Islington. And with Jim on your tail all day you could do with someone like Sally at night—and I don't mean what you think I mean," he added hastily, and flushed again.

Pellew assured him that he understood perfectly, and they continued on their way.

They picked their steps cautiously across innumerable cables, and round TV cameras that gave the impression of large metal grasshoppers. Above the "set" two microphones on booms swung lazily to and fro. Cameramen in shirtsleeves paid no attention to them whatever. A group of actors in one corner looked at them with unabashed curiosity. A young man wearing headphones approached Pellew with an air of ferocity; noticed Toby Scott; made a rude gesture; and withdrew again into the background. Everybody seemed immensely occupied in talking a great deal, and doing nothing in particular. Then a number of red lights flashed on, all movement ceased, and the whole place became silent as the grave. Toby hissed into Pellew's ear that a "take" was imminent.

Whereupon the red lights went out again, and it was clear that it had been a false alarm.

"We'll get up into the gallery while we can," said Toby.

They climbed a corkscrew iron staircase, opened a door, and entered the control gallery. After the lights and spaces of the studio it seemed both dark and crowded. There was no more than standing room between the back wall and the row of padded chairs facing the curved control desk running parallel to the observation window which looked down on to the "set." Plumb centre sat the producer faced by his five "monitor" screens, giving him the immediate output of his various cameras from which to select the forthcoming "shot" at will for transfer to the master screen for actual viewing. At his left elbow was his secretary peering at a script. On his right was a girl vision-mixer, and beyond her a sound-mixer, each behind a battery of knobs and switches. Immediately facing the door was a double bank of gramophone turntables, with a red-haired young man brooding over it with the air of a young mother minding a fractious baby. James Ballantyne was standing behind the producer, frowning. He nodded to Toby and Pellew; then leaned forward over the producer's shoulder, and sprawled one hand like a star-fish on to the opened script. "No, my dear Alan, no—and no—and no again. No dice."

He spoke very quietly. Pellew had expected him to shout.

"What's wrong now, Jim?"

The producer's voice sounded hoarse and exasperated.

"Break 'em—break 'em now, Alan. You've gone on too long. You're not seeing straight. The camera's a positive weapon, not a negative. It's a spear to pierce through to the heart of a play. You're using it like a looking-glass. All I'm getting is a strong smell of grease-paint: imitation theatre. It's partly the actors' fault, I know. But your cutting's too sticky, and you're neglecting your close-ups. Break for half an hour, and we'll try again." His tone was affectionate, caressing, almost hypnotic.

The producer looked at Ballantyne and smiled. Everyone relaxed. It was as if a mass of electrical tensions had been suddenly ironed out.

"Sorry, Jim. You're right as usual, blast you! Break for half an hour everybody. You're coming back, Jim?"

"I am certainly coming back, my dear Alan—as you ought to know by this time," said Ballantyne.

He patted the producer's shoulder, and favoured Pellew with the next thing to a leer as he passed him on his way out of the gallery. "There you are, Mr. Pellew," he murmured. "Now you've seen how it's done—or don't you see? By kindness or by mirrors? Nobody seems able to tell me."

Pellew stared after him until Toby Scott nudged him in the ribs.

"Well—that's that. They're rehearsing some new type of quiz on one of the other stages, if you're interested—"

"Very kind of you," said Pellew, "but I think I should be on my way. You're a busy young man—and you've given me plenty to think about."

Toby Scott cleared his throat; opened his mouth; shut it again.

"Don't bother—er Toby. Just set my feet on the clear road to the way out. I won't forget to give Sally Anstruther your love."

Toby Scott's expression seemed to imply that in his opinion the gift might well be looked in the mouth. But Pellew was not thinking seriously about Toby Scott—not even about Sally Anstruther. He was thinking that James Ballantyne was one of the most unusual men he had ever met.

CHAPTER 10

LILIAN JUKES

Pellew was just sitting down to his breakfast the next morning when his front-door bell rang. Answering it he was confronted by a disillusioned-looking postman, who handed him a large oblong envelope registered, and by Humphrey Clymping, who announced that he would like some coffee and was prepared to cook his own eggs and bacon.

Pellew signed for the envelope, and muttered that in his opinion breakfast was not the occasion for a social call.

"By and large," said Humphrey cheerfully, "I agree with you. You must make exceptions in favour of former undergraduates of Oxford University, where the tradition of going out to breakfast with one's friends is not only preserved but cherished."

"I thought Oxford traditions were civilised," grumbled Pellew.

"This one may not be civilised, Greg. It's necessary. You try the average breakfast in the average college hall."

"I'm sure Kate cooks an excellent breakfast."

"She does," agreed Humphrey. "This morning she's indulging in that agreeable habit of the theatrical profession—a long lie-in. As my mother drinks one cup of China tea in her bedroom, I felt lonely once I'd had my bath. Also I'm curious about your reaction to the Studios and our Jim. Read your mail while I fry an egg." He disappeared into the kitchenette.

Pellew opened the envelope. It was artificially stiffened, and stamped GARGANTUA TV in red both back and front. Inside was a folder—yellow with a zip fastening—marked PERSONAL FILE, PRIVATE AND CONFIDENTIAL, with a label attached on which was written Jukes, Lilian, p/ps. There was also a covering letter from Mr. Rollo Gunn.

Pellew read it slowly. While he did so he became irritably aware of the sizzling sounds of bacon in a frying-pan accompanied by Humphrey Clymping's voice uplifted in the strains of the "Eton Boating Song," loud but hardly melodious.

Dear Mr. Pellew,

During our recent conversation you mentioned that you would probably wish to interview the two secretaries who worked for Simon Hargest in this office. I gathered that you have in fact already seen Miss Anstruther, so I mentioned to Miss Jukes that she would be likely to be approached by you in due course.

I am sorry to have to tell you that Miss Jukes' attitude was the reverse of co-operative. She said that she had already given evidence at the inquest—reluctantly, as the whole business had been extremely painful to her—and that she declined absolutely to answer any questions that might be addressed to her by an unofficial investigator. She added—and I quote—'I know he's already got round that silly little Anstruther bitch with the aid of an expensive dinner and a lot of blarney. I'll have nothing to do with the man.'

As a result of this I felt bound to have a word with the Chairman of our Board, Sir George Farley, and on his instructions—which, I admit, surprised me—I enclose you Miss Jukes' personal file. I shall be grateful if you will return

*it to me, registered and marked Private and Confidential, as
soon as you conveniently can.*

Yours sincerely,
Rollo Gunn

He had finished reading it for the second time, and was
unzipping the folder when Humphrey emerged from the
kitchenette, put his plate down on the table, and reached for
the coffee-pot. "I observe, Greg, the furrowed brow, the ab-
stracted air. I also observe stamped upon that envelope the
hall-mark of the great organisation which I serve. In short I
am Hawkshaw the Detective. What gives?"

Pellew tossed him the letter, and opened the folder.

"What ho! Retort discourteous by the Jukes—hideous
revelations of the private life of a private secretary—the plot
definitely thickens, or does it?"

"You're letting your food get cold, Humphrey."

"What are the attractions of eggs and bacon when compared with the secrets of a confidential file? I'm agog with
anticipation."

"I'm not sure if I ought to show it to you," said Pellew.

"If you don't," retorted Humphrey, "I'm damned if I
don't resign my Watsonship. Your Commander may run you
in blinkers, my dear Holmes. You can't do the same to me.
Share and share alike, or I run out of the course. I'm not
going to publish the damned thing, or sell it to a gossip-
columnist."

"I never thought you would."

"Well then—?"

"And I suppose I do need a sounding-board."

"Echo answers that you do, Greg. Forget your manners
for once. They're not fashionable any longer. You can salve
your conscience by reading me what you think may be important, and leaving out the nubbly bits—if there are any,
which I doubt."

"All right. But I'd be grateful if you'd stop playing the
goat."

"From this moment I'm as serious as a proletarian play-wright. To prove it I shall eat while you read to me. Go ahead."

"Jukes, Lilian Mary," said Pellew after a pause. "Born in Cheltenham. Daughter of Colonel David Jukes, Indian Army, C.M.G., retired, and Mabel Jukes. Educated privately; then at Roedean—reports excellent—and at Somerville, Oxford, where she got a scholarship. Took a first in Modern Greats."

"That," observed Humphrey, "is the hell of an academic record for a secretary, however private. She ought to have become a headmistress, or a top-grade Civil Servant, or a junior Cabinet Minister or something. You don't need Modern Greats to pound a typewriter."

"Came down from Oxford in 1937," continued Pellew. "Travelled in France, Germany and Italy for two years. Fluent French and German. Adequate Italian. Joined W.R.N.S. on the outbreak of war. Transferred after three months to Intelligence Division of the Admiralty. Served later in Malta and the Near East. Excellent record. Commissioned in '41."

"That's more like it," said Humphrey. "I can imagine her pushing the girls around more than somewhat—poor little devils!"

"After the war worked with a publishing firm—reading and translating foreign books. Excellent record. Came to Gargantua with personal recommendation from Managing Director, Mr. Simon Hargest. Attached to his office as personal private secretary. Reports by him, by personnel manager, and by director of administration, all first-rate. (See records, letters, reports, in file.) That's the lot."

"It's quite a good deal," said Humphrey reflectively. "Does it tell us anything we didn't already know? She's obviously an efficient girl, or she wouldn't have had her job with Hargest."

"I'm inclined to think it's worth trying to fill out the picture, Humphrey. There's the retired Service background.

82

There's almost certainly economic stress or she wouldn't have needed that scholarship."

"With two years' travel abroad?"

"Wait a minute. Yes—her parents both died in '37. Presumably she came into a little money, and spent it very sensibly on languages and the general experience of European runaround. The Navy had the sense to make use of her special qualifications—and here's the original tie-up with Hargest. They were both in Intelligence in the Near East. Let's have a look at his letter of recommendation. There you are, Humphrey. 'I was made aware of Miss Jukes' many admirable qualifications and of her record of outstanding service, when we worked together in Malta during 1941.' No doubt he told her to contact him after the war if she ever needed a job. She saw all the publicity about Gargantua, and thought work with Hargest would be more fun than translating French and German textbooks. I'll bet it was, too."

"Rollo Gunn was with Hargest in the Near East, Greg. He hasn't said anything about knowing the Jukes at that time."

"Rollo Gunn was with him in Cairo, not Malta. The Near East covered a pretty big area."

"That's true enough."

"It all adds up, Humphrey. A woman with a family Service tradition, and a Service record of her own. A woman with brains and talent beyond the ordinary, with nothing at all in the way of looks, and now just about the age when she may easily be a little abnormal. There's nothing new or odd in the idolisation of an employer by a secretary. But now and again it becomes an obsession, as I believe in this case it did: the obsession of a hopeless love recognised as being hopeless. That accounts for her attitude when Rollo Gunn talked to her about seeing me. It accounts for the way she spoke of Sally Anstruther. I must say I'm sorry for her. And if she heard me say as much it's long odds that she'd want to murder me."

"It's longer odds that she didn't murder Hargest."

"My dear Humphrey, there's not one jot or tittle of evidence pointing to Hargest's murder by anyone. If there was this job would be a great deal simpler."

Humphrey finished his coffee, and lighted a cigarette. "Well," he said, "that seems to put paid to Jukes, Lilian Mary."

"Not quite," said Pellew. "I still want to talk to her about those tape-recordings which Sally Anstruther mentioned. For the time being I shall have to want. Besides there are other things to think about."

"Jim Ballantyne for instance?"

Pellew shook his head. "Meeting him was an experience I wouldn't have missed. He's certainly a very queer fish. But in this business, Humphrey, he's only a red herring, or I'm much mistaken. No—it's what your mother was saying the other night about Mr. X: the *fons et origo* of this assignment of mine."

Humphrey sat up in his chair.

"Are you on to something, Greg?"

"I may be. When I got back from the Studios yesterday I found a message from the Commander that he wanted to see me—at his house, not at the Yard. He wanted a report on progress. I was in his study, and while we were talking we were interrupted by his wife—a tough little woman—something wrong with the central heating. I was left by myself in the room, and his engagement diary was open on his desk."

"Greg! You horrify me!"

"I rather horrify myself. But the temptation was irresistible. It struck me that if the Commander had met someone just before he sent for me to give me this assignment; and if that meeting was recorded in his diary—"

"You needn't go on. You peeked?"

"I peeked."

"Well?"

"On the day when the Commander sent for me," said Pellew, "he lunched at the Savoy Grill with 'Beetle.' Enlightening, isn't it?"

But for once Humphrey Clymping was quite serious. "It might be, Greg. We must talk to my mother."

"I love talking to Lady Hannington. I don't quite see—"

"Don't you? It might ring a bell."

"You're not going to tell me that Lady Hannington hob-nobs with any character known as 'Beetle.'"

Humphrey leaned back in his chair, and blew smoke-rings at the ceiling. "My dear Greg, in the days when my mother mingled in what was then known as 'Society'—when my poor father was sane, sober, and active in that sphere of life to which it had pleased God to call him—almost every-one was called by some damned silly nickname. A lot of peo-ple still are."

"Obviously," said Pellew impatiently. "We know 'Beetle' exists for one."

"Certainly he exists," said Humphrey. "But you can limit the field in which that sort of nickname registers: clubs, where the members come mostly from the public-schools, and don't want to forget it; the Regular Army, especially the Guards and cavalry regiments. Don't you remember the 1914 generals—'Lucky' and 'The Bull' and 'Bungo' and the rest of them? It's one of the things the young gentlemen who write abusive books about bad leadership in the First War don't seem able to forgive. They line up schoolboy nick-names with shining field-boots and the playing of polo as if they were criminal attributes. Personally, I can't see why it was snobbish to call a field-marshal 'Johnnie,' when it's only democratic to call a Prime Minister 'Clem.'"

"Are you suggesting," inquired Pellew mildly, "that our 'Beetle' is a relic of the 1914−18 High Command? If you are, I don't believe you."

"Now, Greg, you're being deliberately crass. We've got two things—at least we think we have. 'Beetle' equals our Mr. X. Mr. X moves in the higher reaches of the Establish-ment underground. Find someone moving in those reaches who answers familiarly to the name of 'Beetle' and we're home and dry. He must be of a certain age to carry the guns he obviously has. There's a good chance that he's been called 'Beetle' ever since he was at school. There's a small chance that my parents might have heard of him by that nickname, even if they never met him, when they still lived in London. My mother must jog her memory, and look up her old diaries."

"It's a pity," said Pellew gloomily, "that so many people have read *Stalky & Co*. Dozens of bespectacled schoolboys must have been called 'Beetle' in their time. But try the long shot by all means. It comes off occasionally."

"I'll talk to my mother tonight. Incidentally, had your Commander anything to say to you that mattered?"

"Not a thing. I'd next to nothing I could tell him, and he told me to get a move on for God's sake. The atmosphere was not cosy."

"So what next?"

"I'm really not sure. I must find some way to run across Miss Lilian Jukes by mistake on purpose, as my nurse used to say. And I want to follow up your call on Mrs. Hargest, which ended so embarrassingly."

"You're not neglecting the ladies, are you, Greg? Surely you're going to improve your acquaintance with Sally Anstruther? If you're not I'll be delighted to take over."

"You mind your own business, Humphrey. Gargantua calls you—or, if it doesn't, it should. Try and persuade your mother to come out to dinner with me to-night. I can't go on using Seven Dials as a home away from home. No—make it supper. Lady Hannington will enjoy staying up late, and Kate can come on from her theatre. Give me a ring during the afternoon."

"Fine. Will you be here?"

"I shall be here, Humphrey. This, as the Master would have said, is 'a three-pipe problem.' Field-work yesterday, brain-work this afternoon. Run along, and leave me to it."

"Why can't you just say frankly that you want to go back to bed?" said Humphrey maliciously.

He went all the same; went, for once, without slamming the door behind him.

CHAPTER 11

CONCLUSION BY PELLEW

Pellew smoked his pipes and did his thinking. He also made arrangements for that evening's dinner. He had made his first acquaintance with Humphrey Clymping's mother over dinner in the private parlour of The Cunning Fox inn at Hares Green. And one of the many things which he liked about Lady Hannington was her knowledge of food and her appreciation of wine.

Owing to his familiarity with the French language Pellew had found himself occasionally consulted by his colleagues at the Yard when they found themselves involved with French visitors or French resident aliens. And on one such occasion he had been able, quite legitimately, to smooth out a situation threatening to become difficult for a middle-aged lady from Bordeaux who wished to establish a restaurant in Soho. Her gratitude had been immoderate and delightful. Pellew found himself the most welcome of customers chez Babette; was frequently pressed to be the guest of the house; and could always rely on a private room and complete discretion if he needed the combination—which, in the course of his work, he frequently did.

Without hesitation therefore he rang up Madame on the telephone; ordered supper for four at eleven o'clock; agreed to her recommendation of *soles Dieppoises* preceded by the chef's *paté maison,* salad, cheese, and a white wine of Touraine, which he associated fancifully with bottled sunshine; and relaxed in the certainty that he need bother himself no further.

The private dining-room chez Babette had nothing in common with the *cabinet particulier* of romantic fiction. There was no oppressive intimacy about it. There was no sofa; no heavily lush curtaining of the windows. The table was round and unpolished. The glass and china could have belonged to any bourgeois French household. Logs were stacked in an open fireplace against the coming of winter. Candles burned in wooden candlesticks. Madame's father had collected Napoleonana in a small way, and the walls were paved rather than hung with battle-prints by Gerard and Meissonier: Austerlitz, Jena, Wagram, and the campaign of France; an aquatint of Elba; a map of St. Helena; portraits of the Marshals Ney and Davout; a cavalry commission of the Consulate with the signatures "Bonaparte" and "Berthier"; and—in the place of honour in the centre of the mantelpiece —a framed letter of Mme Letizia Bonaparte topped by a small round transparency containing a strand of reddish hair: the hair of Napoleon. This was flanked on one side by a snuff-box in the shape of the famous cocked hat; on the other by a bronze representation of a grenadier of the Old Guard. Favoured clients would find their coffee served in green and gold cups decorated with medallions illustrating the Coronation of 1805.

Sitting back in his chair, his eyes half closed, sipping a glass of Dubonnet while he waited for his guests, Pellew imagined himself back in Paris in the days when, as a very young man, chance acquaintance with a member of the Sûreté had first introduced him to the fascination of police work. Since those days a lot of water had flowed under the bridges of Seine and Thames. But few pictures remained so vivid in

Pellew's memory as the *quais* and the cafés of the Left Bank in the spring; the children and lovers in the Luxembourg Gardens; the smells of coffee and wood-smoke; the glitter and movement of Paris under sunshine; and the first sight of the huge red sarcophagus of the Invalides bathed in the unearthly blueish light from the windows high in the dome. It all seemed so very near, while being in fact intolerably far away. . . .

Lady Hannington and Humphrey arrived punctually. Kate Clymping was ten minutes late, providing as explanation and excuse an interview with an officious stage-manager. She was a tall girl with close-cropped curly hair, features that were attractive rather than pretty, a firm handshake, and a forthright manner. She greeted Lady Hannington with obvious affection, Pellew with obvious pleasure, and her husband with an embrace so uninhibited as to make them both smile.

"Pleasure before business," said Pellew firmly.

They had supper accordingly. Madame served them herself and expressed her gratitude for their comments by producing a bottle of *armagnac* from her private cellar. She placed that and the coffee on the table; smiled comprehensively; and withdrew.

Humphrey pushed back his chair. Lady Hannington poured out the coffee. Kate lighted a cigarette. Pellew reached for the *armagnac*.

"Well, Greg?"

"Don't rush things, Humphrey. I don't know about Kate, but I feel that Lady Hannington might like a minute or two for digestion."

"Thank you—but my digestion is in perfect working order," said Lady Hannington with a suspicion of tartness.

"I know it's my fault," added Kate, "but it's getting on for midnight."

"'When graveyards yawn'—appropriately enough in the circumstances," said Humphrey. "Come clean, Greg."

Pellew took a single sheet of paper out of his pocketbook, and unfolded it deliberately. "Very well. I think I'd better begin at the beginning. First of all, did Simon Hargest commit suicide, or was he murdered? It seems to me there's no doubt that he took his own life. Nothing's come up to contradict or question the medical evidence. No one has suggested to me the likelihood or even the possibility of murder. But, as I've said before, there are other ways of killing a man than by shooting a pistol at his face, or putting arsenic in his coffee."

"You mean," said Kate, "that a man can be driven to suicide by an interested party."

"Exactly. There was no financial or professional reason for Hargest to kill himself. He was rather exhausted, and he'd been working under pressure for a long time. But he was used to that, and physically he was an unusually fit man. A sudden brain-storm is a possible explanation, but somehow I don't fancy it. So what?"

"Blackmail of course," said Lady Hannington crisply.

"Blackmail in some form or other," agreed Pellew. "But in what form? And by whom? I confess that my first idea was that Hargest had involved himself in some scandalous intrigue, and that a man in his semi-public position could not face exposure—"

"Like Charles Dilke and Parnell."

"Exactly, Lady Hannington. There was that improbably good-looking secretary of his. There were indications that Mrs. Hargest was unhappy. The triangle seemed ready made."

"Except that Sally Anstruther isn't at all that sort of girl," said Humphrey.

Kate grinned cheerfully. "I'm beginning to believe," she said, "that if anyone ought to worry about Sally Anstruther it's me—not Mrs. Hargest."

"I'll leave it to you and Humphrey to fight that one out. But I agree that Miss Anstruther is no *femme fatale*. There's no grain of evidence of Hargest's involvement with any other woman, so the notion of a sexual intrigue can go into the discard."

"You can be blackmailed for other things besides adultery," said Lady Hannington. "Things are different nowadays from what they were when I was a girl—the Royal Enclosure—the Cabinet—divorced people get in everywhere. Nobody cares. And a good thing, too," she added rather surprisingly.

"Now let's take a look at the people with whom Hargest worked most closely," Pellew went on. "Sir George Farley, Chairman of his Board. Rollo Gunn, his personal assistant. James Ballantyne, his Programme Director. The two secretaries. How have they reacted to investigation and questioning? Sir George talked quite openly. Ballantyne did likewise, at much greater length. Miss Anstruther was normally forthcoming. On the other hand Rollo Gunn was, to say the least of it, sticky. And the Jukes woman put up a blank wall, through the agency of Rollo Gunn."

"I don't see what you're getting at," said Humphrey, "but I think Rollo's a good chap."

"He may be an excellent chap. Quite probably he merely resents being questioned about a dead man whom he liked and admired. The fact remains. And there's something else that Rollo Gunn and Miss Jukes have in common. They both worked—at different times and in different places—with Hargest in Intelligence during the war."

"Well—why shouldn't they have?"

"No earthly reason. And that they should have was a perfectly good reason why Hargest should have got them both into Gargantua. He'd had experience of what they could do. But while I was thinking things over to-day I got another idea. Isn't it a little odd that of the six principals in our cast—if we include Hargest—three have been connected with Intelligence. It's a big proportion."

"War-time Intelligence was a label that covered all kinds of goings-on," protested Humphrey. "Rollo mentioned as much to us himself. I can't see Hargest and Rollo—and certainly I can't see the Jukes—as spies, in the conventional sense of the word."

Pellew rubbed his jaw.

"What is the conventional sense of the word, Humphrey? Usually it derives from fiction."

"Current fiction at that," said Lady Hannington. "I was brought up on the spies of William le Queux and E. Phillips Oppenheim; Silver Greyhounds; Monte Carlo, and the Orient Express; Balkan diplomats with beards and enamelled crosses hung round their necks, and slinky adventuresses, with plans of fortresses in their *corsages*. Enormous fun—and you couldn't believe a word of it."

"Which is a long way from Eric Ambler and Graham Greene: seedy little men in grubby raincoats skulking in shadowed alleys with half-smoked cigarettes and bad consciences on a salary of a few pounds a month: layabouts game to sell anything or anyone at the drop of a hat, and usually with nasty sexual proclivities. That's the contemporary accepted picture. And that's a long way from the real thing—the thing that matters: spies with solid social backgrounds like Alger Hiss or Burgess and Maclean; atomic spies with outstanding professional attainments, like Fuchs and Ponte Corvo. The most important thing for the genuine spy, the dangerous spy, is his 'cover.'"

"You mean that Hargest was using Gargantua as 'cover' for spying? My dear Greg, what on earth had Hargest got to sell?"

"I'm suggesting, Humphrey, that Hargest was a British spy; that his Intelligence work didn't end with the war. Is there any job that provides so many obvious excuses for seeing and dealing with all sorts and conditions of men as that of a TV tycoon? If he visits a politician, or a Service Ministry, or the T.U.C., it's all part of his normal work. If he contacts a scientist he's following up an idea for a new series of programmes. If he interviews queer characters he's vetting for jobs, or picking their brains. He has justified entrée everywhere. Can you think of a better 'cover' for secret service? And remember that Hargest's advertised career had given him links with the Law, the Services, and with Big Business. Add his acknowledged brains and personality to his record and his position in Gargantua, and you have the picture of an outstandingly able and useful character from the point of view of an Intelligence Service."

"With Rollo and the Jukes to share the secret, aid and abet," said Humphrey slowly. "It certainly adds up. You're an ingenious devil, Greg."

"If I'm right it would account for persons unknown wanting to know a bit more about Hargest's death, and for running me in blinkers."

"But why you? Why not put their own sleuths on the job?"

"That, I admit, beats me."

"I wonder if it beats me," said Lady Hannington.

Pellew and Kate Clymping stared. Humphrey smiled broadly. "Come along, Mother dear. Blow the gaff."

Lady Hannington opened her handbag, and took from it a small leather-covered diary with a lock.

"Humphrey told me of your difficulty about the mysterious Mr. X who got your superior to employ you on his behalf, Mr. Pellew. He said that you had reason to believe that Mr. X was known to his intimates as 'Beetle.' Somewhere at the back of my mind that rang a little bell. In the days when my husband and I went about in so-called Society nearly all the men I met answered to some more or less absurd nickname. One could only suppose that they wanted to pretend that they had never left their schools. It was the period, you remember, when men honestly believed that their schooldays were the happiest days of their lives."

"Before *The Harrovians* and *The Loom of Youth* gave the show away," said Humphrey.

"For a number of years," continued Lady Hannington, "I kept a series of diaries, like this one. I was encouraged to do so by my parents. They said it promoted an orderly mind, and ultimately I got into the habit. Not soul-searching like Marie Bashkirtseff. No record of scandals of the alcove. Just people and places. All very dull and dusty now. I don't know why I didn't burn the whole collection years ago."

She paused; and for a moment looked her real age. It was

as though she contemplated a blurred panorama of luncheons, and dinners, and balls in the London of the Seventh Edward, not altogether without regret. Then she blinked her eyes vigorously, and resumed: "There are two entries in this volume of the diaries, covering the autumn of 1912, which might interest you, Mr. Pellew. They are explained by the fact that one of the most eminent permanent officials of the Foreign Office was a joint master-of-hounds with my husband, and the families were intimately associated accordingly." She unlocked the diary, fumbling a little with the tiny key. "This is the first one:

Luncheon with Mrs. S. in Hyde Park Gate. Small party. Delicious food, but the room terribly hot. Felt rather out of it, and certainly failed to shine, as I was placed between Mungo Deane of the F.O. talking about the *Entente Cordiale*—of which I heartily disapprove—and a War Office colonel laying down the law about the pros and cons of conscription—of which I know nothing. Was introduced to Lancelot (Beetle) Browne, who is generally spoken of as a likely successor to Lord Esher as indispensable maid-of-all-work behind the scenes, and reputed to be as clever as he is rich—i.e., tremendously. A plain young man, fattish, and already balding. Though definitely not attractive, his personality was engaging."

Pellew sat bolt upright in his chair.
"Lancelot Browne," he repeated. "But he's—he's—"
"Just a minute, Mr. Pellew. This is the second:

Dined at Hurlingham with the Seafords preliminary to the Polo Ball. Twenty-four covers. Amazing flowers. The meal over-elaborate and stuffy—conversation nothing but handicaps and ponies and chukkas—but the dance exceedingly well done, and the *valses* divinely played. Supped—rather surprisingly—with Beetle

Browne, who dances admirably, as so many fat men do. I gather I was envied—and may even be talked about! —as he is very much a coming man with his money and his recent appointment as Private Secretary to the latest recruit to the Cabinet. He talked about his collection of stamps, Chinese pottery, and the marriage customs of remote Pacific Islands. Amusing—sometimes witty—but I felt that all the time he was really thinking of something else. Himself?

That's all. Girlish and rather fatuous, I'm afraid."

Pellew was staring straight in front of him as if he had seen a ghost.

"Well, Greg," said Humphrey impatiently, "who is Lancelot Browne? You sounded as if you knew."

"Yes, I know," said Pellew. "He's come quite a long way since those entries in Lady Hannington's diary. He's an additional—and unpaid—personal Private Secretary to the Prime Minister. He pulls more strings behind the scenes than anyone in the country. If the Commander was lunching with him that day—" He broke off.

"It seems to me a likely enough supposition," said Lady Hannington.

"But if so—what?" demanded Humphrey.

Pellew finished his *armagnac* and poured himself another glass. "Right," he said abruptly. "Let's assume that our Mr. X equals Lancelot Browne, and add that fact to my theory about Hargest having been a Secret Service man. If I'm right it wasn't Beetle Browne who's interested in what happened to Hargest. It's the P.M. And why? Because, as I imagine you know, the Prime Minister is technically the responsible head of the British Secret Service. He also has a good many other fish to fry, and therefore has an executive to represent him in dealing with Secret Service affairs, an individual traditionally known as C whose personal identity is known to three people only: the P.M.; the Secretary of State for Foreign Affairs; and the Sovereign. He communicates with subordinates only by telephone or dictaphone. His name—unlike the Directors of Military, Naval, or Air Force Intelligence—is nowhere listed. The names of those chaps aren't actually shouted from the housetops, but you can find them in respectable works of reference, or deduce them with a little knowledge of the world and some common sense. They're certainly in the possession of any adequately staffed foreign embassy or intelligence organisation. But C is faceless. His work is the secret service that is really secret. I was talking about the importance of his 'cover' to any spy. Consider the importance of C's cover. Consider further the questions that must have been asked in Downing Street when the news of C's suicide came through. No wonder an unconventional investigation was called for. No wonder Beetle Browne lunched my Commander at the Savoy Grill. I bet the lunch was a damned good one at that!"

"Always assuming," said Humphrey slowly, "that Hargest was in the first place one of our agents, and in the second that he was C. Isn't your conclusion rather a long jump, Greg?"

"Of course it is—long, and wild. It explains all the things that had me puzzled for all that."

"In particular," said Lady Hannington, "it explains why the Secret Service couldn't do the investigation. Presumably C never dies. A new individual must have taken over. But no one, least of all members of the Service, should know that a former C had killed himself or who that former C in fact was."

"You don't miss a trick, Lady Hannington."

"Perhaps it's as well that I don't keep a diary any longer, Mr. Pellew."

In his turn Humphrey reached for the *armagnac*.

"Well—what do we do now, Greg?"

"Now we start from the proper beginning," said Pellew.

CHAPTER 12

EVIL COMMUNICATIONS

There was a considerable pause, while Kate looked at Humphrey, Humphrey looked at Lady Hannington, and Lady Hannington continued to look at Pellew.

"It's all infernally ingenious," said Humphrey at last. "Do you really believe it, Greg?"

Pellew shrugged his shoulders.

"It was Dupin who said that when you have eliminated the impossible, then whatever remains however improbable must be true. It's a pity that it sounds a little like Oscar Wilde not at his best. It's also a pity that we haven't finished eliminating."

Kate wrinkled her nose attractively.

"Are you being realistic, or clinical?" she inquired.

"I'm sorry if I sounded coarse, Kate."

"You're not in the least sorry," said Lady Hannington. "You mustn't be a humbug, Mr. Pellew, or you'll spoil my excellent impressions of you. Which would be a pity."

"It certainly would," said Pellew. "I'll explain—or try to. Late this afternoon I got another registered envelope from Mr. Rollo Gunn."

"Queer chap—Rollo. Likeable—but I've sometimes thought him a bit mad."

"I fancy there's a good deal of method in his madness, Humphrey. He certainly takes care that his correspondence shan't go astray."

"What had he to write about this time?"

"Very little, to judge by a covering note that was barely adequate and hardly civil. He thought that I might be interested in the enclosures—and he was mine sincerely."

"Get on!" said Humphrey. "Don't be exasperating!"

"I don't mean to be exasperating," said Pellew mildly. "I'm only puzzled. The more so, because one of the enclosures seems to support the rather wild theory we've been talking about with regard to Hargest's real job; while the other pulls us back along much more conventional lines."

He pulled an envelope out of his pocket, extracted its contents with rather delicate care, and laid them on the table. On one side of his coffee-cup he placed a sheet of ordinary quarto typing paper on which was set out an itinerary and a list of names; on the other five sheets of carbon paper, clipped together. Across one corner of the top sheet—it was obviously a letter, marked *Personal* and *Private*—the words "Ballantyne correspondence—Board (?)" had been written in the neatest of longhand scripts.

"Ballantyne," said Humphrey, and held out his hand.

"All in good time, Humphrey. First things first. And in this case the first thing is this itinerary of Simon Hargest's trip to Berlin. Worked out and noted down, unless I'm the proverbial Dutchman, by the admirable and non-communicative Jukes. Everything ship-shape and Bristol fashion including times of planes' arrivals and departures, name of hotel and type of accommodation, time and place of conference meeting, names of delegates with the countries they represented—the whole shooting-match. Even the names of the official interpreters included, together with three recommended restaurants, and a note of warning on the subject of West Berlin night-clubs which Kate is far too young to read."

Kate made a face at him. Lady Hannington picked up the paper.

"No doubt you'll say that I'm too old," she said.

"I shall never say that," said Pellew gallantly.

"Thank you, Mr. Pellew. However, I will confess to short sight." She held the paper close up to her face; peered at it for a few moments; dropped it back on the table with an expression of distaste. "Curious that the Germans retain this passion for a night-life principally depending on men dressed up as women. I remember hearing about it back in the twenties— an unpleasant manifestation of the Teutonic character. And what an exceedingly disagreeable scent! From what you've told me of this Miss Jukes I should not have expected her to sprinkle perfume in her filing-cabinet."

Pellew snatched up the paper and put it to his nose.

"You're right, Lady Hannington."

"Of course I'm right—and you ought to have noticed it yourself."

"Then it didn't come from the Jukes," said Humphrey.

"Then where the devil did it come from?" demanded Pellew. "No—leave that for the moment. From my point of view what matters is the list of delegates' names. I was going to ask for them in any case, needless to say. It's a comprehensive setup: France, Italy, the Scandinavian trio, Holland, Belgium, Yugoslavia, Luxembourg, and even a couple from the other side of the Curtain—Poland and Hungary."

"You've left out the two Germanies, Greg."

"Because, in terms of my theory about Hargest, they're the most important," said Pellew. "At least, one of them is. The West German delegate is a gentleman called Otto von Schramm. I don't know a thing about his standing or qualifications as a broadcasting official. I do know, after making a few inquiries, that at the end of the war he was a captain in the Foreign Armies East department of the German General Staff; that he is at this moment one of Reinhard Gehlen's men, who have been taken over by the Americans in Germany to run their anti-Russian espionage service. Hargest wasn't alone in seeing the value of a broadcasting job as 'cover.'"

"But that clinches it," said Humphrey excitedly, "Hargest went to Berlin to meet von Schramm, with this conference as an excuse."

"That's what I thought, Humphrey. I patted myself on the back, and thought myself rather a fellow. Then I looked at Gunn's second enclosure."

"That's Hargest's handwriting," said Humphrey.

"I know. The bottom two sheets are a memorandum from James Ballantyne to the Managing Director—Hargest—for submission to the Gargantua Board of Directors. It deals, pungently and at some length, with future programme policy in general, and with the definition of Mr. Ballantyne's functions and responsibilities in particular."

"You don't surprise me, Greg."

"Then I needn't bother to read it, though I must say it's quite admirably written. Next we have Hargest's reply—distinctly brusque I'm sorry to say. He merely remarks that he finds his own views so completely at variance with those expressed by Mr. Ballantyne that he finds himself unable to submit the latter to the board. On top of this we find a letter, marked *Personal*, from Ballantyne to Hargest, which I think I will read to you.

> '*Dear Hargest*—
>
> *I don't much like living up to my reputation for being generally difficult, but I feel bound to tell you flatly that your reception of my memorandum is really the last straw.*
>
> *I was prepared for any amount of argument. I was ready to accept a good deal in the shape of qualification and watering-down. Indeed I wrote as I did in the hope of avoiding a head-on clash and subsequent show-down with you. I can't help admiring your know-how and technique, much as I hate your guts for your determining to make Gargantua TV as near a political street-walker as makes no matter.*

What I can't and won't take is this casual brush-off. It proves conclusively, what you've shown again and again in other ways, that you've no conception of the importance or value of Entertainment to Programmes; that you think of me as a clown or a fool—probably both—who has outlived his usefully picturesque accomplishments.

Either you must get rid of me, or I shall almost certainly cut your throat! There's no alternative that I can see. I don't propose to resign, and even with Sir George to back you up I'm afraid you're going to find it difficult to find an adequate excuse for sacking me. So where do we go from here? It's a pity, because if you'd never worn red tabs or a morning-coat I believe we could have got on rather well.

James Ballantyne.'"

"Whew!" murmured Humphrey. "Hot stuff!"

"Finally," continued Pellew, "we have this note from Hargest to Ballantyne, marked *Personal* and *Private:*

'Dear Ballantyne—

Don't be an ass. Your resignation is the last thing I want, and throat-cutting went out with the Borgias—at least as a political solution.

Come and dine with me as soon as I get back from Berlin. Grown men really shouldn't be able to quarrel over dancing-girl troupes, or even over serious subjects like Greek Drama or Quiz Games.

Meanwhile I'll tell Miss Jukes to send you some tranquilizers.

Yours—

Simon Hargest.'"

"And that's the lot?"

"That, Humphrey, is the lot. Two questions arise. Does that correspondence between Hargest and Ballantyne mean literally what it says? What is Mr. Gunn's motive in sending it to me? He had every good reason to send me the Berlin itinerary. There were plenty of good reasons for him being able to lay his hands on it. But this other stuff—"

"Of course it doesn't mean what it says," said Kate Clymping, who never beat about any bushes. "It's a case of a couple of exhibitionists showing off to each other, if you ask me."

"He didn't ask you, darling," observed Humphrey. "And you don't know Jim Ballantyne as well as I do. Mix uncommon efficiency with genuine convictions plus the artistic temperament, and you've got the makings of a murderer. I think Hargest's reference to the Borgias was quite deliberately chosen."

"I confess I find it difficult," said Lady Hannington, "to believe that a grown man could contemplate actually killing another, just because they didn't get along in business. I agree with Kate—in spite of having distrusted the artistic temperament all my life. I've known it go too often with unpunctuality, a strong disinclination for hard work, and a lack of attention to personal hygiene."

"Jim's temperament has nothing in common with Chelsea or Greenwich Village, Mother. And he wasn't in business with Hargest—he was in TV with him, and to an extent under his thumb, which is a very different pair of shoes."

"Shall we bring it in non-proven?" suggested Pellew mildly. "At any rate for the moment. I suppose Gunn had a motive in sending the stuff to me if, as you say, Humphrey, he's devoted to Hargest's memory, and there's no love lost accordingly between him and Ballantyne. But how did he get hold of it? When we saw him he didn't claim access to any private papers Hargest had left."

"The Jukes would have had them. He could have got them from her."

"These, Humphrey? I don't think so. They weren't typed on the machine I saw in Hargest's outer office. I noticed the make—matter of habit. I believe Hargest typed these letters himself on one of those baby Hermes jobs made specially light for executives who want to work during plane trips. Very handy they are, too."

Lady Hannington picked up the papers again, and once more lifted them to her nose.

"I always like it when Humphrey starts contradicting his own arguments," she said tranquilly. "If you really want to know where these came from I think I can tell you."

"Hargest's brief-case, I suppose."

"No, dear boy—from one of the drawers in Mrs. Hargest's bedroom: one used, I imagine, for handkerchiefs or possibly underclothes, though I should have expected her to use something more subtle. She gave me the impression of being a fastidious person."

Pellew got out of his chair.

"You mean that Mrs. Hargest found these papers after her husband's death; hid them in her bedroom; and then on some impulse sent them to Rollo Gunn?"

"Mr. Gunn might have—found them on his own."

"In Mrs. Hargest's bedroom?" said Kate. "What would he be doing there? I'm surprised at you."

"I'm quite serious," said Lady Hannington.

"And probably quite right," said Pellew. "In which case Rollo Gunn, with or without the widow's connivance, has deliberately provided me with evidence leading back towards Ballantyne, simultaneously providing other evidence pointing towards Berlin. I wonder why—and I'm sure he won't tell me if I ask him."

"He'll just say," said Humphrey, "that as an investigator you ought to be interested in any evidence leading anywhere. And I suppose you ought."

He rose laboriously to his feet, and put a hand on Kate's shoulder. "I'm taking the ladies home, Greg. We could talk about this all night and get no forrader."

He looked longingly at the *armagnac* bottle and Kate moved it swiftly out of reach.

"What are you going to do?"

"Stay here for a little, and do some more thinking," said Pellew.

"How about some action?" suggested Humphrey, giving an arm to his mother.

"All in good time. You shall have lots of opportunity to grin like a dog and run about the city. Thank you all no end for coming. Kate, you're the best sounding-board I know. If I told Lady Hannington what I think of her she'd say I was being vulgarly fulsome."

"She's the best mother-in-law I know," said Kate, with an enchanting smile.

"I've had a most interesting evening, Mr. Pellew. By the way, I've just remembered something else about Mr. 'Beetle' Browne—something that I could hardly put in writing even in a diary, as you'll appreciate. He was reputed a homosexual: the elegant and discreet kind, who never get into the papers. Good night." And she had shepherded Kate and Humphrey through the door, and closed it behind her, before Pellew had time to react to this new manifestation of her astonishing personality.

After a few moments he lighted a pipe; rang the bell for Madame; apologised for the lateness of the hour; and asked for a fresh brew of coffee.

"Remain as long as you wish, monsieur. You can let yourself out, and ensure that the front door is fastened, as you have done before. You will excuse me if I go to bed when I have brought the coffee?"

In a corner of the room beside the fireplace, under a print of the battle of Wagram, was a long wicker-work arm-chair stuffed with rather shabby cushions. Pellew lowered himself into it, lay back, and looked at the ceiling.

Taking one thing with another he was as puzzled—and baffled—as he had ever been in his life. There were too many ends about the business, every one of them loose. It was all very well for Humphrey Clymping to talk about "action." To start being active was obviously desirable—or the Commander at Scotland Yard would want to know the reason why not. But which path to follow among the many winding in and out of this particular maze?

Pellew's first instinctive reaction was to go back to the Commander and ask him straight out whether Hargest had in fact been C at the time of his death. Reflection told him it wouldn't do. In the first place the Commander might well not know the answer. Even Beetle Browne might not know. The Prime Minister could, probably would, have preferred to keep his motive for initiating the inquiry to himself. In the second, if the Commander did know, he would be bound to deny it. All that Pellew would get out of it would be confirmation of his trying to be too clever. All the same he would have to follow up the lead to Berlin and Otto von Schramm, which would take time, involve Pellew in a new set of complicated circumstances, and as likely as not prove in the long run the reddest of herrings.

Then there was Ballantyne. Could there be anything really sinister behind the correspondence with Hargest? Pellew did not believe it, no matter what people could find to say about the "artistic temperament." The gap was too wide between a Ballantyne and—for example—a Wainwright. At the same time if not Ballantyne there was Rollo Gunn, with or without Mrs. Hargest, with or without Miss Jukes. In pointing a finger at Ballantyne what was Gunn's motive? Was he covering up for himself? What was Mrs. Hargest's motive, if she had given the papers to Rollo Gunn? How deeply had Gunn and Miss Jukes been in Hargest's confidence? Had he merely engaged them for auld lang syne, or because of their training and experience in intelligence work? In any case he would not have let them know that he was C. Could either of them have found out?

Madame brought the coffee and wished him good-night. Pellew nodded to her absently, sipped with gratitude and satisfaction, knocked out his pipe and refilled it.

Then there were the odd bits and pieces: the tape-recordings in Miss Jukes' filing cabinet; Sally Anstruther—could he be sure that that attractive young person hadn't pulled wool over his eyes?; the solicitude Sir George Farley and Rollo Gunn had expressed for Jane Hargest—natural enough on the face of it, but somehow excessive as her personality come into sharper focus; Lady Hannington's parting shot concerning Beetle Browne—just an arrow from a bow drawn at a venture?

He moved restlessly, and the chair creaked. No use letting speculation run round and round like a squirrel in a cage. He must go to Berlin; risk putting himself out of the main picture for a few days; rely on Humphrey Clymping to hold the fort at Gargantua, keeping his eyes open and his mouth shut.

He finished his coffee, and wrote out a cheque for his bill. In the doorway he stopped and looked back at the room. Its atmosphere of cosy withdrawal from contemporary existence struck Pellew at that moment as peculiarly sympathetic. What was it Napoleon had once said in one of his many moments of frustrated exasperation on St. Helena?

"Mankind must be very bad to be as bad as I think it is."

"I fancy I know just how he felt, poor devil!" muttered Pellew.

PART TWO **WHY?**

Will you, I pray,
  demand that demi-devil
Why he hath thus ensnar'd
  my soul and body?
                    —OTHELLO

CHAPTER THIRTEEN

KATE CLYMPING TAKES A HAND

Forty-eight hours later Pellew was on an air-liner bound for Berlin. Apart from Lady Hannington, and Kate and Humphrey Clymping, the only people aware of his trip were the Commander and Rollo Gunn. To the former he had said no more than that he wanted to look into the background of the conference which had been practically Simon Hargest's last official activity before his death. From him he had asked, and got, the necessary official introductions to the British Occupation authorities and the West German Radio. Rollo Gunn he had merely informed on the telephone that he was going. Gunn had taken the news very much for granted. He had added, apparently as an afterthought, the suggestion that Pellew might find it worth while to be sure and contact the Polish interpreter at the conference.

"This fellow with the curious name?"

"Ladislas Sale—that's the man."

"But why?"

"I don't know." Gunn's voice had sounded impatient. "I can only tell you that he seems to have interested Hargest a good deal. He talked a lot about him when he got back. Made me get his dossier from the War Office."

Pellew, not unreasonably, had asked why on earth the British War Office should have a dossier concerning an interpreter working for a West German radio conference.

"He was a subaltern in our army at the end of the 1914—18 war. He was Polish on his mother's side—hence his queer Christian name—but born and brought up in this country. In 1919, like a good many other people, he couldn't get a job. A war-time yeomanry commission wasn't a conspicuous qualification, I imagine. Anyway he went off to Poland and joined some lancer regiment for the war against the Bolsheviks and the Battle of Warsaw. The call of the blood must have done the trick, for he immediately opted for Polish nationality, promising apparently to do occasional jobs for M.I.6 on the side. Naturally there are no details about those. In September, 1939, he was second-in-command of his regiment, stationed at Grodno. The final words of the dossier read simply 'believed killed.' "

"What an extraordinary story—and he wasn't killed?"

"Obviously not, as Hargest met him in Berlin. I gathered that he'd been pretty badly knocked about. You'll see for yourself."

Gunn rang off. Pellew made up his mind that he certainly would see Ladislas Sale for himself. At the same time he wondered if Gunn's rather over-circumstantial description might not be the laying of a false trail to divert Pellew's attention from more important issues. That possibility would have to be kept in mind.

Meanwhile Humphrey Clymping, interpreting his instruction "to hold the fort at Gargantua" in liberal terms, had made up his mind to approach Sally Anstruther. He salved his conscience, which made him admit ruefully that Sally's extreme prettiness had a good deal to do with it, by making his approach through Toby Scott. That young man, who would have cheerfully entertained the devil if it gave him the chance to include Sally in the company, proved co-operative in the extreme. He jumped at Humphrey's suggestion that the latter should throw a small party in Seven Dials, and that Toby should bring Sally Anstruther.

Humphrey duly informed his wife. She did not show it, but she was not very pleased. She was not the type to be jealous of another girl, not even of a girl as pretty as Sally was reputed to be. Humphrey had proved a completely re-formed character since their marriage, and she had not seen the slightest symptom of any relapse. On the other hand, she was a little jealous of Humphrey's working with Gregory Pellew. She found the inquiry into Simon Hargest's death fascinating. She wanted to be in on it, actively. To act merely as a "sounding-board" was not enough. And now Humphrey would have his party, try to get something out of the An-struther girl—and succeed only in putting his large feet into it as likely as not—while Kate was tied up at her theatre and out of the running.

It then struck her, being both a nice and a sensible person, that she was being unreasonable and rather stupid. What was to prevent her doing some work on her own? There were four days in the week uncomplicated by matinées, during which Humphrey was busy either at the Studios or in the Gargantua Building. She could follow up any line she chose—and there was one line which she felt was being seriously neglected. Kate could not make herself believe that the solution to the Hargest mystery, with all its ingredients of secret agents and Cabinet Ministers and high policy, would be found in the handbag of a private secretary, or even in her private life. It may be, she thought to herself, that I'm a woman and realistic accordingly, while Humphrey and Gregory Pellew are hope-less romantics like all men. But I want to know a great deal more about Mrs. Hargest.

She made up her mind to find out. Her first impulse was to consult Lady Hannington, but she decided against it. Her relations with her mother-in-law were peculiar and excellent. She realised that they were so largely because of a mutual recognition of individual spheres of influence. Lady Hannington had her own rooms; followed a domestic routine of her own, except that she ate meals with Humphrey and Kate whenever she felt so inclined; contributed to the household budget. She never interfered or offered advice unasked. If occasionally she quelled Humphrey's exuberance it was a matter of habit not of right. While invariably interested in Kate's personal doings she never asked questions about them. In short she treated Kate as a person capable of shouldering her own problems and responsibilities. Kate decided that amateur sleuthing was one of those responsibilities.

She said nothing to Humphrey because, while devoted to him and well aware that he was no fool, she knew that it was difficult for him to concentrate on more than one thing at a time. She did not want to distract him from the Gargantua front. And she felt instinctively that any approach to Mrs. Hargest called for the velvet glove rather than the mailed fist.

Upon theatre bills and programmes Kate's surname was still printed "Sempill," as it had been before her marriage. She found that she still had some visiting cards similarly printed; and it was one of these that she sent in to Mrs. Hargest, by the hand of the latter's sloe-eyed maid, about three o'clock in the afternoon of the day following Pellew's departure for Berlin. On the back of the card she had scribbled—mendaciously enough—"Shakespeare Quatercentenary 1964—National Theatre Fund." The sentence contained enough truth, she hoped, to carry reasonable conviction. (A fund was in fact in process of being raised with this particular label.) It was sufficiently vaguely phrased, she hoped also, to provoke curiosity. If her hopes were disappointed she could try some other gambit. She would have given nothing away.

It appeared that the sloe-eyed maid was not impressed by the Glamour of the Theatre. Kate was left to cool her heels on the landing of Mrs. Hargest's flat for the best part of ten minutes, which did not improve her temper. She had almost finished smoking a cigarette when the front door of the flat was reopened. There emerged a moustachioed gentleman

112

wearing an old-fashioned bowler hat with a curly brim and a long overcoat with astrakhan cuffs and collar, the latter turned up to his ears. He walked briskly to the lift without giving Kate so much as a glance. As she turned to look after him she heard the maid's voice inviting her to come in.

She was shown into a room which she recognised from Humphrey's description: the Japanese-gold wallpaper; the modern French paintings; the view across the roof-tops with the top stories of the Gargantua Building in the distance; the single photograph in its silver frame on the escritoire. She would have liked to have studied that photograph at close quarters. Simon Hargest as a name without the attachment of a face had begun to irritate her. But she had hardly entered the room before she found herself settled into a chair—a chair uncomfortably low so that sitting in it she was conscious of showing too much of her knees and of facing the light— with the graceful figure of Jane Hargest between her and the big window.

"I don't think—have we, Miss Sempill?" said Jane Hargest politely.

"No, we haven't met before," said Kate resolutely. "I'm afraid you'll think it pretty brash of me to thrust myself in on you like this—"

"Not at all. It makes a change. I'm getting a little tired of my own society."

"But in the circumstances—"

"Of my husband's death? Is it heartless to confess that I find black clothes and the company of lawyers wearisome? Simon wasn't a devotee of the little black dress, and his opinion of lawyers was unprintable."

So that, thought Kate, explains the curly-brimmed bowler and the astrakhan-trimmed overcoat—or does it?

"I wouldn't have dreamed of bothering you," she went on, "if it hadn't been that Mr. Hargest had expressed so much personal interest in the work of the National Theatre Fund Committee."

113

"I see. I'm afraid I didn't know. He had such wide interests."

"Of course, Mrs. Hargest. Perhaps I'm wrong. Perhaps his interest was less personal than on behalf of Gargantua TV. I know one of his letters mentioned the possibility of a considerable contribution to our fund from Gargantua on the understanding that the National Theatre, when built, would give preferential treatment to Gargantua for televised programme items."

"That would account for it. My husband never discussed that sort of business with me. How can I help you?"

"I'll be quite frank with you," said Kate, who believed—with the late Doctor Goebbels—that the bigger the lie the bigger the chance of its being believed. "The committee I represent is most anxious to know whether there is any likelihood of this contribution to its funds still being available. The sum mentioned, Mrs. Hargest, was a very large one. The committee does not feel itself free to approach any other of the Independent Television Companies until it knows where it stands."

"There's nothing about it in his will, if that's what you mean," said Jane Hargest. "I'd suggest your seeing Sir George Farley. He'd be bound to know if Gargantua, as an organisation, is still interested. He's the Chairman, you know."

"Of course. I'm sorry to have been a nuisance."

"Think nothing of it." Mrs. Hargest held out an elegant cigarette-case. "You're on the stage yourself, Miss Sempill?"

Kate admitted as much, and gave the name of her play and theatre.

"I hope it has a long run. Then I shall be able to look forward to coming to see you. At present, naturally, I don't go out at all."

"Naturally. I apologise again for having bothered you."

"But I entirely understand, Miss Sempill. I'm only sorry not to be able to be more helpful. If Sir George can't tell you what you want to know, there's Mr. Rollo Gunn—my late husband's personal assistant at Gargantua. He might be use-ful."

Kate thanked her, and stood up to go. As she did so she could not resist another glance at the photograph of Simon Hargest.

"My husband," said Jane Hargest, with the suspicion of a catch in her voice. "I think I must put it away. It reminds me of too many things. Would you call it good of him?"

"I don't know," said Kate. "I—" She broke off, realising that she had very nearly admitted to never having seen Simon Hargest, which would have let the cat well and truly out of the bag.

"I suppose you only saw him once or twice at your committee meetings," said Jane. "I think he was unusually good-looking. No doubt I'm prejudiced. Good-bye, Miss Sempill."

Kate went away, considerably relieved but also considerably puzzled. She had found out next to nothing—except that Jane Hargest's attitude to a perfect stranger had been anything but natural: an attitude that could easily be accounted for by nervous strain. She was particularly puzzled by the reference to the photograph. She understood what Humphrey had meant when he had called it a mask. But it was not a good-looking mask, like some photographs of matinée idols. It was certainly not a photograph to remind anyone of anything. Again, why had Mrs. Hargest brought in Sir George Farley's name and then added Rollo Gunn's almost as an afterthought? Surely a subvention to a National Theatre Fund —Kate rather patted herself on the back for having invented that one—would be more likely to have concerned the personal assistant than the chairman? Finally, there was the stranger she had encountered leaving the flat. All Kate could swear to was the big astrakhan collar, the white moustache and—she thought—a pair of dark glasses, apart from the old-fashioned bowler hat. It seemed to her an odd get-up for the lawyer whom Mrs. Hargest had implied he was. Was it fanciful to imagine that the visitor had been at pains to conceal his identity?

As she left the flats Kate noticed on the opposite side of the road a large plate-glass window, framed by startling new blue and yellow paint, advertising **MORNING COFFEE** and **DAINTY TEAS**; the sort of establishment common enough in Chelsea or South Kensington, but rather unusual for Belgravia. She went in, thinking that her imagination might be stimulated by a cup of tea. The place was empty—it was only just a quarter to four—except for the proprietress, a brisk thin middle-aged woman with a mechanical smile and obviously dyed blonde hair. Kate asked for China tea and an éclair. Both proved excellent. Kate said as much, and added a compliment on the decoration scheme.

"I hope you'll tell your friends," said the proprietress frankly. "It looks all right, but so far trade's shocking. I told my——my friend who put up the cash that this place wasn't right for this sort of carry-on. Of course he knew better. He always does. And there you are."

Kate expressed polite sympathy.

"Not that I care, mind you. I'm not all that in love with hard work. But it gets a bit boring, sitting in here and looking out of the window. People who live in flats like those across the road have their dainty teas at home—and I don't blame them."

Kate suggested that she should sit down, and have some tea.

"Thanks—I don't mind if I do. You begin to feel your feet after forty. You don't live around here?"

Kate admitted that she did not.

"I'm on a job," she said.

"Really?"

The tone of the question held profound disbelief.

Kate allowed irritation to master discretion. "I'm trying to find out something about one of the tenants in that block of flats opposite," she said.

116

The proprietress's eyes boiled with excited curiosity. "You mean you're one of those private inquiry agents?"

Feeling that she knew for the first time what it must be like to be a quick-change artist Kate took her cue. "That's about it," she said. "Smart of you to think of it."

The proprietress smirked, and moistened her lips with her tongue. "I know my way about," she said. "I learned it the hard way. Two husbands—and both ran out on me. Vera Mandrake's the name."

Kate appraised the discontented calculating expression and the sensual mouth, and decided to take a chance. "It's a divorce business, Mrs. Mandrake. I don't know if you'd care to help me? I'd make it worth your while."

Mrs. Mandrake shrugged her shoulders. "Depends on what you want to know. The flat porter comes in here for a coffee most mornings."

"Is he a talkative type?"

"He likes his bit of gossip. Don't we all?"

Kate took a five-pound note out of her bag, folded it, and tucked it under the rim of her saucer. "I'll be in here again about the same time the day after to-morrow, Mrs. Mandrake. I'll be very grateful for anything you can tell me about visitors to a Mrs. Hargest—she's the tenant of the penthouse flat in the block."

"Gentleman visitors, I suppose?"

"Particularly one gentleman," said Kate, "who wears an overcoat with astrakhan collar and cuffs and a curly-brimmed bowler hat—and possibly dark glasses."

"Sounds like an actor to me," said Mrs. Mandrake. "I never thought the stage was a respectable profession. You won't expect me to give you any names?"

"I shan't expect anything," said Kate, with perfect truth. She paid her bill and went away. She was beginning to realise—what Gregory Pellew could have told her—that one of the most disagreeable things about detective work was the character of persons prepared to be helpful to the detective. After twenty minutes of Vera Mandrake's society she felt an almost desperate need for a bath: a very hot bath pleasantly scented by Floris.

It was therefore with feelings mingled of distaste and conscious rectitude that Kate returned to the dispensary of dainty teas some forty-eight hours later. However, she was glad to find that on this occasion there were several other customers in evidence, giving Mrs. Mandrake neither leisure nor opportunity for conversation *à deux*. She brought Kate her tea without sign of previous recognition. But under the bill was an unobtrusive envelope.

"We'll call it a tenner, shall we?" muttered Vera Mandrake, under cover of offering a selection of macaroons and *profiterolles*. "You'll find it's worth it."

Kate felt the claim to be excessive—and of a piece with the estimate she had formed of Mrs. Mandrake's character and morals. On the other hand she was in no position to argue. When she paid her bill the envelope had changed places with two carefully folded fivers. She then retired through a bead curtain to where a door marked LADIES seemed to offer reasonable privacy.

Five minutes later she emerged considerably elated, but compelled perforce to admit that her imagination had wronged Mrs. Mandrake. For the porter, always assuming him trustworthy, had produced information which might be confusing but was certainly interesting.

It appeared that the first visit to Mrs. Hargest's flat of the character in the astrakhan-trimmed overcoat had taken place some three days after Mr. Hargest's death. There had been nothing about it to suggest any concealment of identity: no turned-up collar; certainly no dark glasses. The gentleman had been elderly. The porter had particularly noticed his fine white curling moustache. He had taken him up in the lift to the penthouse flat himself, had seen the door opened to him by Mrs. Hargest, "white as a ghost and her eyes all red." The porter had heard Mrs. Hargest address the visitor as "Sir George." The visit had been paid about lunch-time. The porter had recognised the same gentleman arriving at about the same time two days later.

Since then the ashtrakhan overcoat had become a familiar sight, appearing at regular intervals always about the same time each Monday, Wednesday and Friday, and staying for a period between an hour and a half and two hours. Pressed by Mrs. Mandrake the porter had admitted that he had paid no particular attention to the visitor after the first two occasions. Certainly he might have worn his collar turned up. It was possible he had worn dark glasses. To neither fact was the porter prepared to swear. He believed in minding his own business. He was sorry for Mrs. Hargest "who was a real lady." (Mrs. Mandrake had added the cynical comment that Mrs. Hargest was also generous and presumably tipped well.) As far as the porter knew no gentleman had ever called upon Mrs. Hargest in the evenings.

Her producer would have called Kate Sempill's performance that evening perfunctory, and the girl who shared her dressing-room asked her if she was sickening for something. Her elation had faded. All she had found out amounted to the fact that Sir George Farley had been a regular visitor to Mrs. Hargest's flat ever since the tragedy—in itself not an unnatural thing. And during his interview with Pellew Sir George had admitted to his friendship and concern for the lady. It was true that Mrs. Hargest had implied that she had been seeing no one except lawyers. But it was surely unreasonable to find cause for suspicion in her failing to mention to a perfect stranger the routine visits of sympathy by an old friend of her husband's. Kate felt uncomfortable at the prospect of confessing to Humphrey that she had to all intents and purposes thrown fifteen pounds down the drain. Distaste for Mrs. Mandrake was replaced by a positive and aggrieved dislike.

However, Kate was naturally stubborn. She also remembered Humphrey telling her that among Pellew's professional axioms was the necessity to cross-check all evidence, no matter how apparently factual. The next day was a Friday. She would go and see for herself.

Damning the expense—in more senses than one—she secured a hire-car, and was lucky enough to establish it at a parking-meter about fifty yards from the block of flats and on the opposite side of the road at a quarter to one precisely. Five minutes later a taxi drew up at the entrance to the block, and Kate had a brief and unsatisfactory glimpse of the astrakhan coat and curly-brimmed bowler as their wearer hurried up the steps and disappeared within. No two hours had ever seemed to her so long while she waited for his reappearance with a bored and hungry exasperation increased by the knowledge that if on this occasion the visitor overstayed his usual calling period her car might well attract the attention of some officious traffic warden.

She need not have worried. A few moments after half past two another taxi drew up—this time empty. The visitor, who presumably had telephoned for it from the flat, came down the steps, got into it, and drove away—unfortunately not in the direction where Kate was parked. Feeling like a character out of too many novels Kate told her driver to "follow that cab." And the chase was on.

It failed to follow the precedents established by popular crime fiction. Speed was not terrific. Tyres did not screech. Traffic-lights were not ignored. The proceeding was less a chase than a procession: a tedious maddening procession through typical London traffic, moving at perhaps fifteen miles an hour at its liveliest. Also it turned out that the hire-car driver was considerably less expert than the taxi driver. However, the taxi did not sensibly increase its lead. Kate wondered whether its goal was the Gargantua Building or Sir George Farley's office in the City.

When the chase led across Waterloo Bridge she knew. What she did not know was what she could or ought to do next. In her dressing-room the evening before she had decided that the National Theatre Fund could provide her once again with an excuse, this time for an interview with Sir

George. Though what she could hope to get from such an interview she had no idea. In daylight the plan seemed horribly flimsy. Sir George was a man of affairs and a man of the world. To be shown up by him as an imposter—or worse, as an imposter without any apparent motive—would be extremely unpleasant. If her real identity was discovered it might be worse than that. On top of that realisation Kate found her car jammed inextricably between a bus and two lorries just as the taxi nipped past lights that changed remorselessly from green to yellow, from yellow to red. By the time the bus-driver, the lorry-drivers, and the hire-car driver had exchanged appropriate compliments, the taxi had rounded a corner and disappeared. "The Gargantua Building —and get on!" said Kate despairingly.

The hire-car driver did his best. But by the time he had got there, there was no sign of the taxi. Kate jumped out, told him to wait, and hurried into the building. The great entrance hall with its marble flooring and white pillars seemed at that moment particularly cold and forbidding. There was no one visible, apart from the receptionist, except a party of teen-agers shepherded by a middle-aged lady in remarkably ill-fitting clothes, a seedy character clasping a trombone, and an actor whom Kate knew—luckily—only by sight.

Kate stiffened her jaw and walked to the reception desk.

"Sir George Farley, please."

The girl looked blank.

"Now don't tell me that he isn't in," said Kate firmly. "I saw him arrive."

"I don't know Sir George by sight," said the girl patiently. "I'm rather new here. Anyway, he wouldn't come to the desk."

"You must have noticed his overcoat—heavy astrakhan trimmings, and an old-fashioned bowler hat."

"I'm sure he hasn't come in. I'll ring the Chairman's office if you like. What name shall I say?"

"It doesn't matter," said Kate. "I expect he'll be too busy to see me."

Something in her tone flicked the receptionist on the raw.

"You must have made a mistake," she said tartly. "I've not been busy the last ten minutes, and I know that nobody's crossed the hall to the lifts during that time except Mr. Rollo Gunn. He had a coat over his arm and no hat—I remember perfectly."

CHAPTER 14

HUMPHREY THROWS A PARTY

"And what do you imagine you've got out of all that?" was Humphrey Clymping's not unnatural comment.

Kate had made confession of her *sub rosa* activities the same evening before going off to the theatre.

"I don't know," said Kate frankly enough. "I thought you might be able to tell me."

Humphrey grinned. "Don't try and wheedle me into the bargain, Katie. You were lucky not to find yourself in the Farley den. He's not got where he is by being the tenth possessor of a foolish face. He knows his business, and as far as one can gather there's precious little that isn't his business."

"All right," admitted Kate. "Maybe I wasn't so clever. Maybe I should have done things differently. So what? We do know more than we did."

"Do we?" Humphrey yawned. "We know that Mrs. Hargest has been receiving regular visits from a gentleman who seems to like dressing up as the old-fashioned type of actor-manager. It's not a burning or a shining light in the darkness. We don't know whether he is Sir George, or Rollo Gunn, or some third party."

"We know that the original visitor was Sir George, Humphrey."

"Yes—we can assume that much," admitted Humphrey handsomely. "And it was a perfectly natural thing for him to do. It was natural—if perhaps excessive—for him to go on paying visits of sympathy. Elderly gentlemen like an excuse for patting good-looking girls on the shoulder, and letting them sob on their bosoms."

With commendable tact Kate refrained from asking Humphrey how he knew.

"If the man I followed was Sir George," she said, "what happened to him when he got to the Gargantua Building?"

"That," retorted Humphrey, "is where local knowledge comes in."

"Oh, don't be maddening! I'm late as it is."

"The reception girl admitted she was new," Humphrey went on. "It's true that members of the staff go straight across the hall to the lifts. But the Chairman wears another pair of shoes. No mixing with the common herd for him. There's a side entrance to the Building which leads to a private lift, and that lift goes straight up to the top floor and opens on to a tiny landing behind the Managing Director's office. The Chairman uses that lift. He has a hide-out at the other end of the same corridor. That's how he gave you the slip."

"I see. Yes—if it was Sir George."

"Of course it was."

Kate went to the door; opened it; and turned round.

"Suppose it was Rollo Gunn, Humphrey?"

"Why on earth should it have been?"

"You heard him talk—well, sympathetically—about Mrs. Hargest. And it's my experience that men who pat the shoulders of good-looking girls aren't always elderly."

"Come off it, Katie dear. You're implying that Rollo deliberately got himself up so that a casual observer might mistake him for Farley; that he complicated things with dark glasses and—I suppose—a false moustache; that he took off that distinctive overcoat in the cab, and disposed somehow of

124

that equally distinctive bowler hat, in case someone was on his track—you're letting imagination run right away with you."

"I suppose you're right. Damn. Oh, well—have a good party."

"I shall do my best," said Humphrey, and blew his wife a kiss. "You'll be able to see for yourself when you get home."

"I want to find you able to see for yourself when I get home," said Kate coldly.

"That insinuation," retorted Humphrey, "I shall ignore."

Both at Oxford, and later in London, the reputation of Humphrey—in those days the Viscount—Clymping as a giver of parties had been distinctly out of the ordinary. His undergraduate guests had been expected to wear evening dress; to drink with discrimination and without getting drunk; and to amuse themselves without the distraction of feminine company. No denizen of Somerville or Lady Margaret Hall, of St. Hugh's or St. Hilda's, no matter how distinguished for beauty or brains or both, ever entered Humphrey's rooms. Their palates, he asserted, could appreciate nothing more exotic than South African sherry; their society, now that chaperonage rules had become practically a dead letter, implied risks that no sensible bachelor should take.

In Chelsea, on the other hand, Humphrey's parties had been both mixed and uninhibited. True that girls who omitted make-up and visits to their hairdresser were not invited twice. True that a gossip-columnist—or, worse still, any gossip-columnist's leg-man posing as a guest—risked expulsion by the strong hand. The atmosphere had been one of rowdiness, considerable alcoholism, and frequent bonhomous excursions in fast cars ending more than once in the police-courts. The self-conscious Edwardian at Oxford had adopted in London the fashion of the American college campus. It had been a change viewed as one much for the worse by Lady Hannington from the decent seclusion of Hares Green.

Something of this reputation for the eccentric mingled with the disreputable had accompanied Humphrey Clymping when he joined the staff of Gargantua. It was not apparent in his work. In fact all basis for it had vanished with the establishment of his new domestic background. But the aura still clung to him, providing a certain fascination for young men like Toby Scott, whose teens had been enlivened by the viscount's legendary exploits, and who liked to believe that he might still show them a thing or two.

Toby, who put Sally Anstruther on a pedestal whose height would have astonished that young person extremely, had felt it necessary to throw out dark hints of what she might expect in Seven Dials. As might have been expected Sally was both intrigued and excited: a result which Toby had neither anticipated nor desired.

"Of course all those stories are years old," he said. "He was abroad for quite a time before he took the job with us."

"Wasn't he mixed up with a murder case in Italy?"

Toby admitted reluctantly that it was so.

"Anyway," he added, "he's married now."

"I know," said Sally. "She's an actress. I've seen pictures of her in the glossies—not the dowdy intellectual type. I'm looking forward to the evening."

"I shouldn't expect too much," said Toby gloomily.

Sally looked at him with eyes distractingly widened.

"I don't get what you mean, Toby. Is it going to be too wild, or too dull? Better make up your mind."

"All I know is that I wish we were going out by ourselves."

Sally chose to ignore the familiar gambit.

"I don't believe," she said, "that we're in for an evening of charades and 'instant' coffee. Do you think we can afford a taxi—between us?"

"I'll ring for one," said Toby hastily. The dress Sally was wearing would certainly have raised eyebrows in the Tube.

Whatever it was the ingenuous pair expected they did not find it. In justice to Toby Scott it must be admitted that Humphrey's original idea had been to restage one of the parties of his hot youth as a smoke-screen behind which he could make an approach to Sally Anstruther with little risk of being taken seriously by her or anybody else. When it came to the point he found himself up against two obstacles. The first was that when he tried to make contact with the bright young persons who had enlivened his and their nonage he found that they were either respectable *rangés*, hopelessly middle-aged, or abroad for their own or their country's good. The second was Lady Hannington. It was impossible to throw a party in the Seven Dials house without warning the countess. If she did not see, she would be bound to hear. And Lady Hannington did not care to be a witness after the event. The reserve of her judgment when Humphrey told her of his plan could only be described as glacial.

"That, dear," she said, "will be very nice, I'm sure. Who will be coming, did you say?"

Humphrey had not said; and did not say now.

"It's quite time you entertained some of your television colleagues," continued his mother. "There's that Mr. Ballantyne I've heard you speak of so often, and Hamish Rathbone who works you so hard. I shall look forward to meeting them. Naturally an organisation like Gargantua must be full of attractive girls—not to mention those friends of Kate's who seem always to be out of work, poor things. And isn't it rather a long time since you've seen anything of Hugo Bastin and that most attractive wife of his?"

Humphrey choked, laughed, and decided to make the best of it. Lady Hannington had provided him with excuse for inviting Sally Anstruther and Toby Scott. It was any odds that Ballantyne wouldn't and that Hamish Rathbone couldn't come. If Hugo Bastin was rather a bore Joan Bastin—formerly Bathhurst—was as good company as she was an actress, quite apart from having been a very good friend to Kate. And it would be amusing to send invitations to Rollo Gunn and Lilian Jukes. . . .

This amusement was replaced by an apprehension almost amounting to dismay when Ballantyne, Rathbone, and Lilian Jukes all accepted. The Bastins would call for Kate at her theatre, and come along with her. For none of this had Humphrey bargained. Least of all had he bargained for his mother's attendance. Her eyes missed nothing that was worth seeing, as he knew very well. He did not want her jumping to any false conclusions concerning himself and Sally Anstruther. . . .

One of the features of the house in Seven Dials was its attic. From the evidence of a permanent mustiness about its atmosphere it had once been used to store fruit. Its only furnishings were a refectory table (Humphrey had bought it in Sicily, only to find that it was too long for any other room in the house) and a vast Russian stove whose origin was unknown. As a rule it was no more than an invaluable repository for every kind of junk and lumber: suit-cases, books with burst bindings, cardboard boxes, fishing tackle, boots for mountaineering—the flotsam and jetsam of daily living which it is more trouble to get rid of than to hide away. Kate had Hoovered the floor, and stacked most of the junk on top of the stove. Humphrey had dragged up a motley collection of Li-los, deck-chairs, cushions; a mattress under the window; an armchair for Lady Hannington, placed as far from the stove as possible. One pile of plates, another of knives, forks and spoons, hunks of butter on three wooden platters, a big cheeseboard, bottles of beer, *fiascos* of Chianti in their wicker containers, a variety of glasses and tankards, and four tureens of steaming *spaghetti bolognese* completed scene and sequence, lighted by candles in empty wine-bottles. The general impression—as Lady Hannington remarked and Humphrey was obliged to admit—was that of an amateur producer trying his prentice hand at *La Bohème*.

It was this theatricality of setting which principally struck Sally Anstruther and Toby Scott, as they hesitated in the doorway at the top of the narrow wooden stairs which led to the attic. Humphrey stood on the far side of the table, waving a Chianti bottle dangerously in one hand, and dispensing spaghetti into a soup-plate with the other. Wearing a silk shirt open at the neck and baggy corduroy trousers he looked Fal-

128

staffian rather than Vikingesque to Hamish Rathbone who watched him with an expression of mingled indulgence and irritation. Jim Ballantyne, sitting cross-legged on a cushion at Lady Hannington's feet, could be heard above the general babble laying down the law on the subject of television documentaries. ("Absolute sincerity—the individual personal approach—nothing else matters a damn!") Two young actors were discussing a suggested provincial tour. ("The money's all right, old boy, and the part's not too bad. But nine weeks out, I ask you! You can't afford to be out of London these days. You miss too many TV jobs.") Two young actresses were exchanging confidences about an agent. ("No, darling, he hasn't made a sign of a pass—yet. But you know what they say about him. You know Cecilia Thwaites, don't you? She says he jumped over his desk and chased her round it for ten minutes—not that you can believe a word she says!") A group of polo-necked sweaters and dirndls was encouraging an inadequately bearded character with a head bald as an egg, who was plucking inadequately at the strings of a guitar. Over all brooded a haze of cigarette smoke.

"Come right in, Toby," bawled Humphrey through the confusion, "and let me give the pretty lady food and drink."

As Toby and Sally edged their way towards the table Toby became aware of Lilian Jukes on his other side and of her fingers on his sleeve.

"Is Mr. Gunn here?" she whispered.

"I can't see him, but I don't think so."

The pressure on his arm increased.

"Is that Mr. Ballantyne's voice? I see so badly without my glasses. And with all this smoke—"

"That's our Jim all right. Your ears don't deceive you at any rate, Miss Jukes—"

Toby broke off and stared. Lilian Jukes had pulled away her hand as if she had been stung, turned abruptly round, and made for the door.

With surprising agility Humphrey Clymping banged the soup-plate down on the table; thrust the Chianti bottle into

Rathbone's welcoming hands; ducked under the table; and emerging on all fours, like a St. Bernard from a pond, went after the fugitive. She was already on the stairs when he caught up with her and caught her by one shoulder.

"What's the trouble, Miss Jukes?"

"I'm sorry, Mr. Clymping. I never ought to have come. I—I don't feel very well."

"Do you know I don't believe you, Miss Jukes? You're not in the least sorry. And you're perfectly well."

Miss Jukes blinked up at him.

"Very well," she said. "If you prefer an unpleasant truth. I can't stay in the same room with Mr. Ballantyne."

"Why ever not? You needn't talk to him, you know."

"I've my reasons."

"And they're not my business. Quite. All the same—"

Miss Jukes interrupted him.

"Is Mr. Gunn going to be here, Mr. Clymping?"

"I'm afraid not. Would it have made any difference if he had been?"

"It might have. I don't know really. Good night."

"But I'd like to talk to you," protested Humphrey.

"About Mr. Hargest no doubt. I'm afraid you can't. Good night."

She went down the stairs. Humphrey looked after her; rubbed his jaw; went back to the party.

He rejoined Toby and Sally Anstruther in time to overhear the former asking the latter what she thought all that carry-on had been in aid of.

"Jukes has a thing about Jim," said Sally. "She was there one day in the office when he came to see Mr. Hargest, and they had a row—proper up-and-downer, so she said."

"What about? Do you know?" inquired Humphrey.

"Haven't the faintest," said Sally, her tone implying that she cared as little as she knew.

Humphrey urged her and Toby to one of the Li-los, went back to the table, and returned with filled plates and glasses.

"A bit later on—when I've finished feeding the animals,"

he said, carefully lowering his voice, "I'd like to show you my own room, Miss Anstruther. A lot more comfortable than this bear-garden, believe you me."

"Etchings?" inquired Sally, with a flirt of her eye-lashes. "Isn't that rather old hat?"

Humphrey saw Toby wince, and grinned.

"You too, Toby. No need to worry. Relax. I'll be seeing you."

Left to themselves Toby looked at Sally, and Sally looked at Toby. Both had the same impulse: to finish their spaghetti as quickly as possible, which would leave both of them with one hand free.

It was a considerable time before Humphrey came back. To his astonishment, almost to his dismay, the party had settled to go with a swing. The food disappeared. A second case of Chianti was opened. The smoke thickened. The guitarist found his form, and lifted up what proved to be an unusually agreeable tenor voice. Jim Ballantyne was heard to express opinions quite irrelevant to television. Kate Clymping arrived from her theatre in sparkling form, bringing Joan and Hugo Bastin as welcome reinforcements. The room grew steadily hotter. And Lady Hannington demanded a brandy-and-soda.

It was in fact Lady Hannington, who at last gave Humphrey the opportunity to make himself scarce without his absence being immediately obvious.

"Thank you so much, Mr. Ballantyne," she said, when the latter had found her a syphon. "Now you've wasted far too much time on an old woman. There's far more attractive metal handy—for instance my daughter-in-law who's just arrived. Go and exercise your charm on her—and tell Humphrey I'd like a word with him."

Ballantyne obeyed, a trifle bewildered by his own acquiescence.

"So there you are, my dear boy," continued Lady Hannington. "Thank heaven I can relax for a moment or two. Your Mr. Ballantyne—clever as paint no doubt, but exhausting. So positive, like a railway engine on a single-line track. And the room's getting far too hot."

"Is it, Mother?"

"Of course it is. What do you expect with all those candles? In the days when I went to the sort of party where we sat on the floor and everybody talked and nobody listened, we had the sense to know that there's no point in playing Bohemians with all the lights full on. Of course we were used to dancing under chandeliers, and enjoyed the contrast. But the principle's the same. If you blow out half those candles people will be half as warm and twice as comfortable from every point of view."

"You shock me," said Humphrey.

"Humbug," said Lady Hannington placidly. "By this time most people have secured the partners they fancy, and want the opportunity to concentrate without being interrupted or overlooked. Besides, now that I'm relieved of Mr. Ballantyne I rather fancy a little snooze."

Humphrey patted her cheek, and left her to do as he had been told. As usual Lady Hannington proved perfectly right. Within ten minutes babble had been reduced to murmurs. The smoke seemed to thicken with the darkening of the room. The guitarist grew sentimental in the shadows. And Toby Scott had the pleasant shock of finding Sally Anstruther's head resting on his left shoulder. He tightened his fingers round the hand he had been holding, and closed his eyes for a few blissful moments. When he opened them again he saw Humphrey grinning at him.

"Sorry and all that—but duty calls. Come along, the pair of you."

"I'm quite comfortable where I am," said Sally sleepily.

"No doubt," agreed Humphrey. "But I'm in *loco parentis*, and I take my responsibilities seriously. I read the newspapers. I know all about the younger generation, and what lack of supervision leads to."

"Shut up," growled Toby.

He got up all the same, pulled the protesting Sally to her

feet, and followed Humphrey out of the attic and down the stairs. At the bottom of the second flight a door opened into Humphrey's own sitting-room, whose principal features were two leather-covered arm-chairs, a rather shabby sofa, a pair of crossed foils over the mantelpiece, and a complete set of the Badminton Library. Humphrey put Sally and Toby on the sofa; rummaged for and offered cigarettes and whisky; and dropped into one of the arm-chairs.

"Now to business," he said briskly. "I'm sorry to bore you with it, but I must. And we mustn't be too long about it, or people will begin to wonder where we've gone, and to ask each other why."

"Well," said Sally, "why have we?"

Humphrey started to speak; checked himself; looked up at the ceiling. Just how far could he afford to take the two youngsters into his confidence? He ought to have discussed the point with Pellew, but he hadn't.

"You remember Gregory Pellew?" he asked cautiously.

"Of course. He's a lovely man. A real dish."

For a moment Humphrey shifted his eyes away from Sally to consider Toby Scott's expression. It was not encouraging.

"You went out with him one evening?" persisted Humphrey.

"And if I did?" retorted Sally. "What was there wrong about that?"

That remark, thought Humphrey, was addressed more to young Toby than to me. This is rather hard lines on him.

"I believe he asked you rather a lot of questions?"

"Not the only curious one, is he?" said Sally. "Some people enjoy conversation. It can be a nice change from snogging."

"That I can understand," said Humphrey.

He looked again at Toby, who refused to meet his eye and stubbed out his cigarette viciously.

"Gregory seemed to want to know an awful lot about Mr. Hargest," Sally went on. "I told him I thought he must be one of those 'private eyes'—out of one of those 'telly' serials Toby's so fond of."

But to this deliberate provocation Toby did not rise. No doubt he was used to them from Sally.

Humphrey made up his mind to take the necessary plunge: necessary if he was going to get anywhere. So Pellew was "Gregory" to the girl already. It was odds on that she'd be pleased and flattered to be offered a working partnership with him.

"Pellew's making some investigations into the circumstances of Mr. Hargest's death," he said. "He asked me to help him. It's an insurance matter, I believe."

"That doesn't sound very exciting," said Toby.

"I don't suppose it is. But one of the things he wants is to be able to listen to some of the tape-recordings that Hargest had made of interviews in his office."

Sally looked puzzled.

"But I told him about them. I told him that Jukes looked after them——"

"Quite. But Miss Jukes won't co-operate. She won't even begin. I thought that perhaps you——"

"Why hasn't Gregory asked me himself?" Sally interrupted.

"I expect he would have. He's had to go abroad for a few days."

"He'll be back?"

"He'll certainly be back," said Humphrey grinning. "Think of me as an inadequate understudy for him in the interval."

Sally looked at Toby, who sat up and became very practical and decisive.

"Look here, Humphrey. What is it you really want?"

"This is strictly between the three of us?"

"Of course."

"Very well. I'll tell you. Somehow or other I want to see the inside of that filing-cabinet which has the tape-recordings; and I want to borrow some of the recordings long enough to hear them played back. That's all."

"All? It's a large order. Besides the Jukes has the key. How can Sally do anything about it? Hargest had the duplicate key. Why don't you get hold of that for Pellew?"

"The answer to your second question," said Humphrey patiently, "is that I can't. Presumably Mrs. Hargest has that key now, and she doesn't know about this investigation—and mustn't. Sally works cheek by jowl with Miss Jukes all day and every day."

"Good lord!" said Toby. "You're suggesting that Sally—"

"I'm suggesting that Sally should borrow the key long enough for an impression to be made of it. I imagine that filing-cabinet isn't being used at the moment—or is Rollo Gunn keeping up the Hargest tradition, and still having interviews recorded?"

"No," said Sally decisively, "he isn't. It'd be pretty tricky all the same. Jukes doesn't miss much. She's a terror for details. I'd bet she'd spot it if one of her precious keys went adrift."

"You're not thinking of trying this, Sally?" Toby protested.

"Why not? It might be rather fun."

"Fun! If something goes wrong, and you get caught out?"

"Just a minute," said Humphrey. "How about this as an alternative? I expect Miss Jukes goes to wash her hands and what-not just before she goes home in the evenings?"

"Of course."

"Do the two of you go together?"

"Sometimes," said Sally. "Not if I can help it. When I put on my fresh make-up she looks at me as if my next stop would be the streets."

"Capital. Where does she keep her office keys?"

"In the top drawer of her desk. She keeps that key in her bag, and locks the drawer before she leaves."

"Before she goes to the wash-room?"

"She likes to call it the powder-room," said Sally demurely. "No—as a matter of fact she doesn't."

"And if she leaves the office at other times during the day?"

"Then she locks it—if she's going to be away for any length of time."

"That's it then. Snaffle the key of the filing-cabinet while Miss Jukes is in the powder room, use it, *and leave the cabinet unlocked*. It's a good bet that Miss Jukes won't try it before she leaves. It shouldn't take you more than about thirty seconds. And—just to calm Toby's shaking nerves—if Miss Jukes should be madly security-conscious and find the cabinet unlocked she'll put it down to aberration on her part, and get a terrible attack of conscience. There'll be nothing to incriminate Sally."

"Perhaps not," said Toby gloomily.

Sally's eyes were sparkling, and she looked prettier than ever. "What happens after that?" she asked.

"I think," said Humphrey deliberately, "that on that particular evening Miss Anstruther will find she has to work late. Mr. Scott will come along from the Studios to take her home, and Humphrey Clymping will be so amiable as to offer him a lift in his car. I fancy that Humphrey Clymping might happen to have a tape-recording playback machine in his car. Now do you see? The tapes wouldn't even have to go out of the office."

"You won't feel so clever, Humphrey, if Rollo Gunn chooses to work late the same evening."

"Toby, you're being a wet-blanket. Humphrey Clymping might not find it impossible to put it into Jim Ballantyne's head that Rollo Gunn hasn't been down at the Studios lately —in fact, he hasn't—and that it'd do him good to see a transmission in progress. We'll find an evening when one of Jim's bright new ideas is hitting the cameras for the first time. Got it?"

"I suppose it might work," said Toby.

"It's got to work," said Humphrey. "Are you on?"

There was a little silence.

"I'm on," said Sally. "I think it's thrilling. Of course Toby can do as he likes."

Humphrey grinned.

"I do as Sally likes," said Toby. "And she knows that perfectly well. A damned sight too well!"

"That's sweet of you, Toby, darling. Would you like to kiss me?"

"I'll answer that one," said Humphrey. "He would very much—as soon as I've made myself scarce. I must get back to the party. If you don't follow me I shan't draw attention to the fact."

He got up and went to the door.

"Incidentally," he said casually over his shoulder, "I also keep keys. There's one on the inside of this door."

CHAPTER 15

THE INTERPRETER

Pellew had hoped and intended to finish his business in Berlin within forty-eight hours. It took him all of four days, at the end of which he was by no means convinced that he had really got what he wanted. The whole episode was queer, rather macabre, and in retrospect unreal: by no means an enjoyable experience.

To begin with he had had great difficulty in making contact with Ladislas Sale. The man existed all right. The British Military Occupation authorities had and produced a file on him. The West German Radio people confirmed that he had acted as Anglo-Polish interpreter at the recent conference attended by Simon Hargest, and spoke warmly of his professional capacity. But as a human being he remained almost as shadowy as the dossier concerning him which had been provided by the War Office in London. It appeared that he lived obscurely somewhere in the French Zone. His lodging was not on the telephone. And three separate visits by Pellew met nothing more than the shrugged shoulders and blank face of a slattern landlady. Certainly Sale was her lodger. He was not at home. He received no visitors. She knew nothing of his comings and goings. He kept himself very much to himself. He was a sick man.

After each visit Pellew left a note with his own name and the address of his hotel, asking for a reply and a rendezvous. He received no reply.

On the third day, when he had almost decided to cut his loss and go home, he was paying a farewell courtesy call on the Programme *Intendant* of the *Rundfunk*, when an outside-broadcast commentator, just returned from an assignment in Hamburg, was shown in. He was a tubby little man with blond hair cut *en brosse* and a monocle: a flabby caricature of the Prussian officer in innumerable films. His name was Otto Stein. After being introduced to Pellew he stood deferentially rigid in the background, taking no part in the conversation, while Pellew explained to the *Intendant* his lack of success over Ladislas Sale. At the mention of the name Stein came forward, clicked his heels, and broke into rapid German, most of which Pellew luckily was able to follow.

It appeared that Stein also had attended the international conference, and that in the course of it he had made Sale's acquaintance. He had been struck by the interpreter's picturesque appearance, and had admired his refusal to yield to his physical disabilities: a left arm amputated at the elbow, and a twisted foot that compelled him to walk with a crutch. Slowly and with great difficulty Stein had managed to scratch the surface of a reserve and self-containment almost ferocious. By the end of the conference he had even persuaded Sale to share an occasional meal. "It is not surprising you did not find him at his lodgings, Herr Pellew. He is never there—at least not during the day-time, unless the weather is vile beyond the ordinary. You should look for him on the Mountain."

"The Mountain?" Pellew stared at the *Intendant*, who explained.

It appeared that when the town planners tackled the job of rebuilding Berlin after the war, not the least of their problems was what to do with the rubble of the ruins. There were no less than a hundred and fifty million cubic feet of rubble to be disposed of somehow, and it was decided that it must be stacked after some fashion if the ground was to be cleared for the new projected buildings. With a doggedness and laborious determination typically German a vast artificial mountain was created. Not piled up just anyhow, but planned in careful detail to form a natural-looking feature of the landscape, which would ultimately be a pleasure-centre dominating the woods and lakes of Grünewald and Wannsee: a mountain with roads and open spaces, with trees and shrubs and flowers. It was indeed in full process of construction at this moment.

"The place would seem to have for Sale a curious fascination," explained Otto Stein. "I have been with him when he has gone to sit there—to brood, as it were, over the city, looking always out towards the East. He is a Pole—you understand." Stein's shrug and his puzzled eyes were eloquent of his own failure to understand.

Pellew, however, was not conducting an investigation into psychology, German or Polish.

"Can you show me the place?" he asked bluntly.

Otto Stein looked at the *Intendant,* who nodded.

"I will take you there with pleasure—this afternoon."

Stein was as good as his word. It was a day of brilliant sunshine. And as they drove through the city a fanciful notion, which had come to Pellew on his arrival, returned to him: that the place was one vast cemetery, grabbed and divided into building lots by some tycoon operating on a gigantic scale in the field of speculative building. And for what? To raise bigger targets for bigger bombs. And he felt chilly, even under that burning haze-veiled sky.

The Mountain was as the *Intendant* had described it: a wilderness of chaotic activity, curiously impressive. Stein did not attempt to drive his car up what was still little more than a rough track, and was apologetic accordingly.

"You cannot miss your way, I think," he said. "Follow this track as far as the first clearing, and you will find a path leading through a shrubbery to your right. Go along that. It curves left-handed to the very top, where there is another clearing. There they have stopped working, and there are benches. You will recognise Sale by his crutch and his scarred face—he could not be taken for anybody else."

It seemed clear to Pellew that Otto Stein was not anxious to renew acquaintance with Ladislas Sale. For a moment he wondered why—but it was not his business. He thanked the German, wished that he was wearing a thinner suit of clothes, and plodded on his way. Alice entering Wonderland, he thought, must have felt rather like this. . . .

The track was stony and uneven. The German workmen with their jeeps and barrows seemed offensively fit, bronzed and cheerful. Pellew became exceedingly hot, rather ill-tempered, sweated profusely, and with every hundred yards of ascent grew more sceptical of the probable results of his mission. It took him the best part of half an hour's hard walking to get to the top, and his immediate impression was that he had come on a fool's errand. The clearing was there, neatly laid out and tidied, surrounded by a circle of equally tidy flowering shrubs. Several benches were there, of which three were occupied by young couples in obvious love, one by a giggle of schoolgirls with wide blue eyes, stiff straw hats, and flaxen pigtails, and one by two elderly ladies sharing a picnic-basket. The others were bare. However, a placard marked HERREN indicated an almost imperceptible path through a gap in the surrounding shrubs leading to a small green-painted building. Pellew felt that he could at any rate be grateful for one small mercy.

But in the event he never entered the small green-painted building. When he reached it he saw that another and narrower path led off to the right where a pile of rocks stood in the shadow of a clump of little trees, whose recent artificial planting was only too obvious. A man was sitting on the rocks. He was bare-headed with rather long hair that shone silver-white in the sunshine. His back was towards Pellew, but the latter could see that there was a crutch under his left arm-pit. He neither turned nor looked round as Pellew's footsteps crunched on the loose stones.

Pellew stopped, turned, and looked at him in profile. He was immediately reminded of some falcon or sea-eagle caged behind the bars of a zoo: eyes brilliant, restless, and untameable; an arrogant beak of a nose jutting from a face that was all bones and hollows; one big hand with claw-like fingers gripping one knee; a shapeless jacket slung round hunched shoulders; fury desperate and hopeless, chained and forgotten. . . .

Pellew coughed. Ladislas Sale—it was obviously he—turned his head and faced him. His skin was like old parchment, seamed and dusty, and across his forehead was the livid scar of an old wound, a scar that had been botched in the stitching. The jacket, though without shoulder-straps or badges, pathetically threadbare, had once been part of a uniform. The arm supported by the crutch was gone at the elbow.

"Mr. Sale?" asked Pellew in English.

"I would prefer 'Colonel' Sale, if you don't mind. My regiment no longer exists—but I commanded it, though you may find it hard to believe when you look at me."

"I beg your pardon, Colonel." Sale's mouth achieved the parody of a grin.

"You are English? What can I do for you? Or did you come up here, as I do, to enjoy the view? It repays the climb."

"My name is Gregory Pellew. I came to find you, Colonel Sale. A man called Stein told me that you might be here."

"That butter-ball? He can never keep his mouth shut."

"I left notes for you at your lodgings," said Pellew.

"And I ignored them. With only one hand it is too much trouble to open letters you don't wish to read."

Only his natural obstinacy saved Pellew at that moment from ignominious retreat. He opened his pocket-book, and took out the note which the Commander at Scotland Yard had procured for him from the War Office.

"You'll see that this envelope is already open, Colonel Sale," he said, holding it out.

143

Sale took it; unfolded the typed sheet of paper clumsily; read it; returned it.

"I should burn it, if I were you, Mr. Pellew."

Pellew took out his cigarette-lighter, held the flame to the paper, and ground the ashes into dust with his heel.

"Your credentials are in order," said Ladislas Sale. "I warn you I'm not inclined to accept them. What do you want from me? As you see I'm not fit for service—secret or otherwise."

"I only want a little information, Colonel. May I sit down?"

"That rock—like the view—is free."

The invitation was hardly encouraging, but Pellew made the best of it, and himself as comfortable as he could, considering the exceeding hardness of the rock indicated. Ladislas Sale seemed already to have lost interest in his visitor. He looked away again eastwards across the city, as though he watched for the appearance of something on the expanses of the great plains that were no more than a distant featureless blur. The scar on his forehead twitched.

"How long, O Lord, how long?" he muttered.

Pellew started, and dropped the pipe he had taken out of his pocket.

"You think I'm a little mad, Mr. Pellew? You may be perfectly right. You see I have lost everything that is commonly supposed to make life worth living: my country, my health, my friends, my wife, my home. A sane man would have put a bullet through his own head long ago. I sit up here, like the Trumpeter of Cracow, and watch for the Enemy from the East. No doubt it amuses you—as it would amuse most of your countrymen."

Pellew stooped to pick up his pipe.

"England was your country, I believe, Colonel Sale. You were born there. Even after you opted for Polish nationality you worked with our Intelligence Service."

"Before 1939, Mr. Pellew, I believed that England and Poland shared something: distrust of and dislike for Germans. I believed that when Great Britain went to war in

144

September of that year, she meant something of what she said: that when the war was over the freedom and independence of Poland would be guaranteed. When my lancers were shot down in a charge against a German *panzer* brigade I remembered Balaclava as well as Somo-Sierra. When I heard of the Polish pilots who flew in the Battle of Britain, I thought that the debt to them would be paid. The Germans strangled and tortured us. The Russians stabbed us in the back. At Yalta and afterwards you sold us for the sake of Stalin's *beaux yeux:* Stalin—who held back his army's advance on Warsaw while our Home Army was blown off its pitiful barricades, and drowned in the filth of the sewers. I no longer recognise any obligation to England, Mr. Pellew."

"We did what we could, Colonel Sale. Quite a lot of us in England are ashamed that we could not do more. We had to face the facts—"

"Which was not so hard to do in the isolated safety of your island. We faced them on the spot: the ruin of Warsaw, the horrors of Auschwitz, the Katyn massacre, the deportations, the concentration camps. I could tell you—but I apologise, Mr. Pellew. What right to feelings has a wretched cripple like myself? A cripple who is still occasionally a spy—not for a country or a cause, but because his contemptible body cannot deny its need for bread to eat."

There was a silence. The interpreter continued to stare eastwards over the city. Pellew felt, with a certain exasperation that he had wasted his time and his journey. What was he likely to get from a man driven half-demented by an overwhelming sense of grievance?

"It's for your conscience, not mine, Colonel Sale," he said quietly, "to decide whether or not you will help me."

"Help you? How?"

"By answering one or two questions. When you interpreted at the recent international television conference, did you have any dealings with the representative of the British TV organisation Gargantua—Mr. Simon Hargest?"

"What do you mean by dealings, Mr. Pellew?"

"Dealings outside the conference chamber. Did you know, or were you told, that Mr. Hargest belonged to the British Intelligence Service?"

"He told me so. He showed me credentials as you have."

"Why?"

Ladislas Sale turned his head slowly, and gave Pellew a long searching look.

"Mr. Hargest wanted my help, as you do," he said at last.

"To do what?"

"To make contact with a man in the Polish Security Service. His name doesn't matter. He's dead now. He had planned to defect to the West, and had thrown out feelers to London. This planned defection was considered so important that Mr. Hargest came to Berlin to arrange the details of the escape. I was to be the channel of communication. I still have contacts in Poland: a few survivors of my comrades in the Underground of the Home Army."

"The man's dead, you say?"

"If he were still alive, Mr. Pellew, I should not be telling you all this. The scheme failed. Berlin, as you know, is riddled with spies, and there are too few Poles who can keep their mouths shut. I don't know whether it was a case of indiscretion or treachery or—most probably—a mere sale to the highest bidder. Anyway the poor devil was caught in East Berlin by Erich Mielcke's People's Police, and conveniently shot trying to escape. I had to tell Mr. Hargest what had happened. It was not pleasant."

"He was upset by his failure?"

"Upset and angry. It was natural enough. The dead man was to have brought with him a complete list of communist agents operating in Western Europe."

"I see. Thank you, Colonel Sale."

So that was it. No wonder that Hargest had returned from Berlin worried, exhausted, and depressed. The collapse of an enterprise of such importance would have exhausted and depressed anybody. And in one regard Pellew's obstinacy had emphatically paid off. Ladislas Sale had provided very desirable confirmation of Simon Hargest's under-cover role as an Intelligence officer.

Pellew suggested to the interpreter that they might dine together that evening. Ladislas Sale merely shook his head, and he took no notice when Pellew held out his hand. Pellew left him as he had found him: a seated embodiment of failure and defeat, gazing out towards those eastern marshes of Europe which had once found glorious salvation in the lances and chargers and great winged helmets of Jean Sobieski's Polish cavalry.

CHAPTER 16

INTERIM REPORT

In common with a good many other people Gregory Pellew considered flying an over-rated form of travel. In his experience it was always boring; occasionally dangerous; and too often unreliable, owing to the vagaries of weather. He disliked air-terminals with their atmosphere of hygienically perpetual restlessness; their clamant loud-speakers; their hybrid quality of a cross between the rest-room of a department store and its parcel-despatch office; their cups of synthetic coffee consumed perforce for lack of alternative occupation. The bright cheerfulness of air-hostesses failed to carry conviction. Meals served at a height of several thousand feet failed to promote appetite. Pellew found that he tended to drink more brandy than was strictly good for him, and to take a more than normally jaundiced view of human beings. The bird's-eye view of any country was unsatisfactory and unrewarding. One was not travelling. One was being conveyed. It remained necessary somehow to pass the time.

The return flight from Berlin to London did nothing to qualify this point of view. The weather was rainy with a low cloud ceiling. Gatow Airport was a chaos of damp rain-coats, bulging brief-cases; women with streaked make-up and strained expressions; howling children and exasperated parents. A proportion of soldiers and commercial travellers went about their business with a quiet efficiency perhaps too consciously assumed. But the majority were obvious refugees—refugees, thought Pellew grimly, from the wrath that might be expected to come upon one of the Cities of the Plain—with their clumsy ill-tied bundles and packages, their expressions of gloom, of blank despair, of misery or fear. He was never to forget one young woman who stood at the barrier with a young man, evidently seeing him off. The girl had a pretty figure and bright blue eyes. The man was dark, with a sensitive mouth and a fine-drawn intelligence in every feature. They might have been struck dumb as they stood there, staring helplessly at each other. Only the fingers of the joined hands moved, crisping and clasping in mute protest and mutual agony. The frozen emptiness in the girl's eyes came between Pellew and his sleep for a long time.

The plane was uncomfortably full, and Pellew in a seat on the gangway did his best to reconcile himself to some hours of boredom and discomfort. Professional habit led him to throw a searching glance over such of his fellow-passengers as were within sight. None of them excited interest or curiosity. Next to him was a stout woman who immediately swallowed three tranquilizers, closed her eyes and opened her mouth. On her other side a negro in a bright blue suit and a black Homburg hat stared out of the window. Occasionally he hummed to himself. Immediately behind Pellew were three loud-voiced American officers going on leave, and determined that as many people as possible should be aware of the fact. On the other side of the gangway sat a teen-age German girl, very pink and correct; an elderly female relative of hers, wearing a shabby fur coat, and a headscarf over untidy grey hair; and, next to the window, a rabbi with a full black beard and dark glasses. For an instant Pellew fancied something familiar about him: the back of his neck, or the set of his shoulders as he sat down? For a time he watched the rabbi out of the corner of his eye. But there was nothing about him to cause comment, unless it was against custom for a rabbi to read *Life* magazine and drink ginger-ale.

Pellew ordered a large brandy-and-soda; took a writing-pad and a Biro pen out of his brief-case; and appropriated as much of the folding table in front of him as he decently could. He had decided to write a draft of an interim report on the progress of his investigations: a draft which, after revision, he proposed to submit formally to the Commander at Scotland Yard.

"As I see it," he wrote in a shorthand of his own devising "the core of the problem is simply this: Did Hargest kill himself under an emotional strain induced by his professional activities, or alternatively by events in his private life? Or was he driven to suicide by someone with motives professional or alternatively personal? It is of course possible that the answers to these two questions may overlap, to an extent amounting to the same thing. I have differentiated them because, if the answer to the second question is affirmative, the investigation considered in terms of reality and common sense is concerned not with suicide but with murder.

"Taking his personality and temperament into account I find it difficult if not impossible to believe that Hargest would have been 'got down' by purely business activities to the extent of a brain-storm or extreme nervous collapse. He was used to working at high pressure. His financial affairs were in order. He possessed the confidence of his chairman, and the loyalty of his immediate personal staff. (Sir G. Farley, Gunn, Miss Anstruther, Miss Jukes, the latter to a fanatical extent.) The only one of his colleagues in Gargantua with whom he was at odds was James Ballantyne, who was hardly in a position to drive Hargest into an emotional corner. (Can any man believe so passionately in the principles and practice of television as to commit murder or suicide on that account? At the risk of being thought unimaginative I doubt it.)

"But even putting Ballantyne and Gargantua responsibili-

151

ties into the discard there remains an alternative under the 'professional' as opposed to the 'personal' label. My inquiries in Berlin have confirmed a theory which I had previously considered too wild to be possible: that Hargest made use of his position as a high-powered television executive to cover up activities on behalf of the British Intelligence Service— activities stemming from a war-time appointment which had, at different times, introduced both Miss Jukes and Rollo Gunn to him as service colleagues, and accounted accordingly for his having given them jobs with Gargantua. The genuine reason for the visit to Germany immediately before his death was an assignment to arrange for the defection to the West of a prominent member of the Polish Security Service. The go-between was the Polish interpreter to the Eurovision Confer-ence, whom I have interviewed, and whose record as an occasional operative on our behalf is available. This mission of Hargest's was a failure. Its importance was such that the result might reasonably have seriously affected him. (Is an experienced Secret Service man likely to be so affected by, or unused to, a failure as to kill himself on account of it? Again I doubt it.) At the same time I cannot help feeling that the answer to the problem may well be hidden behind the ob-scurities inherent in all Intelligence work: obscurities to which my only further approach can be through Miss Jukes and Rollo Gunn. It is not for me to decide whether, if all the circumstances are considered, it would be wise or profitable to intensify such an approach, which would automatically make Miss Jukes and Gunn aware that I know of Hargest's undercover job."

Pellew put down the pen and lighted a cigarette. He was trying to make up his mind whether or not to add his belief that Hargest had not only been a secret agent, but that he had been C in person. Not to say as much was to deprive the report of a piece of evidence that might easily be the vital factor. To put it in writing—even if in the end it proved a merely fantastic suggestion—seemed to him to violate every normal canon of both security and common sense. He asked the air-hostess for a brandy-and-soda, and waited for inspiration while he drank it. Inspiration did not come. He looked about him wishing, not for the first time, that it was possible to walk up and down in a plane: to stretch one's legs and clear one's brain. Most of his adjacent fellow-travellers seemed to be asleep, except for the Americans who were playing cards rather ill-temperedly. Pellew decided that if the C theory was to be mentioned at all he must raise it verbally with the Commander when he presented the report—and almost certainly have his head bitten off as a result. He stubbed out his cigarette irritably, and picked up his pen again.

"Turning to the possibilities or likelihood of some 'personal' motivation for the tragedy," Pellew continued, "I fear that my conclusions are equally unsatisfactory. Investigation into the background of Hargest's private life has been quite inconclusive, admittedly because circumstances have compelled such investigation to be little more than tentative and superficial. There is evidence that Mrs. Hargest was attached to her husband, and that he was equally attached to her. I believe that any idea of a liaison between Hargest and the unusually attractive Miss Anstruther can be discarded. On the other hand it seems certain that Miss Jukes was frustratedly in love with her employer, and that Sir George Farley probably, and Rollo Gunn possibly, have shown an interest rather beyond the conventional in Mrs. Hargest. To pursue such implications will certainly be disagreeable, but may be necessary.

"At the risk of appearing resigned to falling down on the assignment I am compelled to put my opinion on record that, all things considered, it might be as well to let sleeping dogs lie. There are too many imponderables, too many loose ends, about the case. I feel also that I am working without the complete confidence of my superiors. No doubt there are good reasons for the withholding of such confidences—but without it I see little hope of bringing my inquiries to a satisfactory conclusion."

And if that, thought Pellew, doesn't put paid once and for

all to what I'd once hoped might be a career, nothing will. The assignment might have been strictly an unofficial one. Pellew had certainly undertaken it as a volunteer. He could reasonably expect his report to be read and considered "off the record"; consigned to a waste-paper basket, and forgotten. But he knew perfectly well that as far as the work of special agents was concerned neither reason nor any normal code of behaviour came into it. If a special agent came to grief he must expect to be disavowed. If he fell down on the job— particularly if he implied that the falling-down could be attributed to shortcomings on the part of his superiors—he must expect unpleasant consequences. The only thing of any importance that Pellew had discovered was something that the Commander had almost certainly wished to keep concealed. . . .

He tore the sheets off his writing-pad, and folded them carefully. That, at any rate, was that. Nothing more could be done until he was back in London. Meanwhile he would sleep if he could.

Sleep he did—but for just how long he never knew. The next thing he did know was that he was broad awake; that his next-seat neighbour was screaming like a riverboat's siren; and that he was rolling on the floor of the plane in a flying tangle of arms, trousered legs, skirts, and an assortment of hand-luggage. While he realised that the air-liner had for some reason gone suddenly into a spinning dive, Pellew found himself curiously, almost calmly, aware of various quite ridiculous things: that strands of the rabbi's beard were in his mouth; that his left ear was hurting him consumedly; that one of the American officers was clutching absurdly at the luggage-rack; that the air-hostess, still clutching her tray from which a selection of ordered drinks had been catapulted in all directions, seemed quite oblivious alike of the revelation of almost every inch of her very pretty legs and of a badly gashed chin.

The chaos subsided as suddenly as it had been born. The pilot, who had been wrestling with his controls almost as a rider fights with a momentarily-panicked stallion, found them once more answering to his sweating fingers, and the dive flattening out to normal flight. The "area of totally un-expected sudden atmospheric disturbance"—as it would be officially logged—was cleared. People sorted out themselves and their belongings, shamefacedly or with ostentatiously self-conscious calm according to age and temperament. The air-hostess pulled down her skirt and disappeared for perhaps three minutes, to return with a strip of plaster on her chin and a fresh tray of drinks, cool as any cucumber. A steward followed her with first-aid kit and professionally soothing phrases. And over the loud-speaker from the pilot's cabin came apology and reassurance to quell the uplifted babble of vocal reaction in a variety of tone and language.

Considering its fortunate outcome the episode would have meant no more to Pellew than any mildly unpleasant incident of travel. Everything had happened too quickly to be really frightening, though he found to his disgust that his hand was shaking visibly when he reached out for his brandy-and-soda; that he had emptied his glass in a couple of gulps; and that during the rest of the flight he tended to look unreasonably often at his wrist-watch, and to listen with sharpened anxiety for any variation in the steady beat of the engines. It was only when the plane touched down on the runway of London Air-port that he realised with wry gratitude that for a couple of hours at least he had completely forgotten the tiresome com-plexities of the problem which he had returned to England to face.

And it was only when he had coped with the formalities of customs and passport-control; suffered the boredom of the journey from the airport into London; reached his flat, and telephoned the news of his arrival to Humphrey Clymping —who did not sound as pleased to hear Pellew's voice as he ought to have been; and unpacked his baggage, that he real-ised something else. There was no sign of that carefully folded report which he thought he had tucked away carefully into his brief-case.

CHAPTER 17

EXCHANGE OF DISCONTENTS

The day after his return to London from Berlin Pellew lunched with Humphrey Clymping at the latter's club. If he had hoped to find consolation for his own profound discontents he was destined to disappointment. Humphrey seemed to take no interest in the food—which was unusual—or in his choice of wine—which was unprecedented. He showed little curiosity about Pellew's trip abroad, and hardly reacted to the story of the report lost, stolen, or strayed.

"You probably didn't put the damn thing into your briefcase at all," he said. "If you stuffed it into your pocket it could easily have gone astray when the plane started acting up. Does it matter anyway? You can write it again."

"I can. I don't much want to. It wasn't a particularly edifying document."

"Then why not forget about it?"

"Because," said Pellew deliberately, "I'm inclined to think that someone took the opportunity of the general mix-up to steal it. Fortunately, it was written in shorthand and there was nothing in it he wouldn't have known already, though shorthand—even mine—can be read."

"And your concluding recommendation was to let sleeping dogs lie. If you didn't mean it you may have successfully laid a false scent. If you did mean it—well, I think you're probably being sensible. But I wish you'd told me as much before you went gallivanting off to Germany."

Pellew put down his glass and looked keenly at Humphrey across the table. Humphrey kept his eyes firmly focused on his plate, as though shepherd's pie was something he had never seen before.

"Liver, Humphrey? Or hang-over?"

"I don't know what you mean."

"Then you're being deliberately crass, which is stupid, or sulky, which isn't like you. If I've interfered with your work or your fun by inviting myself to lunch I'm extremely sorry. I'm only too much aware of having made a hash of things—"

"And you sent for Watson accordingly?"

Pellew smiled.

"You might put it like that."

Humphrey continued to stare at his plate.

"I gather you got more or less what you wanted out of the Polish fellow," he said.

"That's true. It's also true that you can never get enough in the way of confirmation. But if that report of mine was stolen, then it means that I was being shadowed. Nothing else was taken, so it wasn't just sneak-thievery. If I'd followed the rules, not to mention my instinct, and concentrated properly on my fellow-travellers, I'd have had a good chance of catching one of them in *flagrante delicto* and getting my hands on our first genuine clue. All I did get was a vague idea that the back of the neck of a gentleman with a beard so bushy that it oughtn't to have been real even if it was, was familiar. I didn't even have a tug at it when we were all rolling about on the floor. I was conscious when I rang you up, my dear Humphrey, of having boobed—badly. I wanted support, moral or otherwise."

Humphrey pushed away his plate with a sudden impatient gesture. "Let's go and have some coffee where we can hear ourselves think," he said. "You know the little library upstairs. There's practically never anyone there after lunch. If you'll go along there I'll pay the bill and order the coffee."

Pellew did as he was told. He climbed two flights of stairs, walked along a dark passage, and entered one of those rooms only to be found in London clubs: a room whose condition no respectable housewife would tolerate for five minutes; its bookshelves dusty, the top of its writing-desk ink-stained, the leather of its arm-chairs and sofa worn and shabby, its window-curtains frayed. The atmosphere was frowsty, redolent of the tobacco-smoke of yester-years. The books were solidly Victorian, for the most part series of the classics: Trollope, Scott, Dickens, Thackeray, translations of Balzac. Above them there stared with grim incongruity a set of steel engravings of generals of the Crimean War: Raglan, Lucan, Cardigan, Pennefather, Airey, His Royal Highness of Cambridge. Everything out of this world, thought Pellew as he sank into one of the battered arm-chairs, and proportionately agreeable.

But what the devil was the matter with Humphrey Clymping? Had he broken away from his unaccustomedly bourgeois domestic routine? Had Kate called him over the coals accordingly? Had something gone wrong with his Gargantua job? Well, presumably he would come clean in his own good time. It was infernally irritating to Pellew, who had never felt more in need of the viscount's cheerfully uninhibited attitude towards people, things and problems alike.

A copy of the *Daily Express* had been abandoned untidily on the sofa. Pellew reached out for it, saw that it was three days old, and was on the point of dropping it disgustedly on the floor when he noticed a headline: INTERESTING NEW TV APPOINTMENT. Beneath it a short paragraph carried the information that Sir George Farley, Chairman of Gargantua Television, had announced the appointment of Mr. James Ballantyne as the new Managing Director of the organisation, in succession to the late Mr. Simon Hargest. Most viewers would be aware of the great services rendered to television by

Mr. Ballantyne as Gargantua's Programme Director, and would welcome the opportunities offered to his remarkable talents in a wider field.

Pellew looked up from the paper to see Humphrey standing over him with a tray which carried two cups of black coffee and two bell-glasses of brandy.

"Every clubman his own waiter in these dear democratic days," he said. "You've spotted it, I see."

"I have. Is that what's given the bear a sore head, Humphrey? I thought you took a good view of Ballantyne. Or has he given you the push?"

"He has not," said Humphrey shortly. "And I do like Jim—though he'll be wasted as a brass-bound executive, and I'd have expected him to know as much himself."

"Then what on earth's the trouble?"

Humphrey took a needlessly long time to put his tray down on a rickety occasional table, light a cigarette, and make himself comfortable on the sofa.

"You'd better smoke a pipe, Greg. You'll probably want something to bite on, and I'd prefer not to be interrupted too often by your calling me names. 'Damned interfering amateur' will probably be the politest of them."

"I am dumb," said Pellew resignedly, and took his pipe out of his pocket. "Tell me the worst."

Humphrey gulped down his coffee, picked up his glass of brandy, swung his feet up on to the sofa, and spoke to the ceiling.

"Too much bloody initiative, Greg, that was my trouble. I thought I was being rather smart. Quite honestly I believed I could save time, and a certain amount of trouble for you, by some operating on my own while you were away. And I'll admit that as the scheme implied working considerably outside the rules I thought it might be as well if you knew nothing about it."

"I suggest," said Pellew mildly, "that you cut the masochistic self-reproach and get to the point."

"You would. Very well. I'd come to the conclusion that it

might be helpful to get hold of those tape-recorded interviews which Hargest entrusted to the guardianship of Miss Lilian Jukes. As she hadn't been exactly co-operative from any point of view I worked out a plan for a spot of amateur burglary, pulling Sally Anstruther and Toby Scott in on the party."

Humphrey broke off, and looked at Pellew. The latter's expression was not encouraging, but he did not interrupt.

"Sally jumped at it, Greg. I don't know what you've been up to in that quarter, but to judge from her reaction when I said that we'd be working on your behalf you haven't wasted your time. And young Toby would cheerfully fling himself under a bus if by doing so he could save Sally from having her stockings splashed."

"Shall we take the sentimental relationships as read, Humphrey?"

"You're a great help, Greg. Anyway, I remembered reading somewhere about the merits of simplicity. We steered clear of anything fancy. The notion was this. Sometime during the working day Sally would get hold of the key of the filing-cabinet where the tapes are kept. Jukes has that key on a ring in her bag, and doesn't always take that bag with her if she's only going to be out of the office for a minute or two. Originally I thought of asking Sally to make a wax impression and having a duplicate key cut. But in practice that sounds a lot easier than it is when you don't really know the drill."

"Quite. Well?"

"All I wanted was for Sally, during that minute or two, to borrow the key, unlock the filing-cabinet, leave it unlocked, and put the key back in the bag. It was long odds against the Jukes noticing that the cabinet was unlocked. Sally told me that nobody's called for the tapes since Hargest's death. The Jukes works like a slave. She's also a bit of a clock-watcher— whipping the cover off her typewriter at half past nine in the morning; powdering her nose and putting on her coat as Big Ben strikes half past five, in the evening. Sally was to find an excuse for staying late in the office—something that

161

Rollo Gunn had asked her to do for him at the last moment. The Jukes would go. Sally would stay. The filing-cabinet would be unlocked. And a little before six Toby Scott would arrive to take Sally home, accompanied by her humble servant who had given Toby a lift in his car from the Studios, and happened to have also in his car a portable play-back machine. Toby and Sally would play cat's cradles—or its contemporary equivalent—while yours truly had a private session listening to a play-back of various selected tapes. After which the tapes would be returned to store. The party would break up. And the following day Sally would re-lock the cabinet if she got the chance. If she didn't, and if the Jukes spotted that it was unlocked, she would reasonably suppose that the last time she'd opened it she'd failed to turn the key properly."

"Cutting butter," murmured Pellew.

"That's what I thought."

"Except that you'd forgotten that Mr. Rollo Gunn might also have had some reason for working late on that particular evening."

"Damn you, Greg!"

"Am I right?"

"No. I didn't forget. I suggested to Jim Ballantyne that it was about time Rollo put in an appearance at the Studios, and covered an evening's transmission *in propria persona*. Jim thought it was a good idea, and fixed it up by telephone. I was there when he did it. That settled our date, and we went ahead accordingly."

"So everything was gas and gaiters—except that Mr. Rollo Gunn changed his mind. Was that it?"

"It's a waste of time talking to you, Greg."

"I'm sorry," said Pellew. "I know it's a shame to spoil a good story. Go on. What happened?"

"Everything," said Humphrey gloomily, "happened like the proverbial clockwork. Lilian Jukes found her afternoon tea much too strong, and left the office—and her bag on the desk—while she had words in the passage with the character

162

in charge of the tea-trolley. Sally snaffled the key; opened the filing-cabinet; and reverted to her normal form, mentioning to the Jukes that she was properly fed up and would have to work late. Smartly at half past five the Jukes departed, without noticing a thing. Smartly at a quarter to six—trust young Toby to get me to risk my neck!—Messrs. Scott and Clymping arrived. There followed congratulations all round, and—I regret to say this in case it wounds you, Greg—a prolonged embrace between Toby Scott and Sally Anstruther."

"You can leave out the trimmings," growled Pellew.

"Just as you like. I confess the sight warmed my withered heart. It is, of course, exasperating how youth will be served. However—there it was, and there we were. Barometer set fair. Only remained to walk across the office; slide open the drawers of the filing-cabinet; select any tapes that looked interesting from their labels; relax, lean back, and listen."

"A delightful tableau, Humphrey. Too bad that Rollo Gunn should have ruined it by choosing that moment to walk in."

Humphrey swung his legs off the sofa and scowled. "I said there was no point in talking to you, Greg."

"My dear Humphrey, the climax was bound to be a bit obvious considering the look on your face. What I really want to know is whether Gunn came into the office before or after you'd opened the filing-cabinet."

"Before—worse luck."

"Now," said Pellew, and knocked out his pipe as if to emphasise the word, "you are being really stupid. Or did you give yourselves away?"

"Of course not. Not in the sense you mean. Naturally Toby and I looked silly, being in an office where we had no business to be, and after working hours into the bargain. We did our best to cover up for Miss Pretty. Toby had just looked in to offer her a lift home in my car if she happened to be working late. It sounded damned unconvincing, and poor Sally didn't quite know how to play, being as it were unre-

163

hearsed. Personally, if I'd been in Rollo's shoes, I think I'd have sacked the three of us for choosing the wrong time and the wrong place for a bit of slap and tickle—if you'll forgive the vulgarism, Greg."

Pellew ignored vulgarism and breeziness alike. "How *did* Gunn take it, Humphrey?"

"Without a blink of an eye, let alone an unkind word. He practically apologised for butting in. He had some report to make out for the Chairman, and had heard our voices from his office. He must have come into the building by that private entrance and lift of his. As Miss Anstruther was there he'd be glad of her services—if Mr. Scott would be so kind as to spare her. All this without a hint of irony, and a wink to me that was better than any nod. He wouldn't keep her for more than an hour or so, if Toby and I cared to go out and have a drink and then wait for her in the entrance hall downstairs. So that was that. I've seldom wanted a drink more or felt quite such a fool."

Pellew started to refill his pipe.

"Did you think to find out from Sally," he said slowly, "whether she got the impression that the report was a genuine article or a spur-of-the-moment invention?"

"My dear Greg, the average girl taking down dictation doesn't bother her head about its meaning, let alone its significance."

"I wasn't asking about the average girl. I was asking about Sally Anstruther, whose head I believe to be screwed on very much the right way."

"She didn't say anything about it to us," said Humphrey sulkily.

"Then perhaps she will say something about it to me, Humphrey. The point has its importance."

"Even I can see that."

"Capital. I don't think I shall take you with me when I go to see her all the same."

Humphrey heaved himself off the sofa, walked over to the

fireplace, and stared into the empty grate with his back to Pellew.

"I'm sorry about the whole thing, Greg. I'd feel happier if you damned me into heaps. I know I deserve it. I was trying to be smart on my own—much too damn smart. I wanted to have something on a plate to hand you when you got back. Not to put too fine a point upon it I hoped to do you in the eye and bring something off for you simultaneous. And a pretty mess I've made of it!"

A subdued chuckle made him turn round. Pellew was grinning through the smoke of his relighted pipe. "I doubt if you've done much real harm, Humphrey. It's a pity you didn't get a hearing of those tapes. But you were quite right in so far that sooner or later we've got to get at them some-how. That apart—well, we've a new slant on your friend Rollo Gunn—who's interested me more than somewhat from the beginning—and you've provided me with the best possi-ble excuse for seeing Sally Anstruther again. Bless you, my dear fellow. You can sleep to-night with a clear conscience—which is more than I'm likely to be able to do. I shall have a busy, and probably a beastly, day to-morrow. Many thanks for lunch. I'll be seeing you. So long."

He went on his way. Humphrey, oblivious of his duty as a host to see his guest off the club premises, picked a volume at random off the nearest shelf and went back to the sofa. When he found that he had selected *Futility*—that admirable novel of William Gerhardi's—he had to repress a strong impulse to hurl it across the room. Then he laughed, and felt better. In the circumstances there was obviously only one thing to do. Humphrey Clymping did it.

He went to sleep.

165

CHAPTER 18

THREE CHINESE BOXES

In prophesying for himself a probably disagreeable tomorrow Pellew had been perfectly correct. It began not too badly, as his telephoned suggestion to Sally Anstruther that he might call upon her during the evening was received by that young lady with an enthusiasm which she did not bother to conceal. She added that if he didn't mind taking pot-luck, and would give her time to tidy up after getting home from the office, she would be delighted to give him some dinner.

This was satisfactory. What Pellew wanted to say to Sally could be said far more easily in her flat than in a restaurant. But he had hardly put down the receiver when he had to pick it up again to receive a second invitation more accurately to be construed as an order: to lunch with the Commander in the latter's private house at one o'clock precisely. The fact that Pellew could foresee pretty well what would be said over that luncheon table did little or nothing to improve the prospect. He spent a gloomy morning mulling over the notes he had collected in his file marked H, and went off to see his superior in a frame of mind that he remembered from his school-days when summoned to the presence of the headmaster.

When he put on his overcoat, which he had not worn since his flight back from Berlin, he found in his left-hand pocket his missing report. Whether to be relieved or exasperated by the discovery he did not know.

His apprehensions were justified. The meal was Spartan, the Commander barely civil. Pellew found himself driven to the bald admission that such progress as he had made was disappointing; that, all the circumstances considered, he felt he ought to recommend that the investigation should be abandoned.

"Is that all you've got to tell me as a result of this presumably expensive trip of yours to Berlin, Pellew?"

"I had to go to Berlin, sir. It wasn't entirely that——"

"Then what the devil is it? What's going on? I hate beating about bushes, as you perfectly well know."

Pellew did know. But he disliked even the suspicion of being bullied. The risk was considerable, but he decided the moment had come for shock-tactics. "I don't think you've treated me quite fairly, sir."

"Not fairly! How not fairly?"

"It would have saved a lot of time, and made things a lot simpler for me, sir, if you'd told me in the first place that Simon Hargest worked for our Intelligence people."

The Commander stared. His expression was now bewildered rather than angry.

"He worked for Intelligence during the war, certainly. There was no secret about that."

"And since, sir."

"I suppose it's possible. How do you know?"

"There were various indications. My Berlin trip confirmed it."

"Of course that would explain——what else have you found out?"

"I don't know this for certain," said Pellew delicately, "but I suspect that my assignment didn't really initiate with you, sir."

"I told you as much, didn't I?"

"You didn't tell me that the inquiry came from the Prime Minister's Private Office."

The Commander flushed.

"I told you as much as I could tell you—as much as it was considered necessary for you to know. Your job was to investigate Hargest's death—not to ferret into why the investigation was ordered, or by whom."

"Unfortunately," said Pellew, "the investigation involved the ferreting. I feel I'm getting into pretty deep waters. I don't swim well with my hands tied. I'm sorry, sir, but that's how it is."

There was a short silence.

"You're working in a private capacity," said the Commander at last. "If you're determined to throw in your hand I can't stop you. You're quite free."

Pellew managed a not very convincing smile. "And you're quite free, sir, to draw what conclusions you like if I do opt out. It won't exactly improve your opinion of me, will it?"

"If you're thinking of your career at the Yard, Pellew—"

"If you'll forgive my saying so, sir, I'm thinking more of human nature and natural reactions. I couldn't blame you."

There followed another silence.

"You've got nerve—I'll say that for you, Pellew. I got you here to give you a rocket, and you start tearing a strip off me! Do you want an apology? You can have one if you like. Of course, I knew where the original inquiry started. I didn't know about this cloak-and-dagger complication. And, frankly, I don't like being used as a stalking-horse any more than you do. Now—do you still want to chuck the whole thing? At any rate you know now that you're not working for peanuts, or just to satisfy idle curiosity."

Pellew looked round the dark little dining-room. There was no inspiration to be drawn from a couple of indifferent family portraits, some dubious blue-and-white china, and faded crimson brocade curtains. He had taken one risk, and it had paid off. Should he take another, a considerably greater one? The Commander's bark had certainly been a lot worse than his bite. Within his normal limitations indeed, he had behaved rather well. Pellew drew a deep breath.

"If you still want me to go ahead, sir, I will—on one condition."

"Blackmail, eh?"

"I want you to answer one question, sir. It's rather a peculiar one."

"Well?"

"Without mentioning any names, is the individual who first mentioned this business to you, sir, included in a certain list at the Yard?"

"I don't follow, Pellew."

"I think you do, sir. After all we're all immensely broad-minded these days—particularly since the Wolfenden Report. I'm not concerned with so-called morality, and I'm not being idly curious, I promise you."

The Commander got up, went to the window and fingered one of the curtains. "This brocade's worn damned badly—my wife was right about it." He turned round suddenly. "You win, Pellew. Yes, he's queer all right. He's also one of my oldest friends, and it's never made a ha'porth of difference and never will. Don't let's have any mistake about that. Why the devil do you want to know?"

"It may have a bearing—quite indirectly. You still want me to carry on?"

The Commander nodded abruptly. Then he went to the sideboard, picked up a decanter, and brought it to the table. "I don't drink in the middle of the day, Pellew. It makes me sleepy. But I'd like you to try a glass of this port. It might be worse. Good luck to you, and remember that I rely on you to keep me informed how things go—and be discreet for God's sake!" His hand, as it lifted the decanter, was not quite steady.

Pellew sipped his port with feelings curiously mixed. He was grateful for the port—which was excellent. He could, he supposed, congratulate himself on the outcome of the interview and confirmation of that startling entry in Lady Hannington's old diary. Not that it actually got him much further.

And some successes could be embarrassing, and unrewarding in proportion. Watching the Commander's lined face—the face of an ageing man with too many responsibilities who gets too little sleep—Pellew felt that this was one of them. He was relieved to get away.

The afternoon proved unprofitable. He rang up Humphrey Clymping, only to be told that the latter was out on some job, and would be tied up in the Studios all evening. He rang up Rollo Gunn, only to be told by Lilian Jukes that Mr. Gunn was in conference, could not be disturbed, and was likely to remain in conference for a period that could not be specified. He asked Lilian Jukes to meet him outside the office at any time and place that suited her, and she hung up on him. He would have liked to talk to Lady Hannington but he knew that it was her habit since her return to London from Sussex, to take a nap after lunch followed by a cup of China tea in bed. And he could not decently put in an appearance at Sally Anstruther's flat before half past seven at the earliest.

He had almost made up his mind to waste a couple of hours in a cinema, and was looking half-heartedly at the list of films currently showing in the vague hope of finding one that did not include rape, space-fictional horrors, the amours of French beatniks, Italian layabouts or the English redbrick-student fraternity, when he noticed that the theatre in which Kate Clymping was acting was playing a matinée. Just after five o'clock he presented himself accordingly at the stage-door, and found himself in due course in a room whose size and temperature reminded him more than anything else of a large refrigerator.

Kate received him with enthusiasm tempered only by the requirements of make-up removal.

"I'm glad you're back," she said through a flurry of Kleenex. "With luck and a little help from you, Humphrey will become a human being again. He's been impossible these last few days."

"I gathered as much when I saw him," said Pellew.

171

"I suppose he told you about the hash he made of his private burglary stunt. I told him it wouldn't work out."

Pellew nodded.

"I'm sorry I can't offer you anything more comfortable than a stool, Greg. Now you see how a small-part-player-plus-understudy lives in a whirl of theatrical glamour! By the way I think you'll find a tooth-glass and half a bottle of gin somewhere on that shelf in the corner."

"No thanks, Katie. I just wanted to talk to you."

"That's nice. But you look rather depressed."

"I am rather depressed. This case is getting me down. It's like one of those nests of Chinese boxes. You go on opening and opening and there's always another inside."

For a few moments Kate concentrated her attention on the proper application of lip-stick. Then she turned round from her mirror and dropped her hands in her lap.

"As a matter of fact I wanted to see you, Greg. It's probably only one more of your Chinese boxes. But I may have got something."

"You've been up to some private investigating, have you?"

"I have," said Kate crisply. "And just because Humphrey's ham-handed it doesn't mean that I'm necessarily half-witted."

"I never imagined you were," protested Pellew.

"The tone of voice was unmistakable. However, I'll forgive you."

"I can't claim any credit. It just happened."

"What just happened?"

"One of those things."

"Katie, dear—aren't you being the least bit in the world obscure?"

Kate wrinkled up her nose after an endearing fashion which reminded Pellew of his adoration, persisting through the years, for Miss Ginger Rogers.

"Now listen, Greg. You know the particular bee that I've always had in my bonnet about this whole business, and still have—in spite of the fact that neither you nor Humphrey

ake it seriously: that the solution's far more likely to be found
n Mrs. Hargest's flat than in the Gargantua offices."

"It's the normal woman's approach," said Pellew cau-
iously.

"Thank you for nothing! At least thank you for not com-
ng back at me with 'feminine intuition' or some equivalent
guff."

Pellew shifted uneasily on his stool.

"All right," Kate went on. "It won't take long. And we're
afe from interruption in here, which may be as well."

"Go ahead."

"I've kept on thinking about Jane Hargest, Greg, ever
since that faintly ridiculous Keystone Comedy chase of mine
after the astrakhan-collared visitor to her flat which ended in
fiasco. When I went to see her I had the idea that there was
something familiar about her face; that I'd seen it before,
though I was sure I hadn't met her before. I expect you know
that Humphrey had collected a whole set of cuttings of Hargest's obituary notices?"

"I should know. I gave them to him."

"None of them carried any photo of Hargest, which struck
me as a bit peculiar—"

"Not at all, if Hargest was really a high-powered Intelligence operative. He'd naturally fight shy of photographers."

"Let's skip that side of it for the moment, if you don't
mind. What interested me was that several of those obituaries
carried photos of Jane Hargest. The notion that her face was
familiar went on nagging at me, and three nights ago I
stuffed the cuttings into my bag, and brought them down to
the theatre with me to go through them in peace and quiet
without Humphrey breathing down my neck and asking me
silly questions about what I thought I was up to."

"And what *were* you up to, Katie?"

"I wasn't sure—then. I was sitting in here, with the cuttings spread out all over my dressing-table, when Millie
Cresswell came in. She's the new character-woman who
joined the cast a fortnight ago when Zoe Parfitt went off to

173

Rome on a film job: rather a sweet old thing, who's spent almost all her working life in provincial reps. She thinks I need a bit of mothering. And I'm not sure she isn't right, with my husband in Gargantua TV—not to mention this lousy dressing-room."

"And the motherly Miss Cresswell recognised the photos of Jane Hargest, and supplied the missing link."

"You're not so dumb, Greg. Jane Hargest had been a six-teen-year-old—and much publicised—local beauty queen in a town in the Midlands where Millie Cresswell was at the time leading lady in the rep. Presumably as a result of the beauty competition—she couldn't apparently act for sour apples—Jane was brought into the company as the *ingénue*. She stayed there for nearly a year. Then she dropped out. According to Millie she was supposed to have gone abroad. She'd heard nothing more of her until she saw the cuttings."

"If that's all, Katie, we're not much forrader. It's not a crime to have won a beauty competition. It's not suspicious, though it's certainly unusual, for a girl to have a crack at show-business and chuck it realising that she had no talent. It's surely comprehensible that once married to a man like Hargest she would want to leave that episode buried in the oblivion of Midland newspaper files."

"All quite true. But there's more to come. And this is where I'd ask you to look the other way if only there was room."

"Scandal, Katie? I'm surprised at you."

"I'm a little surprised at myself. I'm not fond of the whis-pering-behind-hands-in-corridors brigade. Nor is Millie, to judge from what little I've seen of her—"

"Suppose you get it off your chest," interrupted Pellew.

Kate shrugged her shoulders.

"Right. Well—it seems that Jane Hargest, who was then Jane Duncan, was what Millie in her dear old-fashioned way calls a man-eater; even at the age of sixteen. She worked through the company steadily, from the assistant-stage-manager, who had milk behind his ears, to the leading man

174

who was sixty-odd with false teeth and a toupee. She showed a marked preference for the middle-aged and married. That's no more than fact, Greg. I'm not going to repeat the rumours that followed and pretended to explain her ultimate departure. You've plenty of imagination."

Pellew rubbed his jaw.

"She and Hargest were married abroad, and without beat of drum," he said. "This certainly gives one to think—though along what lines I'm hanged if I see."

Kate stood up and reached for her coat. "Try this one," she said, as Pellew hurried to drape it round her shoulders. "The domestic felicity of the Hargests was a pious fraud. To maintain it may have suited both their books. But if Mrs. Hargest hadn't changed her spots—if she had set her cap successfully both at Rollo Gunn and Sir George Farley—doesn't that open another of your boxes?"

"With nothing inside it as usual," said Pellew exasperatedly. "Many thanks all the same, Katie. You may have started more than you ever imagined. It's just struck me—"

"What's struck you, Greg?"

"That there's one outstandingly good reason for a man pretending to be happily married when he's nothing of the sort."

"And what's that?"

"The best explanation—and a pretty good excuse into the bargain—for a married woman seeking consolation elsewhere."

Kate opened the dressing-room door.

"I'm not sure if I know what you mean," she said. "And if I do, I'm not sure that I want to."

"*Entendu.* I won't elaborate. But I've an idea that this Chinese box of yours might fit rather neatly inside the one I opened at lunch-time to-day."

"Always happy to be of service, Greg. Shall we go?"

They went. Both were unusually silent in the taxi on the way back to Seven Dials: Kate because, contrary to all common sense, she more than half regretted not having held her tongue; Pellew because, while the boxes might fit, their ultimate content remained as elusive as ever. He refused to go in for a drink; begged Kate not to discuss what she had told him either with Humphrey or Lady Hannington; and walked the whole way to St. John's Wood, hoping perhaps to draw inspiration from the trees and open spaces of Regent's Park. He got some fresh air into his lungs, and developed a blister on his left heel. Inspiration did not materialise.

The blister may have had something to do with it. Certainly his visit proved a considerable disillusionment for Sally Anstruther. She had taken a lot of trouble: changed into a cocktail-dress that was chic without being in the least gaudy; prepared a meal that was simple without being dull; and dispatched her girl-friend firmly to a West End cinema, at her expense, with instructions on no account to come back early.

Pellew failed to pay her compliments on the dress, hardly seemed to notice what he was eating, and altogether showed a distressing lack of personal interest in his hostess. His manner was rather brusque, and completely matter of fact. Sally, who had cheerfully endured what had almost amounted to a scene with Toby Scott when she told him how she proposed spending the evening, was not pleased. Of course, she wanted to be helpful. Of course she was prepared to answer Pellew's questions. But there were ways of doing things. Pellew's approach made her think of the type of man who makes a pass at a girl in a taxi almost before he has slammed the door. The preliminaries can make all the difference. Worst of all, Pellew seemed neither to notice nor care that he was spoiling things.

The fact was that, although inspiration might fail, Pellew was beginning almost unconsciously to see light through the wood. Here and there a pattern of possibility, however blurred by fantastic or even perverted elements, was beginning to take shape. With awareness of such a pattern the instinct and discipline of the trained police officer was renewed. The "private eye" with his opportunities for private indulgence, his weaknesses for alcohol and attractive young

176

women, receded into the background. The bloodhound replaced the human being. Sally Anstruther could not be blamed for not realising what had happened to the man whom she had found originally so attractive.

"I suppose," she said, as she poured out the coffee, "that you're cross with me because that business over the tape-recordings went all wrong. It wasn't my—"

"I'm not in the least cross with you. And, of course, it wasn't your fault. If it was anyone's fault it was Humphrey Clymping's. He knows my opinion about amateur detectives. They're almost bound to come to grief when they don't know the form."

"You look cross," pouted Sally. "And you sound cross."

Pellew failed to rise to the invitation implied.

"I'm sorry. I've had rather a tiring day."

"Then why didn't you put me off? I'd have understood."

"I had to see you, Sally."

The sentiment was satisfactory. The tone of voice in which it was expressed was not. Sally lighted a cigarette, and became dignified. "Why did you have to see me, Gregory?"

Pellew leaned forward in his chair, with his hands clasped between his knees.

"I want you to think back carefully," he said. "I want you to tell me just what happened when Rollo Gunn came into your office and caught you and Humphrey and Toby Scott together."

"Nothing—really."

"How do you mean—nothing?"

Sally looked—and felt—honestly bewildered.

"What I say. Besides we hadn't been caught. We weren't doing anything. We hadn't had time to get at the filing-cabinet. We were just there."

"What do you imagine Gunn thought you were up to?"

"Snogging," said Sally simply; and grinned at the recollection.

"With Humphrey there to play chaperon?"

"I don't know about that. I saw the inner office door open

177

and Mr. Gunn coming in, so I threw my arms round Toby's neck and held on tight. I think he was surprised, but he didn't seem to mind."

"I don't suppose he did. And then?"

"Well—Mr. Clymping laughed, and Mr. Gunn coughed, and we broke it up. I expect we all looked pretty silly."

"What I'm wondering," said Pellew grimly, "is whether or not you looked convincing. What did you expect Mr. Gunn would do?"

"Quite honestly I shouldn't have been surprised if Toby and I had been given the sack. They're pretty hot on that sort of carry-on in the office—and quite right, too," added Sally unexpectedly. "Lilian Jukes talked to me about it. Down at the Studios the set-up is quite different of course."

"Due to the corrupting influence of a lot of actors, or the breadth of mind of Mr. James Ballantyne, do you think?"

"I wouldn't know about that, Gregory."

"What *did* Gunn do?"

"He just laughed it off, with some crack about it being too bad that him and me were the only people in the office who took their jobs sufficiently seriously to work overtime. I'd always thought him rather stuffy before. Then he called Toby a lucky young so-and-so, and told Mr. Clymping to mind his own business in future, and said that personally he had to work late, but he wouldn't keep them. So they cleared out."

"And no reactions while you stayed to take down his dictation?"

Sally shook her head.

Pellew rubbed his jaw; took his pipe out of his pocket, and put it back again. "Now, Sally, another thing. When you talked to me before, you told me that when you worked for Mr. Hargest it was your job to take care of his personal arrangements: lunch dates, hair-cutting, theatre-tickets and what-not. Usually a private secretary with those responsibilities keeps a duplicate engagement-book. Did you?"

"Of course."

"Have you still got it in the office?"

Sally flushed.

"Actually I haven't. It's here."

"Here?"

The flush deepened.

"It was silly of me, Gregory. But somehow I didn't want to use the same book for Mr. Gunn's engagements after Mr. Hargest died. I got a new book for the office, and brought the old one home—to keep."

"Can I see it?"

"If you really want to—"

"Please."

It was a relief to Sally to have an opportunity to go into her bedroom and spend a good many more minutes by herself than it needed to find the engagement-book tucked away at the back of the drawer in which she kept her stockings. She wasn't sure whether she wanted to cry, to laugh a little hysterically, or to make a scene, though she certainly felt entitled to do one of the three. She hadn't defined what she had expected from this second visit of Pellew's, but she certainly hadn't expected him to behave rather like Perry Mason—one of her least favourite TV characters—questioning a hostile witness. It wouldn't do him any harm to be left by himself for a little, and to wonder—she hoped—what she might be up to. She renewed her make-up, made a face at herself in the mirror, and felt better. When she came back into the sitting-room she found Pellew standing by the window. He had pulled back the curtain and was looking down into the street.

"Here it is," said Sally.

He turned towards her abruptly, and held out his hand. "Thanks. I'll borrow it, if you don't mind. I promise you shall have it back."

"Aren't you going to look at it here?"

Pellew smiled.

"I don't think so, Sally. You're going to have another visitor, if I'm not mistaken."

"Whatever do you mean?"

179

"Toby Scott's kicking his heels down there on the pavement. I don't suppose he's come to admire the view."

"The nerve of that boy!" said Sally indignantly. "I told him you were coming here this evening."

"And he's probably hoping for a chance to save you from worse than death. More seriously, I know when I'm in the way. I'll put him out of his misery, and send him up to you."

"I don't want to see him, Gregory."

"You do. You may not think so, but you do. Thank you very much for my dinner, and thank you even more for the book."

He patted her shoulder, and left her standing quite still in the middle of the room, biting her lip. As he came out of the main entrance to the flats he was amused to see Toby Scott move hastily away to take what was apparently absorbing interest in the nearest lamp-post.

"The coast's clear," said Pellew as he passed him; and hurried away leaving the young man looking after him with an expression in which astonishment was mingled with relief.

CHAPTER 19

THE ENGAGEMENT-BOOK

Back in his own flat Pellew got out the Hargest file, and took
from it his notes on Hargest's movements during the last
week of his life. Then he opened Sally Anstruther's duplicate
engagement-book and found the two pages which covered the
same period. The entries—Biro-written in Sally's rather
schoolgirlish script—were quite clear.

WEDNESDAY:	Back from Berlin. Time(?)
THURSDAY:	2:30—Studios
	5:00—Carton's
FRIDAY:	10:15— Executives' Meeting
	11:30—Mr. Ballantyne
	12:45— Lunch—Club
	2:15—Chairman
	3:45—P-B. Mr. Gunn

That was all. On the Saturday morning Hargest had been
found dead.

On the face of them three of the entries called for further
consideration. *Carton's?* Pellew recalled that Carton's was a

well-known hairdresser's establishment in Duke Street, St. James's, and told himself that there was nothing odd in a man visiting his hairdresser as soon as possible after a trip abroad. *The interview with Ballantyne on the Friday morning?* Almost certainly part of the normal routine of picking up the threads after absence. All the same a word with James Ballantyne on the subject might be worthwhile. *P-B?* Who was P-B? Presumably Rollo Gunn would know. Was he a member of the Gargantua staff or an outsider? Pellew riffled through the Gargantua staff list, of which he had a copy in the file. Yes —among the junior assistants in the Talks Department appeared the name of one, Pleydell-Bouverie S.N. There would almost certainly be an obvious explanation. But some sort of explanation of the presence of a junior talks assistant at such a meeting was clearly called for.

The likelihood of a new lead so far seemed remote. But there was another thing about the entries over which Pellew smoked a pipe with increasing exasperation in that he couldn't see its significance—if any. The left-hand of the two pages covered the Monday, Tuesday, and Wednesday of the week. On the Wednesday there was the one entry regarding Hargest's return from Berlin, written in the same handwriting that had made the entries on the right-hand page covering the Thursday and Friday, and the blank Saturday. But there were a number of entries on the Monday and Tuesday spaces in a script altogether different: tiny, neat and precise. First of all, why were there entries at all for those two days? Hargest was still in Germany, so they could not refer to him. The diary revealed blank pages for the rest of the period during which he had been in Germany. For whose benefit then had the Monday and Tuesday entries been made? And, as Sally Anstruther had clearly not written them, who had?

MONDAY: 11:00—Board Meeting
           1:30—Lunch. United Universities
           3:00—Mr. Ballantyne
           4:30—Mr. Gunn

182

Pellew sat up suddenly and called himself an evil name. Sally Anstruther was bound to know who had been taking liberties with her book, and if he hadn't been in such a hurry to throw her into young Toby Scott's arms he could have had the answer before leaving her flat. He looked at his watch. It wasn't quite eleven o'clock. No doubt Toby would still be there. It might be tactless, even unkind, to interrupt whatever they might be doing, but this was a clear case of duty versus inclination. He picked up the telephone.

Rather to his surprise he got through almost at once, made a perfunctory apology, and asked his question. The reply was unhesitating. Jukes had written the Monday and Tuesday entries. Why? Sally had been out of the office during those two days. No, she hadn't been ill. With Mr. Hargest away she hadn't really had enough to do to keep her fully occupied, and Mr. Gunn had suggested she should take a couple of days leave before Mr. Hargest came back. Whom had the entries concerned? Sally wasn't sure about that. It might have been Mr. Gunn. It was more likely to have been the Chairman, who had been using the Managing Director's office during the early part of the week. Was that all—because it was getting late and Sally was just going to bed?

Pellew assured her that it was all, and apologised again. Presumably Toby Scott had not been received with open arms after all. Unless of course—but Pellew declined resolutely to pursue that hypothesis. It was rather gross, and not his business. He rang off and went back to the engagement-book. By hook or crook Lilian Jukes must be cornered, and persuaded, induced or forced to speak. And as one of the Monday entries was an appointment with Rollo Gunn it was reasonable to assume that his appointment was with someone else. The possibility of that someone being Sir George Farley seemed confirmed by the entries relating to a board meeting and the

Advertising Manager. In which case who was J.H. in whose flat the Chairman had lunched on the Tuesday? It was surely not too long a shot to construe J.H. into Jane Hargest. It all added up.

On the other hand why the deuce shouldn't the Chairman use Hargest's office in his absence if he wanted to? Why shouldn't he get Lilian Jukes to note down his appointments for him in Hargest's book if Sally Anstruther was away? Why shouldn't he lunch with Mrs. Hargest in her flat, instead of possibly causing gossip by taking her to a restaurant when her husband was known to be out of the country? It was the height of stupidity to invent evil motives and melodramatic explanations, when everything could have happened in a perfectly normal and simple way. The pieces composing the background of the puzzle were gradually falling into place to form a reasonably clear pattern. What still showed no sign of emerging was any reason for Hargest's death that made sense.

Pellew had just reached this depressing conclusion when Humphrey Clymping battered on his front door, demanding whisky and news of the latest development in the intervals of bemoaning the lot of "any miserable bastard who ties himself to the chariot-wheels of that blasted goggle-box." He appeared to have quite recovered his normal ebullience, and gaily disregarded alike his own hideous mixing of metaphors and Pellew's air of weary preoccupation.

"Take your drink—read through this last lot of notes of mine, if you can read them—and for God's sake simmer down!" said Pellew. "I've had a long day, I'm thinking in circles, and I'm not feeling sociable."

"The patient," said Humphrey, "is clearly irritable. Tongue furred? Temperature rising? Spots before the eyes? The obvious prescription—"

"Is bed and a good night's sleep, if you'll let me have it."

"All in good time, Greg. I know you've got your troubles. What about mine? How would you like to spend all day and half the night shooting interviews in a travelling circus? When I wasn't on a trapeze platform I was on the back of an

184

elephant, or exchanging confidences with a lion-tamer with a couple of tigers breathing down my neck, or dodging a mixed team of Shetland ponies and muscular young ladies in sequins. One of my camera-men twisted his ankle, and another ran out of film. And when I got back to the Studios Hamish Rathbone—blast him!—was kind enough to imply that I didn't know how to organise a unit for that sort of assignment."

"If you expect me to burst into tears of sympathy, Humphrey, you can think again. Let's exchange, shall we? I'll take your camera-crews, tigers, flying-trapeze-artists, and an assignment to dive off a pier on a flaming bicycle—if you'll accept Miss Sally Anstruther, Miss Lilian Jukes, my Commander at Scotland Yard—and your enchanting wife. Incidentally you may care to know that I found that shorthand report of mine. Not stolen—merely strayed, blast it!"

Humphrey put down his whisky untasted and picked up the Hargest file. "You know, Greg, I spend quite a lot of Gargantua's time mislaying things like this by-mistake-on-purpose. They don't know it—but that's really how I earn my salary. We're both damn tired. I'm not going home to bed until you've given me the form at the latest time of asking. It's less exhausting to listen than to read your handwriting. So forget that I'm here, and just talk to yourself." He leaned forward, and laid the file gently on Pellew's knees.

Pellew's reaction was to close his eyes. Humphrey, whose susceptibility to "atmosphere" was hardly acute, realised that there are moments when a bull in a china shop ceases to be amusing and becomes purely destructive.

"Tuck yourself into bed, Greg, and take a couple of aspirin. I'll bring you some hot milk, and be on my way."

"No," said Pellew.

He spoke with decision, though without opening his eyes.

"Just listen, and don't interrupt. 'Look here upon this picture and on this'—why do these bloody quotations always come up? Take the picture of Hargest's death as presented in the papers, and as presented to me when the case was opened:

185

Simon Hargest, brilliant television executive, with a back-ground of unbroken success in a sufficiently variegated career, commits suicide. He was, admittedly, overworked—as anyone in his position was bound to be. He was on the best of terms with the top brass of his organisation, notably with Sir George Farley his Chairman. His personal staff was devoted to him. He lived happily with his wife. His health was good. He had no money troubles. A harmless necessary detective-inspector, with a slightly unconventional record, is invited to investigate the affair unofficially, while being given to understand that the Establishment is sufficiently concerned for the inquiry to be routed through Scotland Yard, with all that that implies for the investigator. All right so far?"

"Go on," said Humphrey quietly.

"Now take the picture as it's emerged in the light of our ferretings, yours and mine. Hargest was not only an important television executive. He was a top Intelligence operator —and quite possibly the very top of that particular tree, using Gargantua as his indispensable and admirable 'cover.' In that field he had just experienced a serious and mortifying set-back. (*Evidence—my meeting with the Polish interpreter in Berlin.*) Two of his personal staff owed their jobs to having worked in Intelligence with Hargest during the war. (*Evidence—Rollo Gunn's own statement, and Lilian Jukes, personal file.*) Hargest's relations with his Chairman were probably less cordial than they seemed. (*Evidence—the appointment as his successor of James Ballantyne.*) Hargest's relations with Ballantyne were anything but satisfactory. (*Evidence—Ballantyne's own statement, and correspondence between him and Hargest.*) Hargest's domestic felicity was, to say the least of it, questionable. Circumstances point to the possibility of Mrs. Hargest being involved with Rollo Gunn and/or Sir George Farley. (*Evidence—Vera Mandrake, Millie Cresswell, and Kate Clymping.*)"

"What the devil has Kate been playing at?" exclaimed Humphrey.

"I said—don't interrupt," said Pellew calmly. "So much

186

for the revised picture. There are also a number of curious loose ends, which may or may not have a bearing. First, Lilian Jukes was in love with Hargest. (*No evidence, but reasonable assumption based on her attitude and Sally Anstruther's observation.*) Second, Sally Anstruther hero-worshipped Hargest. (*Evidence—her own statement.*) Thirdly, the original inquiry into Hargest's death was, if not initiated, at any rate entrusted to the appropriate policy authority by a homosexual. (*Evidence—Lady Hannington's diary, and the police authority's admission.*) Fourth, during Hargest's absence in Berlin his office and his secretary were made use of by Sir George Farley. (*Evidence—Sally Anstruther's statement, supported by entries in her duplicate engagement-book.*) Fifth—and in my opinion most important—Sally Anstruther was given leave during the last two days of Hargest's absence abroad. (*Evidence—her own statement.*) Sixth, during those two days and in Hargest's office Sir George Farley interviewed James Ballantyne, and Rollo Gunn among other people, and lunched with 'J.H.' in the latter's flat. (*Evidence—entries in the duplicate engagement-book. Assumption, not too far-fetched, that J.H. equals Jane Hargest.*) Seventh, and last, Hargest's final interview in his office on the Friday after his return, and during the afternoon before his death, was with Rollo Gunn and a certain P-B. (*Evidence—the engagement-book. P-B unidentified, but a junior talks assistant on the Gargantua star list called Pleydell-Bouverie would seem to qualify.*) And that, I think— and as far as I can remember at this time of night—is the lot."

Pellew opened his eyes, and reached out a hand for his pipe.

"I'm surprised at you, Humphrey. You haven't touched your drink. You might give me one. I think I've earned it."

"For once I agree with you. Apart from waiting on you hand and foot do you want comments?"

"Surely."

"Then I'll work backwards over your seven loose ends to begin with."

"Pleydell-Bouverie?"

"Doesn't make sense to me. He's one of Jim Ballantyne's bright young men at the Studios; promising and all that, but very new. I can't imagine what would take him to a meeting with Rollo and Hargest, He's out of their world."

"J.H.?"

"That makes sense if your other line on Jane Hargest is correct. If Katie's awake when I get home to-night there's a clear case for a curtain-lecture."

"You leave Kate alone, Humphrey. Compared with you — and me — she'd not done at all badly."

"No wonder the girls all love you, Greg. Get on with it."

"That leave of Sally's?"

"What's strange or significant about that?"

"Possibly nothing. Let's leave it for the moment. Perhaps the Chairman's use of Hargest's office strikes a chord?"

"If it does," said Humphrey gloomily, "the chord's lost. I imagine that in Hargest's absence the old boy wanted to be in closer touch with the works."

"Imagination is of course a wonderful thing. Would you care to exercise it in respect of your mamma's homosexual boy-friend?"

Humphrey took longer than seemed strictly necessary to refill his glass before he answered.

"From what I've read," he said cautiously, "I've gathered that blackmail in that particular field is one of the commonplaces of Intelligence activities. If Hargest was one of the fraternity it might explain his domestic set-up — if your ideas about that are justified. It seems a bit far-fetched to me."

"And to me, Humphrey. What about the two secretaries and Hargest?"

"My dear Greg, you know a lot more about Miss Pretty than I do. As for Miss Plain I expect you're right. She was frustratedly in love with Hargest and has probably erected a shrine to his memory, which would account for her non-cooperative behaviour. It doesn't get us any place."

"Nor does it get us much further towards tying up the loose ends, Humphrey."

"What about the ends that aren't quite so loose?"

"I've thought about them too much and too often," said Pellew, "to start talking about them again at this time of night. The facts—and the evidence for what it may be worth —are all in that file. You can take it home and sleep with it under your pillow if you like. I shouldn't much care if you lost it on the way."

Humphrey heaved himself out of his chair. "You sound as if you were pretty well all in, Greg."

"I usually am—at this stage of any case."

"What stage?"

"When I've made up my mind, and don't know what to do about it. It sounds a little absurd, but it's as if virtue had gone out of me."

"You mean," said Humphrey heavily, "that you know the answers to this Hargest business?"

"I mean that I know who caused Hargest's death."

"Well—who?"

Pellew shook his head and smiled faintly.

"I can't prove it, my dear Humphrey. Nor do I know yet how the trick was done. Guessing is the Sin against the Holy Ghost in criminal investigation. I'm not giving even you the chance to accuse me of committing it. Besides, you know as much as I do. Your guess is as good as mine."

"That's all very fine," said Humphrey irritably, "but what do we do next?"

"The details can wait," said Pellew. "But I propose to ask our delightful mother to exercise her wiles—and her charm —upon the elusive Miss Lilian Jukes. I think I shall have to find some excuse for another talk with Sir George Farley. And from you I want two things, or rather two dates: first when Mr. Ballantyne is to take over the Managing Director's office; second when you can conveniently take Rollo Gunn out to dinner, and—if at all possible—make him drunk. Now will you please go home to bed?"

189

"All right, damn you," said Humphrey amiably.

"Thanks. One other thing. Are you going into the Gargantua office to-morrow?"

"As a matter of fact I've got to—on my way to the Studios."

"Good. Then will you give Sally Anstruther her engagement-book back—at some moment when Miss Jukes is looking the other way? And ask her—from me—to keep it carefully under lock and key?"

"Can do," said Humphrey. "All the same I'd like to know—"

"You can't. Good night. And sleep well."

PART THREE # HOW?

'Tis sure enough, an you knew how. . . .

—TITUS ANDRONICUS

CHAPTER 20

LADY HANNINGTON PAYS A CALL

The working alliance between Lady Hannington and Detective-Inspector Gregory Pellew was a singular one. Kate Clymping explained it to Humphrey, as kindly as possible, by pointing out that as an only son Humphrey had always shown considerable limitations, and that the countess had come almost to regard Gregory as a substitute. Humphrey retorted that there might be something in Kate's theory but that Greg's real attraction for Lady Hannington lay in his having been orphaned in his teens and having lost his wife within six months of their marriage. Needless to say no one put the question to Lady Hannington. She would probably have replied that Mr. Pellew was almost the only one among Humphrey's friends of whom she could approve; that she liked his punctuality and good manners and obvious admiration for herself; that she was interested in his work. Similarly questioned, Pellew would have shrugged his shoulders, and muttered something about a natural sympathy between devotees of common sense as the cure of this world's ills.

In fact, their principal bond was a mutual detestation of humbug. Lady Hannington disliked liberal humanitarians, whose liberalism excluded their own country, and whose humanitarianism embraced everyone except their friends. She distrusted lawyers, and loathed psychiatrists. Pellew understood criminals, and often sympathised with them. He despised workers-to-rule, and hated medical witnesses. Also he was a lonely man, walking by himself as much by choice as from necessity. In Lady Hannington's well-bred certainty he found comfort. From her unobtrusive intelligence he drew stimulation. In a world so largely composed of self-conscious exhibitionists, self-induced neuroses, and dissolving standards, her brisk tubby little figure and improbably auburn hair embodied sanity qualified only by kindness. The gentleman might have perished with the Empire he had done so much to win. As long as Lady Hannington lived there would always be a gentle woman. Without knowing how to admit it, Pellew loved her.

So, when he asked her to tackle Lilian Jukes and explained why, Lady Hannington showed no embarrassment and made no difficulties. She knew, perhaps better than Pellew, that no one is so irresistible as an elderly lady who knows her own mind, and has been used for the greater part of her life to getting her own way; a knowledge shared to their cost by doctors, theatrical managers and publishers. She saw no reason to invent a bogus excuse for her visit, as Pellew had done with Rollo Gunn, and Humphrey and Kate with Jane Hargest. Having decided that Sunday afternoon was the most likely occasion to find a hard-working woman at home Lady Hannington called at Lilian Jukes' flat a little after four o'clock; introduced herself with a beaming smile and the most casual of references to Humphrey and Gargantua; and asked if Miss Jukes would give her half an hour of her time and a cup of tea.

Miss Jukes' reaction was not exactly welcoming. But when you have been brought up in a Service family, and live in Queen's Gate, you can hardly slam the door in the face of someone old enough to be your mother—especially when you have visited that someone's house, however briefly. Lady

Hannington found herself in the vast bed-sitting-room of one of those flats into which the former mansions of the prosperous Kensington bourgeoisie have been converted so uncomfortably. Miss Jukes disappeared into the tiny kitchenette adjoining to make the tea. She was sorry it wasn't China. She had lost the taste for China tea during the war.

Lady Hannington settled herself into an upright but comfortable chair and looked about her. It was no doubt an old-fashioned idea, but women really ought not to live alone. Except for its size the room might almost have been a cell. There was a narrow divan that would have suited a nun. There was one small bookcase. There was a desk as depressingly neat and featureless as the furnishing. The wall-paper was neutral, the paint a dull green. Above the gas-fire hung three W.R.N.S. service groups, and facing them two large and abominably painted pictures of a country-house with its garden. There was neither sewing-basket nor dog-basket; neither parrot nor budgerigar, nor companionably lingering smell of tobacco smoke. Scene and sequence were completed by a typewriter carefully cased and a filing-cabinet obviously locked.

Miss Jukes returned with a table-cloth over one arm; set an occasional table conveniently at Lady Hannington's elbow; went out again, and came back with a silver tea-pot, two cups, and half a seed-cake on a rather charming silver tray. Her movements were deft and controlled. Her hands were certainly too big, but she had pretty legs and feet. She sat down in a stiff-backed chair facing the light, and gave Lady Hannington her first opportunity to study her hostess's face.

Yes, she was plain. Humphrey would have made no mistake about that. But she was not featureless like the room she existed rather than lived in. There was character in the high-bridged nose, the dark thick eyebrows; obstinacy in the narrow forehead; intelligence in the eyes; and sensuality in the full lower lip. If she did not face determination and discipline Lady Hannington had never recognised the combination. This was no case for wheedling or bullying, still less for

195

bluff. Only the direct approach would serve. And, unless she was much mistaken, the defence would be almost carefully sited, and in depth.

To her surprise it was Lilian Jukes who opened fire— with a rather stilted apology for her behaviour at the party at Seven Dials when she had gone away almost as soon as she had arrived.

"I suppose I should have written, and said I felt ill or something of the sort. It wouldn't have been true. There was someone there I didn't want to meet."

"I gathered as much from my son," said Lady Hannington tranquilly. "It seemed to me a most sensible thing to do."

"Thank you."

"Nothing's more tiresome or such a waste of time as trying to be civil to people you can't bear. Surely you agree?"

"I suppose so."

"Of course you do. So if you don't feel inclined to be civil to me, Miss Jukes, I shall perfectly understand. This visit's an intrusion and can't be called anything else. We must go on from there—unless you tell me to go away and mind my own business."

Miss Jukes poured out the tea with a perfectly steady hand. "If I could have done that," she said, with the suspicion of a smile, "I should have done it on the doorstep. Milk and sugar?"

"A little milk, please, and no sugar."

"I hope you can eat seed-cake. I don't like it, but we always had it at home on Sundays and I got into the habit. I even missed it when I was abroad and couldn't get it for love or money."

Lady Hannington sipped her tea.

"Just a small piece. It reminds me of the country. I don't know why. Now—aren't you going to ask me why I've come to see you?"

Lilian Jukes put down her cup. "I know," she said.

"Really?"

"I've got eyes and ears, Lady Hannington. I've even got

eelings, though most people don't realise it—which, of
ourse, is my fault. You've come to ask me questions about
Mr. Hargest, haven't you? Whoever thought of that one was
clever. It's no use being defiant or even dumb with a person
like you. Besides, I'm so tired."

She cupped her chin in her hands, and stared past Lady
Hannington at the plane-tree outside the window.

"It's not just idle curiosity you know, Miss Jukes."

"Oh, yes—I know that. But I've been trained to do my
work and not to talk about it. That inquiry agent had no right
to try to break me down. Any fool could have seen that his
story about Mr. Hargest and insurance was rubbish. And
even if it wasn't—"

"Well?"

Lilian Jukes stood up. "I was in love with Mr. Hargest,"
she said. "I fell in love with him the day I met him in Malta.
I'd never been in love before. When he sent for me after the
war and gave me the job to work for him in Gargantua it was
the most wonderful thing that had ever happened to me. I
was happy for the first time in my life. Now, I've nothing but
his memory and his reputation. No one else cares, except
Lollo Gunn—a little. And then people want to ask questions,
and probe about, so that they can talk and smear. They don't
know the sort of man he was, and they mustn't know. He's
dead, and he has the right to rest in peace."

Lady Hannington finished her tea and looked up. "Even
if it was murder?" she said gently.

"Murder? I don't know what you mean! He killed himself. I suppose you could say they killed him, considering the
work and the responsibilities they piled on his shoulders—"

"'They,' Miss Jukes?"

"That man Ballantyne. Sir George Farley. They all exploited him."

"By 'all,'" said Lady Hannington, "you mean people in
addition to Mr. Ballantyne and Sir George, don't you?"

Lilian Jukes turned her back, and moved over to the fireplace. Lady Hannington noticed with interest that she stood staring at the framed W.R.N.S. service groups.

"I can't answer that," she said.

"A uniform helps, doesn't it?" said Lady Hannington quietly. "All the same the job goes on. And the job and working with Mr. Hargest were one and the same thing as far as you were concerned."

Miss Jukes spun round. "How much do you know?"

Lady Hannington swallowed a mouthful of seed-cake and coughed delicately. "I know that you worked with Mr. Hargest during the war, and that Mr. Gunn worked with Mr. Hargest during the war. I've an idea that that work didn't end with the war. What that work was, I've no idea. You won't tell me, and I don't really want to know—except from natural curiosity. The point—the real point of my coming to see you like this—is that there's quite good reason to believe that Mr. Hargest's death can be attributed somehow to that work; not to any anxieties connected with Gargantua Television. Of course I understand why you hate what you call this 'probing about.' I believe—and you've only got my word for it—that the reason for it is the vital importance of that work's future and what it means to the country. That sounds pompous I know. I'm sorry."

"But I don't know anything. It wasn't my business to know things. I did what I was told."

"And I'm asking you," said Lady Hannington, "what you were told to do, and by whom."

"If you know as much about the work as you seem to know," said Miss Jukes stubbornly after a pause, "then you ought to know that I can't talk about it."

"Of course, in normal circumstances. These circumstances aren't normal. At any rate you can answer this. Were Mr Hargest and his wife happy together?"

There was another pause. Then Lilian Jukes laughed. It was not a pretty sound. "Why should I know the answer to that, Lady Hannington?"

198

"Because you were his secretary, and you're not a fool," said Lady Hannington tartly. "Of course you know."

"He was happy enough to ruin any chance I might ever have had. He was happy enough not to realise she was making a fool of him. Now are you satisfied?"

"Not quite. Who was the *tertium quid?*"

Miss Jukes shrugged her shoulders. "I was taught at school not to tell tales, Lady Hannington. And I'm still employed by Gargantua."

In her turn Lady Hannington got to her feet. "You're an admirable—and most exasperating woman, Miss Jukes. I'll change the subject and try again. I believe you were responsible for the tape-recordings that Mr. Hargest had made of some of the interviews in his office?"

"I suppose you got that from Sally Anstruther. I always said it was a mistake to have a little idiot like that around. From the day she was taken on, half the men in the building started finding excuses to come into the office. You can't expect sense and discretion from a face and figure like hers—not that she isn't a nice enough kid in her own way."

"Why do you think Mr. Hargest took her on, Miss Jukes?"

"Not from any personal interest. You can be sure of that. I don't think he noticed her. I believe it was Rollo Gunn's idea. I imagine he wanted to keep me in my place by drawing the contrast."

The bitter truth of that last sentence affected Lady Hannington strangely. She had to repress a strong impulse to put an arm round Lilian Jukes's shoulders and tell her to have a good cry. She reminded herself with difficulty that in Gregory Pellew's estimation at any rate, Miss Jukes was to be regarded as a hypothetically hostile witness, if not an actual suspect. She forced herself to remember that she was there as Pellew's mouthpiece; that she could not afford to indulge her natural sympathy with a lonely, middle-aged, and unhappy woman.

"In fact, Miss Jukes, you were, and still are, in sole charge of those tape-recordings in your office?"

"Yes, Lady Hannington."

The reply came without a shadow of hesitation, and in a tone clearly implying that the last word on the subject had been said. But Lilian Jukes' eyes had flickered for a second towards the filing-cabinet beside the desk in the window, and Lady Hannington saw that flicker.

"Why do you dislike Mr. Ballantyne so much?" she asked.

"He was always intriguing against Mr. Hargest behind his back. He wanted his job. And now he's got it. Much good may it do him!"

"How could you know that, Miss Jukes?"

"You said yourself that a personal secretary who isn't a fool knows a lot of things that aren't strictly her business. I couldn't help knowing. I saw the correspondence between them. I saw them together. Mr. Hargest refused to take Ballantyne seriously. He thought he was just a fanatic about his programmes. I knew better. And when he got at the Chairman—"

She broke off, biting her lip. But she had gone that half-sentence too far, and Lady Hannington pounced.

"But you're not the Chairman's secretary, Miss Jukes."

"I—I worked for him occasionally. When Mr. Hargest was away."

"I see." Lady Hannington had not forgotten what she had been told by Pellew about the entries in Sally Anstruther's duplicate diary. "You mean you worked for Sir George during the last few days of Mr. Hargest's absence in Germany?"

"Yes."

"And it was then you discovered that Mr. Ballantyne had 'got at' the Chairman?"

"I'd suspected it for ages. It was the obvious thing for him to do."

"It was during those few days," persisted Lady Hannington, "that your suspicions were confirmed? I happen to know

that on the Monday afternoon Mr. Ballantyne had an interview with Sir George. Was that when you found out?"

"I wasn't there, Lady Hannington."

"You were in the outer office surely?"

"I don't listen at keyholes," said Miss Jukes contemp-
tuously.

"Of course not. But sometimes you do listen to tape-
recordings, don't you? And you know how to manage a tape-
recording machine. And there's a tape-recording machine in
your outer office. Are you going to deny that you made a
recording of that interview between Sir George Farley and
Mr. Ballantyne?"

"You can't prove that I did."

"I think I can, Miss Jukes, if you'll open that filing-cabinet by your desk."

Lady Hannington sat down again. Miss Jukes lifted her
chin and stared at her defiantly.

"You know, I'm not blaming you in the least," said Lady
Hannington quietly. "Curiosity plus loyalty provide a pretty
strong motive for anything. I suppose you brought the
recording home with you for safety. At the office it might
have got into the wrong hands."

Miss Jukes continued to stare. But her lips quivered, and
Lady Hannington remembered having read somewhere that a
liar is betrayed by his mouth, not by his eyes.

"On the afternoon of the Friday—the day before his death
Mr. Hargest gave Mr. Ballantyne an interview. Did you
tape-record that interview, Miss Jukes?"

"Certainly not!"

"You weren't curious any longer?"

"I only took recordings on instruction from Mr. Hargest."

"But when Mr. Hargest wasn't there? You're not going to
tell me that Sir George Farley instructed you to record that
interview of his with Mr. Ballantyne. Who did? Mr. Gunn
was Mr. Hargest's personal assistant, and acted for him in his
absence. Was it Mr. Gunn?"

Miss Jukes' almost terrifying self-containment suddenly cracked. She began to cry, noisily, shamelessly, with convulsive movements of her throat and helplessly twitching hands. Then she moved uncertainly to the desk, opened a drawer, and took out a key. She turned round, with tears pouring down her cheeks, dropped the key into Lady Hannington's lap, blundered across the room into the kitchenette, and slammed the door behind her.

Lady Hannington was fingering the key, and wondering what with decency and humanity she could and should do next, when the door reopened.

"They were all I had to remember him by," said Miss Jukes. "I've been a fool and a coward. Please take them away."

The door was shut again. This time it was locked.

CHAPTER 21

LAST ROUND-UP

Pellew reached the house in Seven Dials late that same evening in a pretty disgruntled frame of mind. Lady Hannington had been guarded on the telephone, but from what she had felt able to tell him he felt reasonably certain of being able to put two and two together. He had got in touch accordingly with Scotland Yard, and suggested that the Commander should meet him, if he had nothing better to do. The reply, delivered through a secretary, was that the Commander was expecting a report in writing to be delivered personally by Inspector Pellew, and saw nothing to be gained by a meeting until that report was delivered.

Kate and Humphrey Clymping were on the doorstep when Pellew's taxi drove up, and it quickly became obvious that neither was on top of the world. Kate had been "called" to play the lead she understudied that evening, only to be told five minutes before the curtain went up that she wasn't wanted after all. Humphrey, who had called for her on his way back from the Studios, had been late. Instead of being properly contrite he had grumbled about having been given futile assignments by Pellew, and the difficulties various people had raised to his taking a tape-play-back machine out of the Studios without official sanction.

"They talked as if it was fun for me to cart the damned thing about London," he said indignantly. "Seemed to think I was going to play it for pennies in the street, like a blasted barrel-organ. And frankly, Greg, I don't think you ought to have sent my mother to see the Jukes. Why did you?"

"We had to get hold of those tapes, Humphrey. You weren't so successful when you had a shot, were you?"

Kate laughed. Humphrey grunted, and opened the front door.

"You think she's got them? The right ones, I mean?"

"I think so."

"You might have told me beforehand, instead of making me waste my time inventing a reason to get in to see our Jim, and talking hot air to that blazing young ass, Pleydell-Bouverie. Let's go upstairs."

"Yes," said Pellew, as they stopped on the landing outside Lady Hannington's sitting-room. "I apologise about Pleydell-Bouverie. That was stupid of me."

"What do you mean?"

"I don't think I do apologise after all. I ought to have seen it admittedly. But so ought you. You've got it in your hand."

Humphrey glared.

"P-B—Play-Back—simple, isn't it?"

Kate opened the door hurriedly.

Lady Hannington was sitting in an arm-chair playing patience. She was wearing a pale blue dressing-gown, and with a frilled cap over her hair looked like a character out of Beatrix Potter. At the other end of the table was a bottle of red wine, glasses, a large cheese, and some long French rolls.

"There you are at last," she said, without looking up from the cards. "Make yourselves comfortable, and help yourselves, while I just finish this. I think it's coming out."

"Black knave on red queen," said Kate, bending over to kiss her.

"Thank you, my dear—but never help anyone to play

tience, if you value their affection. Don't you agree, Mr.
llew? I made it a picnic as we're getting down to business.
ose tins on the chair in the corner—I hope they're what
u want."

"We shall all look pretty fools if they're not," growled
umphrey. He opened the bottle with more force than was
ictly necessary.

"You get that machine of yours operable," said Pellew. He
nt over and examined the tins. There were four of them,
ain, circular, three small type-written gummed labels.

"Are these all there were, Lady Hannington?"

"They were quite enough for an old woman like me to
ry, Mr. Pellew. I must have looked most peculiar getting
o the taxi. Luckily I got one in Queen's Gate almost at
ce. There—out. Most satisfactory." She swept the cards
ay. Pellew brought the tins to the table. Humphrey, his
uth full of French bread and cheese, grumbled that he
uld like to be brought up to date.

"Don't be impatient, Humphrey. You come first. I sold
u a pup over P-B—"

"You mean you know that means Play-Back, Mr. Pellew?
ow disappointing of you. I'd looked forward to giving you
urprise."

Pellew made her a little bow.

"But what about Ballantyne, Humphrey? You saw him?"

"I did. It wasn't easy, as you can imagine, with the whole
-up buzzing about his new appointment, and all the ca-
er-boys trying to get on terms with the risen sun. But I
ked up a story—and it wasn't altogether a fake—about my
t much wanting to go on with my job once he was out of
e Studios. I could usually rely on him to keep Hamish
athbone out of my hair."

"How did he seem?"

"Bright as a button. Lively as a cricket. He's under the
pression that a genuine programme man turned executive
n solve all Gargantua's problems. He's raring to go."

"Did you manage to bring Hargest into your convers‐
tion?"

"He brought him in himself. His attitude was that Ha‐
gest's only mistake was having involved himself in televisi‐
at all below board-room level. About Hargest's general abi‐
ties he couldn't have been more emphatic."

"Not too emphatic?"

"Now look here, Greg. I know I haven't exactly sho‐
over this business, but if you've still got Jim Ballantyne
your sights as suspect you're making a big mistake. I do‐
say he couldn't do murder for the sake of a programme. I'‐
positive he wouldn't for the sake of a step up the ladder. I
simply not on."

"Good enough," said Pellew. "I don't think I wasted yo‐
time to-day after all. I'm honestly grateful."

Kate, who had been watching her husband's face with ‐
occasional side-glance at her mother-in-law, turned sudden‐
to Pellew.

"I'm like Humphrey," she said. "I want to be brought ‐
to date."

"Then I'll do my best," said Pellew. "Let's start with wh‐
we actually know. And by 'know' I don't mean facts whi‐
could be supported by evidence in a court of law. Some cou‐
be, but most of them couldn't. Perhaps we're lucky in so f‐
that my business is to inquire and report; not to bring a case‐

"Well," said Humphrey impatiently, "what do we know‐

"We know that Hargest killed himself. We know th‐
Hargest was an important Intelligence operative. We kn‐
that under the Gargantua cover he carried on his Intelligen‐
work with the help of Rollo Gunn and Lilian Jukes, who h‐
both worked in Intelligence with him during the war. ‐
know that Lilian Jukes was in love with Hargest. We kn‐
that Mrs. Hargest has been carrying on an intrigue wi‐
another man. We know that there was a fierce professio‐
conflict for final effective control of Gargantua programm‐
between Hargest and James Ballantyne. We know that t‐
inquiry into Hargest's death was set on foot by a homosexu‐

We know that—setting aside physical or nervous collapse, neither of which are out of the question—there is only one reason for a man of Hargest's calibre to kill himself: blackmail, financial or emotional. We know that Hargest was a rich man. Hargest was blackmailed emotionally into a condition of mind in which he believed that life was no longer worth living. He was peculiarly susceptible to such pressure because—we know this, too—his last extremely important Intelligence assignment in Berlin had proved a failure. Anything to add, Humphrey?"

"Only that in terms of your use of the word 'know' I know that Jim Ballantyne can be counted out."

"How about you, Katie?"

"I don't pretend to know anything, Greg. But if Jane Hargest isn't as two-faced as they come, I'll eat the sort of hat Humphrey can't afford to buy me."

"Lady Hannington?"

"I know that Lilian Jukes is the perfect subordinate, the ideal faithful-bitch type, Mr. Pellew. She always does precisely as she's told. I know that the people who told her to do things were Mr. Hargest, Mr. Gunn, and Sir George Farley. Just once she acted on her own initiative, when on that Monday afternoon she took a tape-recording of the interview between Sir George and Mr. Ballantyne. She took it out of loyalty to Mr. Hargest. Presumably that tape-recording is in the tin there that's unlabelled."

"Finally," said Pellew, "I know—I think I know—who applied the blackmail screw. I don't know how, but I believe those other three tins of tape-recordings contain the answer."

"Who was it, Greg?"

"We'll listen to the tapes first, if you don't mind."

"If I remember rightly," said Lady Hannington, "the three labels are marked: Ch—G, Ch—JB, Ch—JH."

"Exactly. The Chairman and Rollo Gunn. The Chairman and James Ballantyne—"

"Wait a minute, Greg. You said that the Chairman-

Ballantyne interview was the tape in the unlabelled tin."

"No, dear," said Lady Hannington mildly. "That was *my* idea."

"I don't get it," said Humphrey. "That means there are two recordings of the same interview."

"Well?" said Pellew sharply. "Is that impossible?"

"Not impossible. That recording machine takes duplicate tapes automatically, in case there's a technical flaw in one of them. But only one is kept as a rule, once they've been checked."

"Then, though I don't like to suggest it, Lady Hannington may be wrong. We shall know when we've heard them played back."

"I'm sure we shall," said Lady Hannington. "And the last one?"

"The Chairman and Jane Hargest," said Kate triumphantly. "What did I tell you, Humphrey?"

"Too much," growled her husband. "Let's hear the damned things. They'll probably prove us all liars."

"I'm beginning not to like this very much," said Kate.

"You can always go to bed, darling."

"As long as we're married we go to bed together," said Kate firmly.

"Kate's common sense," said Lady Hannington, "is remarkable. Are you going or staying, Humphrey?"

Humphrey looked at his wife and grinned. "Oddly enough, I'm staying."

He held out his hand for the first tape.

"Before we start," said Pellew, handing it over, "I want you all to imagine yourselves in Simon Hargest's shoes, hearing these recordings for the first time."

Lady Hannington sat up very straight in her chair.

"The first time," she repeated slowly. "I see. P-B—Play-Back—3:45, Friday afternoon. But why—?"

"Questions later, if you don't mind, Lady Hannington. Go ahead, Humphrey. Switch the thing on."

Lady Hannington leaned back resignedly, and closed her eyes.

"I don't suppose we shall be listening as long as all that," said Humphrey consolingly. "You can bet these tapes have been edited—on the same principle as programme recordings: the bit that matters kept, and the rest into the wastepaper basket. Here goes Ch—G: old Farley and Rollo."

He pressed down the switch. There was a click, followed by a brief silence. Then the voices came through, clear and unmistakable.

Farley: Come in. Sit down. Can't bear people standing about. Now, Gunn, why did you want to see me?

Gunn: I won't take up much of your time.

Farley: I hope not. Much too busy as usual. Well, what is it?

Gunn: I've completed those inquiries on the advertising side.

Farley: You have, have you? You've taken your time, considering that the original suggestion came from you.

Gunn: I'm sorry, sir. I couldn't be too blatantly obvious about it.

Farley: Naturally not. Well?

Gunn: I was perfectly right. Both our own advertising people and the most important agencies outside would prefer Ballantyne in the job.

Farley: Hum! I see. Been thinking for some time that Hargest was losing his touch. Pity.

Gunn: He's allowed himself to be over-influenced by the Eurovision angle, sir, if you ask me.

Farley: Don't ask you. Whole business most distasteful and unpleasant. What I don't understand is why you didn't put yourself forward for the succession, hey?

Gunn: I owe Hargest a good deal. And I think I know my own limitations.

Farley: Will you be able to work with Ballantyne? Thought you didn't like him much, hey?

209

Gunn: I've the greatest respect for his professional abili
ties.

Farley: Suppose Ballantyne won't work with you?

Gunn: Over that, sir, I'm relying on you. If I hadn
brought the situation to your notice, the consequences to Gar
gantua would have been pretty serious in the long run.

Farley: I shall tell Hargest on Friday afternoon. I mus
see the Advertising Manager again first.

Gunn: Naturally, sir.

Farley: Arrange that for eleven o'clock to-morrow morn
ing, will you?

Gunn: Certainly.

Farley: Can't quite understand Ballantyne's attitude. No
very consistent, hey?

Gunn: He's an unusual personality you know.

Farley: Of course I know. Anything else?

Gunn: I don't think so, sir. Thank you.

Silence. Click. The whirring sound of the tape being re
wound. Lady Hannington kept her eyes closed. The othe
three listeners stared at each other.

"Next one please, Humphrey. Ch—JB, isn't it?"

"Sir George and Jim—that's right," said Humphrey
changing the tapes with surprisingly deft fingers. "Comin
up."

Again the click and the silence, followed by Ballantyne
voice.

Ballantyne: I suppose you're not pulling my leg, Si
George?

Farley: And why should you think that, hey?

Ballantyne: It's a complete reversal of what I'd understoo
to be Gargantua policy.

Farley: Policies, Ballantyne, are conditioned by circum
stances. I've reason to believe that circumstances hav
changed.

Ballantyne: And that the advertising agencies are now gen
uinely interested in the content of programmes?

210

Farley: We're now in a position to make them so—and you're the man to do it.

Ballantyne: Then I'll make my own position perfectly clear. I'll take the job. Hargest's a stubborn bastard—I loathe his guts—There's nothing I wouldn't do to get him outed. Can we go on from there?

Farley: Certainly. I quite agree with you about Hargest.

Ballantyne: You'll let me know when you've seen him?

Farley: Probably Friday.

Click. Silence. Then Humphrey turned on Pellew.

"Look here, Greg. This just doesn't add up! I'll be damned if it does!"

"I'd rather you didn't swear quite so vigorously, dear."

"I'm sorry, Mother, but Jim's not that sort of man. He's an enthusiast, almost to the point of mania, if you like. But he's not a back-stabber or a four-letter man."

"I suppose," put in Kate, "it was Mr. Ballantyne's own voice?"

"Voice—and manner—yes. I simply don't understand it!"

Lady Hannington opened her eyes. "Don't you think it might be a good idea," she suggested, "if we heard the duplicate tape of that interview? The tape Miss Jukes kept in the tin without a label? Always supposing that we're right and it is a duplicate."

"I don't see how that's going to help," grumbled Humphrey.

"But I think I do," said Pellew. "Let's have it."

He reached for the unlabelled tin. Humphrey turned back to the machine with a shrug, and almost immediately there was repeated the sound of Ballantyne's voice.

Ballantyne: I suppose you're not pulling my leg, Sir George?

Farley: And why should you think that, hey?

Ballantyne: It's a complete reversal of what I'd understood to be Gargantua policy. *And it's pretty rough on Hargest.*

Farley: Policies, Ballantyne, are conditioned by circumstances. *I'm sorry for Hargest but* I've reason to believe that circumstances have changed.

Ballantyne: And that the advertising agencies are now genuinely interested in the content of programmes? *Hargest knows more about that aspect than either of us.*

Farley: We're now in a position to make them so—and you're the man to do it.

Ballantyne: Then I'll make my own position perfectly clear. I'll take the job—*on the terms specified in my letter to you*—but only if Hargest agrees. Hargest's a stubborn bastard. *Outside this office I admire him no end. Inside it, I admit,* I loathe his guts. *But don't get the idea that* there's nothing I won't do to get him outed. Can we go on from there?

Farley: Certainly. I quite agree with you about Hargest. *Every consideration possible, and, I hope, a seat on the board, if he'll stay.*

Ballantyne: You'll let me know when you've seen him?

Farley: Probably Friday. *I don't look forward to it.*

Click. Silence. This time it was prolonged almost unendurably.

"You see," said Pellew at last. "More accurately, you heard."

Humphrey banged his fist down on the table. "Greg, I ought to be in a home! I was almost on the ball when I talked cheerfully about editing tapes. But I never imagined——"

"That the second tape was the recording of the interview in full. That the first had been carefully snipped to give the interview a completely different slant. It was diabolically ingenious. Cutting out about ten sentences turned normal procedure into the filthiest kind of conspiracy."

"I can understand that," said Lady Hannington dryly. "But surely what we want to know is who did the snipping, and why?"

"There's one more tape," said Pellew. "Let's have all the evidence before we start making deductions."

Humphrey had gone over into a corner of the room with the two tapes already played back laid carefully across his

rm, and was peering at them closely under a standard lamp.
I can tell you two things," he said. "The first tape wasn't
dited; and the cutting and rejoining of the second was done
y someone who knows his business—a neat job."

"I'm sure that's very clever of you, darling," said Kate,
but I've already stayed up as late as this because I'm madly
urious to know what Sir George Farley and Jane Hargest
ad to say to each other, which was worth recording. I'm still
ollowing that hunch of mine." She picked up the tin labelled
h—JH and held it out to her husband.

"You don't let up, do you?" said Humphrey. "Greg—
hen do you imagine this tape was recorded?"

Pellew shrugged his shoulders. "Sir George had a lunch
ppointment with Mrs. Hargest on the Tuesday. I don't think
's too wild a guess to assume that she called for him at the
argantua office, in which case there was the opportunity for
nyone who wanted it. Anyway, let's hear it."

Click. Silence. Then Jane Hargest's voice, well-bred,
uriously remote:

Mrs. Hargest: You don't look very pleased to see me,
eorge.

Farley: I'm sorry.

Mrs. Hargest: You don't look sorry. You look stuffy—al-
ost stuffed.

Farley: I've a good deal on my mind.

Mrs. Hargest: You said you wanted to talk to me about
mething important.

Farley: Can't we leave it until after we've had lunch?

Mrs. Hargest: I've never fancied the atmosphere of the
entist's waiting-room, George. Better get it over.

Farley: Very well. D'you know that people are talking—
bout us?

Mrs. Hargest: People are always talking. Does it matter?

Farley: It might—if they talk to Simon.

Mrs. Hargest: Simon wouldn't listen.

Farley: Something's got to be done, Jane.

Mrs. Hargest: I really can't see why.

213

Farley: Can't you? During all the years I've known you, I've loved you. I've kissed you. I've held you in my arms. And Simon loves you. We both know that. This is our point of no return.

Mrs. Hargest: I had no idea that you had a poetic streak, George. But for once I agree with you. I don't think an office is the proper setting for this sort of conversation. We'll leave it till after lunch.

Click. Silence. Lady Hannington shook her head vigorously.

"No," she said. "No, I don't believe a word of it."

"Out of her own mouth," protested Kate.

"I don't care. The tone's all wrong, somehow. That man isn't in love with that woman. I don't believe he ever has been. That scene's been faked, Mr. Pellew."

"How on earth could it have been?" Kate demanded.

"The tape's been edited," said Humphrey. "There are three distinct cuts. I still don't see—"

"Perhaps I do," said Pellew. "Run the tape again—slowly—and point out where the cuts come in the dialogue."

Humphrey did as he was told. It appeared that all three cuts had been made in one speech of Sir George Farley's before the word "loved"; before the word "kissed"; and before the word "held."

"It sounds to me like the Lord Chamberlain," said Kate.

"Don't be frivolous, dear," said Lady Hannington. "Tell her, Mr. Pellew."

"You mean you know the answer, Lady Hannington?"

"I think so. But you're the professional."

"And professionals aren't supposed to guess. I'm going to do that all the same. Suppose Lady Hannington is right—as she always is. Suppose Sir George and Mrs. Hargest, in spite of appearances are not and never have been lovers. I suggest you slip in the word 'never' before 'kissed' and 'held,' and a qualifying phrase of some kind before 'loved.' The speech would read: *During all the years I've known you, I've never done anything to give you the impression that I loved you. I've*

214

never kissed you. I've never held you in my arms. Instead of the guilty confession of the 'cut' version you have a sentimental old gentleman, worried by gossip and his conscience, trying to screw himself up to telling a rather hard-boiled young woman that their avuncular relationship must end."

"Precisely," said Lady Hannington with emphasis.

"It makes sense, I admit," said Kate. "That woman's a bad lot all the same."

Humphrey Clymping poured himself out a glass of wine; drank it off in one gulp; and proceeded carefully to put the tapes back into their tins.

"You've heard what you waited up for," he said to Kate. "You run along, while I help Greg to tidy things up."

"While Greg delivers judgment, you mean? Not on your life!"

"As far as that goes, Mr. Pellew," said Lady Hannington, "it's quite time I was in bed. We've heard the evidence. What's the answer?"

Pellew shook his head and smiled. "I've got a report to write about this whole business. And it's not the sort of report that can be written off the cuff. I promise you that you three shall read it before I send it in. But I've still quite a lot of thinking to do. As far as what Lady Hannington calls 'the answer' goes, I fancy that you're all now in as good a position as I am to produce it. However, I'll commit myself to this extent. Only three individuals were in a position to have those tape-recordings made and edited: Sir George Farley; Lilian Jukes; and Rollo Gunn. I don't believe that Sir George would have done something that on the face of it proved him a false friend, an adulterer, and a fool. I very much doubt his having the technical know-how to cut and edit tape-recordings, and it's almost inconceivable that he would have risked getting hold of anyone else to do such a job for him. I'm pretty certain that Lilian Jukes effected the actual recordings—but under orders. And in Hargest's absence, who could give her such orders except Sir George Farley and Rollo Gunn? I've eliminated Sir George. Snap!"

215

Humphrey splashed more wine into his glass. "It's all very slick and ingenious, Greg. You haven't explained Hargest's death. You're implying that Rollo Gunn is the villain of the piece. What was his motive, and how was Hargest killed? We're almost back where we started."

"You're forgetting," said Pellew, "that I'm still a private inquiry agent, not a policeman. All the same I want the answers to those two questions as much as you do. I propose to ask Mr. Gunn to give them to me."

"You're raving mad!"

"I don't think so. I very much doubt his having put himself within reach of the law. And refusal to answer will be as good as an admission. Have you got his telephone number?"

"My dear Greg—it's almost midnight, and it's Sunday."

"I don't mind waking him up. I don't even mind his trying to sleep on it."

Humphrey looked at Lady Hannington, who nodded.

"There's always a high-level executive on duty for Gargantua over week-ends," he said reluctantly. "I happen to know that this week-end it's Rollo Gunn's job. It was one of Hargest's ideas, as a matter of fact. The office switch-board will know where he's to be found in an emergency."

"Then will you ring them, Humphrey—or shall I?"

"I'm afraid I'm leaving that to you, Greg. You see, I've—I've known Rollo for quite a time—and I like him."

Again Lady Hannington nodded.

Pellew picked up the telephone. Kate took out a cigarette and seemed to have difficulty in lighting it. Lady Hannington fiddled with the rings on her plump fingers. "Gargantua Television? I want to make contact with Mr. Rollo Gunn—yes—an inquiry of some urgency—of course—I'm speaking for Mr. Humphrey Clymping. I see—thank you very much."

Pellew rang off. His face, when he looked up at the others, appeared suddenly haggard. He swallowed a couple of times before he spoke.

"What's the matter, Greg?"

"Gunn was working in his office this afternoon."

216

"He often did," said Humphrey. "He said that the week-end was the only time when he could count on working comfortably without a lot of damned silly interruptions."

"He left the office about six, Humphrey. He told the switch-board that he was going to see Miss Jukes in her flat in Queen's Gate, and would be back in about an hour. He hasn't been back. A message came in from the Studios—from James Ballantyne—and the switch-board rang Miss Jukes's number. They could get no reply."

"So what?" demanded Humphrey.

"It's the end of the case, dear," said Lady Hannington quietly.

"Yes," said Pellew. "I'm afraid that's what it is."

There was a little silence.

"Yes," said Kate Clymping simply, "that's what it is—I'm afraid."

CHAPTER 22

FINAL REPORT

Submitted herewith my report of conclusions reached concerning the death of Mr. Simon Hargest as the result of the investigation undertaken by me on your personal instructions.

(Signed) Gregory Pellew

I feel compelled to point out in the first place that the earlier stages of my inquiry were seriously hampered by what would appear to have been a lack of confidence on the part of the authority which initiated the investigation. No doubt there were good reasons for the carrying of discretion to such extreme lengths. It is merely the fact that until I became aware of Mr. Hargest's connection with the Intelligence Service I was not in a position to make useful progress. On the face of it this discovery made the problem infinitely more complex. Apart from it, however, there was really no problem to solve. Taken by themselves neither Mr. Hargest's business responsibilities, nor emotional disturbance arising out of his domestic circumstances, provided adequate reason for a man of his abilities, experience, and calibre to commit suicide.

The link with an Intelligence background once established, the perspective of the whole business naturally changed. The canvas was widened. The field of motivation possibilities was immensely enlarged. It seems to me that the first link in the chain of significant events was Mr. Hargest's acceptance of the suggestion made to him at the end of the war that he should continue his Intelligence activities, working no longer under the War Office, but in that organisation known for convenience as the Secret Service. His success in this new sphere was outstanding, and his rise rapid. Whatever my personal opinion may be I have no certain knowledge of the position in the Service he finally achieved. It was certainly an important one.

The second link in the chain was Mr. Hargest's appointment as Managing Director of Gargantua Television: an appointment providing the finest and most ingenious "cover" for his secret work. He decided that he needed a small "cell" within the Gargantua organisation, whose members would be aware of his dual identity, and upon whose loyalty and capacities he could rely in both fields. This "cell" consisted of his Personal Assistant, and his Private Secretary. It was entirely natural that to fill those jobs he should wish to recruit individuals known to him personally and with previous experience of Intelligence work. He found them in Mr. Rollo Gunn, who had served him on the M.I. staff in Cairo during 1943–4; and Miss Lilian Jukes, who as an officer in the W.R.N.S. had worked under him in Malta in 1941. He trusted both of them implicitly. Until about a year ago this trust was completely justified, in spite of the fact that ever since the Malta period Miss Jukes had been in love with Mr. Hargest, frustratedly and desperately. Mr. Hargest was married, and his marriage was generally considered a successful one.

As one of the top-grade executives of Gargantua Television Mr. Hargest completely justified his appointment. No doubt is position was considerably helped by the fact that Sir George Farley, the Chairman of the organisation, was a friend of his wife's of long standing, with a relationship approximating to that of an uncle for a favourite niece. As far as Gargantua was concerned Hargest's main difficulties arose out of his relations with Mr. James Ballantyne, the Programme Director. Mr. Ballantyne is a man of unusual gifts, forceful personality, and considerable ambition, combined with strong and even violent prejudices and enthusiasms. Disputes and tensions between Hargest and Ballantyne were frequent, complex, and occasionally bitter. They were, however, mitigated by a mutually acknowledged respect. There can be little doubt but that Ballantyne hoped to step into Hargest's shoes, with the wider scope and responsibilities involved should Hargest disappear from the scene.

The third link in the chain was forged some eleven months before Mr. Hargest's death, when Rollo Gunn fell in love with Mrs. Hargest, and found that love returned. It is, I think, fair speculation to assume that Mrs. Hargest—whose reputation before her marriage had been a trifle "wild"—had found the marriage unsatisfactory. The multiplicity of her husband's interests and responsibilities left her very much alone. She knew herself not to be entirely in his confidence, which, for obvious reasons, she could not be. In the event she and Rollo Gunn became lovers. The resulting effect upon Rollo Gunn's attitude to Hargest was immediate and crucial. Gunn was a man whose ambitions had always outrun his accomplishments. His background was that of a rolling stone. He was victim alike of strong passions and an inferiority complex. To live daily almost cheek by jowl with the husband he was cuckolding—a man to whom, incidentally, he owed everything—and to take orders from him became an intolerable strain.

An equivalent strain—though she successfully and creditably concealed its effects—was borne by Miss Jukes.

It should be mentioned at this point that one of the practices introduced by Hargest into the Gargantua office was that of having tape-recordings made of many of his personal interviews. Knowledge of this practice he shared only with Gunn and Miss Jukes. As a rule such recordings were actually made by Miss Jukes on instructions from either Hargest or Gunn. Most were destroyed. But some—also on instructions from either Hargest or Gunn—were kept in a locked filing-cabinet in Miss Jukes's office to which only she and Hargest possessed keys.

Naturally in the circumstances Mrs. Hargest and Gunn went to extreme lengths to keep their affair a secret. They were never seen in public together and Gunn only visited Mrs. Hargest at her flat when he was certain, from his particular knowledge of Hargest's movements, that he could do so in perfect safety. As a further precaution use was made of Sir George Farley's affection for Mrs. Hargest. He also visited her at her flat when she was left alone. He went unconventionally often—so often indeed that a certain amount of gossip began to circulate, which caused Sir George to become uneasy—but he always went quite openly. It was his habit to wear an unusually noticeable overcoat, rather of the type once generally attributed to theatrical managers, with a heavy astrakhan collar and cuffs. Made aware of this, Gunn got hold of a similar coat and wore it whenever he paid a visit to Mrs. Hargest. With the collar turned up, a pair of dark glasses and a false white moustache of Sir George's unmistakable dragoon type, it was long odds that anyone curious concerning the identity of the visitor to Mrs. Hargest's flat would be satisfied that he was Sir George. One example of such a mistake of identity was brought to my attention in the course of my inquiries.

So much for the general background to Hargest's affairs at the time of his visit to Berlin which preceded the week of his death. It must be remembered that, while he appeared to be in good physical shape, he had been working under great pressure for an indefinite period. Also—though of this there is no concrete evidence—it is likely that he was conscious of definite malaise if nothing worse in his relations with his wife.

The ostensible reason for the German trip was an international conference of television authorities regarding Eurovision, an aspect of the work in which Hargest was known to be peculiarly interested. It was excellent camouflage for his real mission, which was to arrange for the reception and escort to this country of a highly-placed operative in the Polish Security Service, who had planned defection from the other side of the Iron Curtain. That Hargest went himself to Berlin is sufficient proof of the importance attributed to his journey. It was not only the rank of the individual himself. He had guaranteed, in return for promised security and asylum, to bring with him a complete list of communist agents operating in NATO countries. Something went wrong. The defector was trapped by the People's Police in East Berlin and liquidated. And Hargest came back to London with the consciousness of having failed in what must have been one of the most vital assignments with which he had ever been entrusted. It is not difficult to imagine his consequent state of mind.

During Hargest's absence—possibly even some time before he went abroad—Rollo Gunn had made up his mind that something definite had got to be done. To begin with it seems likely that he did not go beyond some scheme which would eliminate Hargest from the Managing Directorship. With the help of facts and figures supplied unwittingly by the Advertising Department of Gargantua, and of arguments based on his knowledge of James Ballantyne's theories of programme values, he opened a campaign to persuade Sir George Farley that there were signs of Hargest's methods becoming out-dated, and that he should be replaced by Ballantyne. Sir George proved amenable—partly because he had thought that Hargest had been showing signs of strain from overwork, and probably also because his feelings had been played upon by Mrs. Hargest, prompted by Gunn. A confession by Mrs. Hargest that she was unhappy with her husband, that she had covered a breaking heart with a brave face for years, would have profoundly affected a sentimentalist like the Chairman. Ballantyne was brought into the picture. He wanted the job, and professionally he had always been at odds with Hargest. But he would have no part in anything to be construed as an underhand intrigue: an attitude with which Sir George agreed. Gunn found himself up against a blank wall. If he was to get what he wanted—and what he wanted was freedom in the long run to marry Mrs. Hargest—he had to find some method more effective and more brutal.

He found that method by combining the technique of the secret tape-recordings with Miss Jukes's habit of blind obedience. This she was accustomed to give automatically to Gunn whenever Hargest was away from the office.

During the first three days of the week when Hargest was due back from Berlin Sir George was using the Managing Director's office, and Miss Jukes as secretary. Rollo Gunn took care to give the second secretary, Miss Anstruther, special leave over those days so as to get her out of the way. Miss Jukes made and noted Sir George's various appointments, which included meetings both with Gunn and Ballantyne regarding the possibility of the latter's succession and Hargest's future. Gunn, hinting to Miss Jukes that an internal office intrigue against Hargest might be in the wind, instructed her to tape-record the interviews in Hargest's own interests. Miss Jukes did so—but out of natural curiosity kept for herself the duplicate recording of the interview between Ballantyne and the Chairman, and took it home with her. Gunn knew also, from Miss Jukes's engagement-book which she had taken over from Miss Anstruther, that Sir George had a lunch date with Mrs. Hargest on the Tuesday. She called for him at the office, and Gunn—Miss Jukes had already gone to lunch—seized his chance to tape-record their conversation. He edited that tape, and the tape of the Ballantyne—Sir George interview to such effect that from the recordings it seemed clear that Sir George and Ballantyne were engaged in a conspiracy to get rid of a man whom they disliked not only professionally but personally; and secondly that Sir George was, and had been for years, Mrs. Hargest's lover.

Hargest returned from Germany in the frame of mind to which I have already referred. He was depressed, rather exhausted, and suffering from the after-effects of a bad bumpy flight. That was late on Wednesday. He rested in his flat on Thursday morning, and spent all the afternoon in the Studios. On Friday he held an executives' meeting; saw Ballantyne before lunch; and the Chairman immediately afterwards. The atmosphere of those interviews must have been distinctly strained, as the possibility of Hargest's being kicked upstairs and Ballantyne's succession must have been discussed, however vaguely. Then at 3:45 Hargest found that Gunn had asked for a special appointment, and against the noting of that appointment the cryptic letters P-B: cryptic, because Hargest must have wondered why Gunn had arranged a play-back session so soon after his return.

(I feel it is only fair to put into the discard one suspicion which I was obliged to entertain during the earlier stages of the affair. No one—as the Foreign Office has good reason to know—is more vulnerable to blackmail than a government servant engaged on secret work. Once I found out that the first inquiries concerning Hargest's death had come through the medium of someone who can reasonably be described as a member of the homosexual establishment I was bound to ask myself whether those inquiries might not have been prompted by anxiety on behalf of a fellow-member. Nothing whatever came to light to justify such a theory which, incidentally, offered a reasonable explanation of the breakdown of the Hargest marriage.)

It is necessary at this point to envisage Simon Hargest as he was on that Friday afternoon a little after three o'clock: a man still exhausted from his journey, bitterly chagrined owing to the failure of his mission, and with suspicions piling up remorselessly in his mind in connection on the one hand with his wife's attitude, on the other with the possible implications of the hints dropped by his Chairman and James Ballantyne. To him enters Lilian Jukes, bearing the inevitable tea-tray and three tins of recorded tape. Behind her Rollo Gunn, carrying the play-back machine. (Gunn—as the most important member of Hargest's private intelligence "cell" within Gargantua—would have known of the under-cover reason for Hargest's mission to Berlin. He was therefore in a particularly favourable position to render that mission abortive. An anonymous message to the Polish Embassy in London, naming the hypothetical defector and giving warning of his intentions, would have been enough for the appropriate police authorities in East Berlin to have been put on their guard. This, I believe, to have been Gunn's first shot.)

His other three—Miss Jukes having gone back into the outer office—Gunn now proceeded to fire at close quarters. He told Hargest that certain recordings had been made in his absence which it was vital for him to hear. The tapes were then played back. It is a pity that no equivalent tele-recording of the expression on Gunn's face during those play-backs is available. The first tape—perhaps the most cruel sublimation of ingenious devilry—must have gone far to convince Hargest that Gunn, whom he had trusted implicitly both as colleague and friend, was involved in, and had to some extent inspired, a conspiracy against him with the Chairman. *That it implicated Gunn himself was brutally sufficient guarantee of authenticity.* The second—in its edited version—revealed Sir George and James Ballantyne not only planning his supersession, but speaking of him in terms of dislike and contempt. The third tape—also edited—told him in the Chairman's own voice that he was, and for years had been, the lover of Hargest's wife. The façade of domestic felicity, which he had been at such pains to preserve, together with his faith in friendship were utterly destroyed.

Simon Hargest had lived three lives simultaneously; one personal, one professional, and one secret. During that half hour on that Friday afternoon he was compelled to face the

226

ending of all three—ended by Rollo Gunn with no more deadly weapons than some yards of electro-magnetic tape and his imagination. When Hargest walked out of that office nothing remained for him to do apart from disposing as swiftly and tidily as possible of the only thing he had left; a life that had become hateful and beyond endurance. The bottom had fallen out of his three lives. Late that night, or early the following morning, he killed himself.

Rollo Gunn had succeeded. But he made one mistake, and he had one bit of bad luck. He did not know that Lilian Jukes had, from personal motives of her own, taken the duplicate—and of course unedited—recording of the interview between the Chairman and James Ballantyne. And he failed to destroy the other tapes. Probably Hargest, automatically following his usual practice, told Miss Jukes to lock them away before he left the office. Only he and Miss Jukes had keys to the filing cabinet, and Gunn could not risk arousing suspicions in Miss Jukes's mind by asking for her key, nor by telling her to destroy the tapes herself. Still less could he afford to do so once Hargest was dead. Gunn knew all about Miss Jukes's devotion to Hargest. All he could do was to play on that devotion and tell her that for the sake of Hargest's reputation it would be best for her to keep the tapes safe outside the office. So they joined the fourth tape in Miss Jukes's flat, where all four were ultimately discovered.

I hope that the above account may be deemed to cover all the relevant aspects of the case. A file containing my day-to-day notes during the course of the investigations; the names of various individuals prepared to answer questions relating to and confirming my account; and the four tape-recordings, are available should they be called for.

Having regard to the unusual background and circumstances of the whole affair, and the contents of the press-cutting attached herewith, I assume that no further action need or will be contemplated.

G.P.

ATTACHMENT.

A tragedy, involving two members of the staff of Gargantua Television, occurred yesterday in the flat of one of them
in Queen's Gate, S.W. A neighbour of Miss Lilian Jukes, a
secretary in the Gargantua Organisation, noticed a strong
smell of gas coming from Miss Jukes's flat. Unable to obtain
any answer to ringing and knocking, she became alarmed and
contacted the police, who broke into the flat. Miss Jukes was
found dead with her head on a cushion on the floor in front of
the gas oven in the kitchenette. Beside her, also dead, was
Mr. Rollo Gunn, Personal Assistant to the Managing Director of Gargantua. The tragedy is intensified, and may even be
explained, by recalling the sad and comparatively recent
death of Mr. Simon Hargest, the brilliant and well-known
Gargantua executive. Miss Jukes and Mr. Gunn had worked
closely with Mr. Hargest for many years. Their personal
devotion to him was common knowledge among the Gargantua staff, and they had been greatly affected by his death.
Foul play is not suspected.

AFTERWORD

_____

venty-four hours after he had delivered his report Pellew
s summoned to the Commander's office. He obeyed with
thusiasm considerably tempered. The case had certainly
en out of the common run. Pellew was far from certain that
e unconventional form of this report would be excused ac-
-dingly. When he went in the Commander was standing
se to the window, his back to the light. It was almost im-
ssible to deduce anything from the expression on his face.

"You sent for me, sir."

"I did. Thanks for all that."

The Commander made a vague gesture towards his desk.

"Your final assumption is perfectly correct, Pellew. No
ther action is contemplated."

"Poetic justice?" ventured Pellew.

"You can leave out the poetry. I've seen the medical re-
-ts. The woman killed herself. There's no doubt about that.
.ooks rather as if Gunn walked into it unawares. He had a
" of the flat."

"She must have let him know that she'd handed over the

229

tapes, sir. Once he'd heard that he must have known he wa‍s for it."

The Commander shook his head. "I don't see how a ca‍se could have been brought. That report of yours—I don't see ‍it being read out in court, do you? Not even if it was discreetl‍y —er, edited. I may as well tell you that I propose to do som‍e editing before I pass it on."

"Quite so, sir."

The Commander went over to his desk and sat dow‍n. "You'd better take a fortnight's leave before you resume duty‍."

"Thank you, sir."

"I've been thinking about your future. You've never real‍ly fitted the Yard pattern, have you? Poetry and justice as be‍d fellows—this report of yours—"

"I was afraid you might come to that conclusion, sir."

"Were you, Pellew? I don't get the impression that you'‍re afraid of much, and I'm damned certain you're not afraid ‍of me! I seem to remember some quotation about 'contemplati‍ng with appropriate emotions.'"

"Yes, sir. The Greeks had a word for it."

"They had. A classical education's out of fashion, but th‍ey knew a thing or two in a quiet way. I wanted to ask you ‍if you'd care for a transfer."

"I suppose I've as good as asked for it, sir," said Pelle‍w gloomily.

"Well," said the Commander briskly, "you've got it. T‍he Prime Minister seems to have got the impression that liais‍on between his Private Office and Scotland Yard could be i‍m‍proved. Run along. Take your leave. Come back—and i‍m‍prove it. Good morning."

By the year 2000, 2 out of 3 Americans could be illiterate.

It's true.

Today, 75 million adults...about one American in three, can't read adequately. And by the year 2000, U.S. News & World Report envisions an America with a literacy rate of only 30%.

Before that America comes to be, you can stop it...by joining the fight against illiteracy today.

Call the Coalition for Literacy at toll-free **1-800-228-8813** and volunteer.

**Volunteer
Against Illiteracy.
The only degree you need
is a degree of caring.**

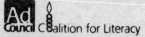

Ad Council Coalition for Literacy